The Piano Player's Son

LINDSAY STANBERRY-FLYNN

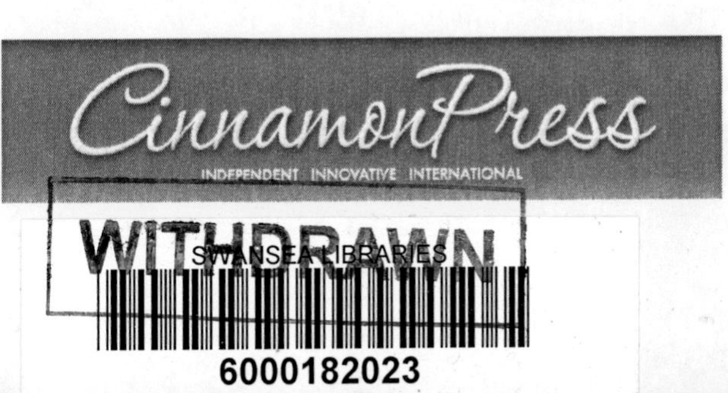

Published by Cinnamon Press,
Meirion House,
Tanygrisiau,
Blaenau Ffestiniog,
Gwynedd LL41 3SU
www.cinnamonpress.com

ISBN 978-1-907090-93-6

British Library Cataloguing in Publication Data. A CIP record for this book can be obtained from the British Library.

Designed and typeset in Garamond by Cinnamon Press. Cover design by Cottia Fortune-Wood & Jacob Hull from original artwork 'meditation of piano' by Jozef Sedmak © Jozef Sedmak, agency dreamtime.

Cinnamon Press is represented by Inpress and by the Welsh Books Council in Wales.
Printed in Poland
The publisher acknowledges the support of the Welsh Books Council

The Piano Player's Son is a work of fiction, Any resemblance to any person is entirely co-incidental.

Acknowledgements

I would like to thank Jan Fortune for her belief and encouragement, and everyone at Cinnamon Press for their hard work and dedication. My thanks also to my writing group who read the early chapters and gave me good advice and to Cornerstones Literary Consultancy whose guidance helped strengthen both characters and plot. Elisabeth Drake's help with Italian was invaluable, and Judith Selby's eagle-eye pinpointed some discrepancies. I am also grateful to my writing students who keep me exploring the craft of writing and to friends for their support. My love and gratitude goes to my family whose belief and pride in my writing mean so much to me. Above all, I owe a huge debt to Trevor – without his love and encouragement none of it would be possible.

To find out more visit my website
www.lindsaystanberryflynn.co.uk

About the Author

Lindsay Stanberry-Flynn writes novels and short stories. She published her first novel *Unravelling* in 2010, and it went on to win three awards. She won the Cinnamon Press Novel Award with *The Piano Player's Son*, her second novel. A number of her short stories have also been published by – amongst others – Cinnamon Press, Rubery Book Award and Fish Publishing. Lindsay worked as an English lecturer in further and higher education before leaving to take an MA in Creative Writing at Bath Spa University. She now works as a creative writing tutor.

Book Groups: A free guide to 'The Piano Player's Son' is available for reading groups. The guide contains discussion topics and background to the book. To receive a free copy of the guide, please go to
www.lindsaystanberryflynn.co.uk/contact

For Gavin, Hugh and Hannah

One

By four in the morning, the vigil was over. Isabel's lips touched his forehead. He already felt cold. 'I love you, Dad,' she whispered.

The others had said their goodbyes and would be waiting in the car park. Their impatience tugged at her, but she couldn't go. It didn't seem right to leave him on his own. She gazed at the bristles spiking his chin. How long does a beard keep growing?

There was a noise behind her and she glanced round.

A nurse was standing in the doorway. 'I thought you'd all gone.' She indicated the trolley in front of her. 'There are one or two things I need to do.'

Isabel clamped her fists to her sides as the nurse's hand, reddened and capable, touched her father's pale arm. 'What will happen to him now?'

'I'll make him comfortable, and then he'll be taken to the mortuary.'

Isabel frowned. *Comfortable*? What on earth was that supposed to mean?

He looked so peaceful, you heard people say. *He could have been asleep*—platitudes to ease the pain. But never, ever, would she have thought her dad was asleep. Sleeping people wake up, they come back to you: *I had a bad dream*, they'll say. *I love you*, they'll murmur. But this was different. This awful quality of absence slashed a gulf between you and them, between sound and silence.

The glass doors slid open and Isabel stepped out. The early morning air stung her cheeks after the fug of the hospital. She hesitated at the top of the steps, looking down at her mother and brother waiting at the bottom, their faces blobs in the shadow cast by the sodium light. Her mother clung to Rick's arm.

Isabel started down the steps and joined them. Closer, Rick's eyes were bloodshot. Before he arrived at the hospital last night, she hadn't seen him for several months and was surprised to see his hair streaked with grey. Her mother's mouth was pinched and lifeless without its red lipstick.

The three of them formed an awkward little circle. No one spoke. Isabel's fingers searched for the ring on her left hand. She couldn't get used to its absence.

She settled her mother into her old Volvo and followed Rick out of the car park. As they passed St Joseph's, Isabel glanced at the statue of Mary, baby Jesus cradled in her arms, which stood in the church forecourt. Her mother made the sign of the cross and lowered her head. When Isabel was young, she would sprinkle holy water on them all, or offer up Hail Marys as they left for school when they had exams or something big happening. But the Blessed Virgin hadn't come up trumps this time, had she?

Rick was already in the kitchen when they arrived at the house. He was tapping numbers into his mobile.

'Sit down, Mum,' Isabel said. 'What can I get you?'

Her mother, usually so talkative, so loud, shook her head.

'Brandy's good for shock. Dad's got a bottle somewhere.'

Rick looked up from the phone. 'I've sent Georgie boy a text.'

'Saying what?'

'No point driving like a maniac. Dad's gone.'

Isabel glared at Rick. 'You told him that in a text?'

'Credit me with some sense. I said *no rush now*.'

Isabel turned away. She glanced at the wall where her father's old station clock hung. Over the years, the long black hands had announced when it was time for school, piano lessons, her driving test, and the moment she and her father left for church on her wedding day. 'The clock,' she said. 'Look. It says five to four. That means it stopped when Dad—'

'I'll sort it out.' Rick pulled open the glass front.

'No!' Isabel caught his wrist as his fingers reached towards the clock. Only her father was allowed to wind it. It had been one of his rules.

Rick shook off her hand. He searched around on top of the case and Isabel heard the staccato clicking of the mechanism as the key turned. She stared at her brother's back, his outstretched arm as he closed the front again and returned the key to its home. He was taller, slimmer, but it could almost have been her father standing there.

She crouched beside her mother's chair. 'What about some tea?' Her voice sounded bright and artificial.

Rick turned from studying the clock, which now showed twenty past five. 'Not for me. I'm shattered.'

'Go to bed, *caro*,' her mother said.

'And you, Mum. Isabel can bring tea up to you.'

Their mother stood up, catching hold of the back of the chair. She suddenly looked much older than sixty-eight. 'You won't forget about Grace?' she asked, from the doorway.

'I'll ring her now.'

While she waited for the kettle to boil, Isabel dialled Grace's mobile. When they'd realised their father's condition was serious, she'd phoned her sister in Italy. She would leave immediately, Grace had said. She wanted to be there. But a few moments before he died, the nurse had come in with a message. There were technical problems: Grace was stuck in Naples.

Grace took an age to answer. Isabel pictured the airport: lights dimmed; row upon row of travellers trying to sleep, whiling away the hours that held them suspended between one moment in their lives and another. It was the worst of settings to receive such news.

*

The bedside light was on in her mother's room and she was sitting up, tiny against the plumped up pillows. Isabel tried not to look at the empty space beside her.

'When I first came to England,' her mother said, sipping the tea, 'I hated this dreadful stuff.' She pulled down her mouth at the memory. 'I was nearly sick more than once.'

'I phoned Grace,' Isabel said.

'Poor baby. All on her own.'

'Flights resume in the morning. I'll pick her up from Heathrow.'

'And *mi tesoro*?'

Isabel took the cup from her mother's hand and put it on the bedside table. 'George will be here soon.'

Her mother closed her eyes. Isabel watched the rise and fall of her chest. When she was sure she was asleep, she leant forward and kissed her cheek.

Her mother's eyes shot open. 'Isabel! Why are you here? Where's your father?'

'Mamma…' These days Isabel rarely called her mother that. She'd left the name behind with toys and dressing-up clothes. It was her father who would say *Ask Mamma*; *you'd better tell Mamma.*

Her mother reached up and stroked her cheek. 'You're a good girl, Isabel. A good daughter.' She smiled. 'Tell Henry I want him.'

'Mamma. Dad's gone.'

'But he hasn't said goodbye. Henry always kisses me goodbye.'

Isabel put an arm round her shoulders. A pad of flesh covered the bone. 'Mum, you remember. You went in the ambulance with Dad.'

Her mother's fingers clutched at the bedcover, her long nails red against the cream material. 'Gone. He's gone,' she repeated as if she was learning a new language.

'Mamma…'

Her mother dropped back on to the pillow. 'I'll be all right on my own.' She pushed Isabel's hand away. 'You get home. Brian will be wondering where you are.'

'I doubt he will.'

'Why? Has Brian gone too?'

'We split up, didn't we?' Isabel said.

'Did you?'

'I'm in that flat now. Dad helped me sort it out.'

Her mother slapped her palm against her forehead. 'I'm all confused.'

'It's shock.'

'I can't manage on my own.'

'I'll help you.' Isabel hoped she sounded confident. Her father had been a saint when it came to dealing with her mother.

'Henry did everything for me.'

'I know,' Isabel said. Too much, people used to say. 'You and Dad were perfect together.'

'*Perfetto*.'

'I wish I'd been half as lucky with Brian.'

'He'll come back. They always do. Make him pay a little and then forgive him.'

Isabel stared at a brown stain on the wallpaper above the bed. It looked like tea, or blood. She'd never noticed it before. 'It's not so easy.'

'Forgiveness. Isn't that what marriage is all about?'

'You should know, Mum.'

'What makes you say that?' Her mother's voice was sharp.

'You and Dad were married a long time, that's all.' Isabel felt for the words as if she was negotiating a route on a rocky path. 'You must have had to forgive a few things over the years.'

Her mother's face wrinkled into a smile. 'You were his favourite.'

'Dad didn't have favourites.'

But you have. Isabel watched her mother. *And it's no secret who.*

On the landing, a strip of light shone from underneath Rick's old bedroom door. She tapped and waited. No answer—he'd probably fallen asleep with the light on. She pushed the door open.

Rick was sitting on the narrow bed, his laptop open on his knees. He looked up. His face was grey in the computer's bluey glow. He kept his fingers poised over the keyboard. 'What?'

'I thought—'

'What do you want?' His voice rasped as if he'd just smoked a pack of twenty.

Isabel smoothed down the edge of the carpet with her foot. It always caught on the door. 'Someone will have an accident on that one day,' her mother used to say. Dad had never got round to sorting it out. 'I thought you might want to talk.'

Rick's heavy eyebrows dived towards each other and a furrow appeared. 'What's to talk about?'

For a second, Isabel was a little girl hovering at her big brother's door: *Do you want to play? Shove off! I'm busy.*

She shrugged, the urge to communicate shrivelling away like melting snow. 'What are you doing?'

'Making a list.' Rick's gaze had returned to the screen.

'A list of what?'

'What is this? A catechism?'

Isabel edged the door shut with her heel. 'Ssh. You'll wake Mum up.'

Rick sighed and laid the laptop on the bed next to him. 'Right. You've got my attention. What do you want?'

A prickling sensation started in Isabel's nose, and she bit her lip hard. 'Why do you have to be so vile? Dad's just died. I thought there might be things to talk about.'

'Isabel.' Her mother's voice called from across the landing.

'Mum's awake.' Rick lifted the laptop back on to his knees.

'Isabel.'

'You'd better see what she wants.' His fingers raced across the keyboard.

A lamp burned on the bedside table, and her mother was sitting at the dressing table, plaiting her hair.

'I thought you were asleep, Mum. What are you doing up again?'

'You know I can't go to bed without doing my hair. You shouldn't have made me.'

Isabel sat down on the bed and looked at her mother's reflection as she wound the long, thick hair round her fingers. At one time it had been the colour of burgundy, but now there was more white than anything else. She looked different in the mirror. There was something about her eyes, the shape of her mouth with that slight droop in the corner that made her seem a stranger.

'He used to love watching me do this.' Her mother smoothed a stray strand of hair. 'Morning and night, he'd sit on the bed and hand the clips to me. Except yesterday. He didn't want to get up.' She gripped Isabel's hand. 'If I'd called someone then, he might still be with us.'

'It was a major heart attack. Nothing could have been done.'

'I should have known. He was always up first.'

Her mother's eyes had a distant look as she contemplated some private world Isabel couldn't begin to imagine. Isabel followed her gaze across the room. Her father's dark suit, the one he wore for best, was hanging on the wardrobe door.

'We were going out for his birthday next week. He'd got his suit out to be cleaned.' Her mother turned back to the mirror. 'I didn't deserve him.'

'He adored you.'

'Sometimes I think he loved me too much.'

Her mother's voice was a whisper, so at first Isabel thought she must have misheard. Surely, her mother could never have too much adoration?

'He'd have done anything to make you happy.'

'That was the trouble.'

'How do you mean?'

Her mother shook her head and the newly wound plait twisted snake-like on her shoulder. 'It doesn't matter.' She sat on the edge of the bed and swung her legs round. 'I'm tired, Isabel. I think I could sleep now.'

'You can't say something like that, Mum, and then shut up.'

'Your father made me promise not to tell anyone.'

'If there's something I should know about…'

Her mother lay back against the pillow and closed her eyes. 'Perhaps it would be better.'

'It's no good bottling things up. Isn't that what Dad always said?'

'My eyes hurt. It's too bright.'

Isabel switched off the bedside light. For a few moments darkness and silence coalesced, and then her mother began to talk.

Isabel hung her key on the hook in the kitchen. The flat was cold and silent. She went back into the hall and hesitated outside Rose's room. The door was ajar and she could hear the soft sound of her daughter's breathing. She hadn't expected Rose to wait up, but still she felt disappointed, like a child coming home from school to an empty house.

In the kitchen, she fished around in the back of a cupboard and found the bottle of gin. She poured a large measure. There was a time after Brian left when she drank every night. It got especially bad when Josh went to live with his dad. After the first couple of glasses she hardly felt the pain. She used to fall asleep at the kitchen table, waking up cold and stiff in the early hours, to climb into Josh's bed and cuddle his pillow.

One night when Rose was staying with a friend, she'd phoned to say there'd been a row, and she wanted to come home. Isabel tried to persuade her to get a taxi but she wouldn't hear of it, sobbed down the phone. Isabel went. It still made her shudder to think what might have happened.

She hardly drank after that. But tonight was different. She rested her forehead against the cold wet glass of the back door. The blackness of the night was creeping away. A soft grey had edged in. The hedge bordering the garden stood hunched against the darkness of the sports field beyond. A shape streaked across the lawn: Samson. Isabel opened the door and he shot in, arching his back and rubbing against her legs.

She picked him up, burying her face in his warm fur. His weight made her arms ache and she slumped on to the rocking chair. Her father had given it to her when she moved into the flat. 'Very comforting, rocking chairs,' he'd said.

Samson initially tolerated her embrace, but began to struggle. He stood over her, paws kneading her chest. She smelt the sardines Rose had given him for supper. His purr vibrated against her ear and her breathing slowed in response. She pushed her toes against the floor and rocked back. Forwards. Back. Forwards. Back.

Two

Isabel spotted Grace as soon as she came through arrivals. With her silver jacket, her long legs in tight jeans, and her sunglasses, her sister might have been a celebrity arriving at the airport. The other passengers streaming through the barrier looked insignificant in comparison.

Isabel waved and Grace turned and strode towards her. The knot lodged in Isabel's stomach eased its grip—she'd always been close to Grace, wedged as they were between two warring brothers.

Close up the celebrity persona was frayed. When Grace pushed her dark glasses up on her head, Isabel noticed her eyes were puffy and shadowed. She hugged her. Despite the jacket, Grace felt thin and fragile.

'Let's go somewhere we can talk,' Grace said.

'Don't you want to get out of here?'

Grace shook her head. 'I want to know what happened.'

'Okay.' Isabel steered her towards a café area away from the crowds.

Grace sipped her cappuccino. She made a face: 'Dreadful stuff.'

'I forgot you've become more Italian than Mum.' Isabel slid the plate of pastries across the table. 'What about something to eat?'

Grace took a croissant and began to cut it into slices. 'Tell me. Was it terrible?' Her dark eyes were glassy with tears.

'More unreal. It hasn't sunk in.'

'What was it like?'

'Mum phoned about four o'clock in the afternoon—'

'I mean at the end. What was it like at the actual moment… you know… when he died?'

Isabel stirred her coffee. 'It's hard to describe.'

'Try—I need to know.'

'It was…' She shook her head: that hospital room… sickly mustard walls… the smell, something bad, something rotten, disinfectant failing to mask it… the machines… their incessant bleeping… the next beat of her father's heart, the only thing that mattered –

'Isabel.'

Isabel forced herself to talk: 'At first we expected him to come round. Then his breathing changed: it was shallower and there were gaps between each breath…' Those gaps… longer and longer… waiting… wondering… the next breath… when would it—'

'Isabel!'

'Can we talk about it later? I can't now.'

'He's my dad too—I've got a right to know.' Grace pushed crumbs around the plate. 'It's horrible being the only one who wasn't there.'

'George hasn't arrived yet.'

'Really?' The sharp lines of Grace's face relaxed. 'I'm glad I wasn't the only one.' She tried another sip of the cappuccino.

Isabel stared at the line of froth on her lip. She had longed for Grace to get here. She'd imagined them comforting each other. But this? She didn't recognise this less-than-perfect sister.

Grace rubbed her hand across her mouth. 'It's always me that's left out.'

'How?'

'Middle child and all that.'

'Grace, there are four of us—you can't be the middle one.'

'Rick's the eldest, you're the first girl, and George is the baby… Mamma's darling.'

'But you're the beautiful one. You're so much like Mum when she was younger—Dad adored you.'

'Because I look like her?'

'Dad was proud of you, all that you've achieved.'

'Achieved!' Grace shoved her cup to one side. Liquid slopped over the edge and made a brown pool on the table. 'But he loved you for you.'

Isabel closed her eyes. The blackness inside her lids was like a balm. If only she could shut out the past forty-eight hours as easily. She forced her eyes open again and found Grace watching her. 'Let's not argue. At the moment I don't care who loved who more and why.'

Grace caught hold of Isabel's hand. 'Sorry.'

Isabel looked down at her sister's long pale fingers entwined with her plump ones, already bulging at the knuckle. 'I seem to be everyone's whipping boy at the moment. I've had Mum telling me all sorts of stuff—'

'What stuff?' Grace's hand tightened on Isabel's.

'You know what she's like.' Isabel felt her cheeks growing hot. 'Always rambling on about the past and her beloved Italy.'

'At least you had the chance to say goodbye to Dad.'

Isabel's hand itched to fly up in the direction of Grace's cheek. She imagined the sting in her palm as she slapped her sister's smooth skin. The red weal erupting over its serene beauty. What was this harping on about not being there when he died? He was dead. Gone forever. Never again would she feel his hug; never again hear his voice: *Don't upset yourself, love*; never again sit beside him on the piano stool and—she tried to pull her hand from Grace's, but Grace clung on.

'If I'd been there, I'd have known one way or the other.'

Grace's voice, usually so light and musical, grated on Isabel like chalk on a blackboard. *Known one way or the other.* What was she talking about? Known what? Did she want to hold the mirror up to see if he was still breathing? Wait while the nurse made him *comfortable*? Words screamed up through Isabel's chest into her mouth, like exploding fireworks: *It's okay for you on your beautiful island, with your beautiful husband and your beautiful life.*

Oh God. What was happening to her? This was Grace she was about to heap abuse on. Grace, the baby sister she'd adored from the moment she'd first seen the black curls, the dark eyes peeping out of the crocheted shawl. She'd helped change her nappy, pushed her pram, rattled her toys, lifted her out of the cot each morning. Until that day. The day when the big black taxi arrived and Mamma climbed into it carrying little Grace in her arms. 'Italia,' Mamma had said in response to Isabel's anguished cry. 'We're going to Italia.' And she waved as the taxi pulled away. The shops. Playschool. The park. Even Yorkshire, where her granny and granddad lived. Isabel knew where they all where. But where was *Italia*?

She clutched her waist with her arms and clenched her hands into fists.

'Don't go all silent on me.' Grace's accusation sliced across her thoughts. *Going silent.* It was what people said she did. When things were difficult, when she was angry or unhappy and wanted to explain her feelings, she formulated, rehearsed, reorganised the words she would say, but before she could open her mouth, the gibe always came: *You've gone all silent again.* Moody, Brian called it.

Okay, she wouldn't be silent. 'Why haven't you been over for so long?'

'You know it's difficult to get away. The restaurant…' Grace sounded different, her voice smaller, more diffident.

'It's not easy looking out for Mum and Dad either.' Tears pressed at the back of Isabel's eyes 'And all the stuff with Brian as well.'

She felt Grace's fingers stroking her wrist. 'I'm sorry.'

She wanted to answer, say she understood, to mend the breach in her love for her sister, but the sides of her throat felt glued together.

'I am sorry about Brian, Bel.'

Bel: her family's pet name for her. Only her father and Brian had used it recently.

'Are you okay?' Grace asked.

'Josh has gone with him.'

Grace's eyes opened wider. 'What? You mean Josh is living with Brian?'

'And *her*.'

'Oh, Bel. Talk to me.'

So Grace wanted her to talk: she'd tell her all right. Tell her what it felt like when your husband fucked someone else, gave away what was precious between you to someone else, had a baby with someone else, and worse, took away your child and gave him to someone else to look after. Isabel searched in her handbag for the photo. At first she'd looked at it constantly and it was dog-eared. Now she rationed herself. She held it out to Grace. 'That was in Majorca. Our last holiday,' she said. 'We'd been fooling about in the pool and Brian asked the man from the next-door sun lounger to take a photo. Look how happy Rose and Josh are. You can't believe Brian was sleeping with that bitch even back then, can you?'

Grace frowned. 'Perhaps it would help if you let go of the anger, Bel.'

Isabel shoved the photo back in her bag. Josh was Grace's godson and she'd always had a soft spot for him, but she didn't have any children. How could she know what it felt like? Only her father understood. 'It's tough, lass,' he used to say. 'When you put the pieces of a broken heart together, it never goes back quite as it should. But these things happen, and we get through them. Somehow.'

'Play the piano for me, Dad,' she'd pleaded, when she couldn't cry any more.

His fingers were poised over the keys. 'What would you like?'

'Do you need to ask?'

'Debussy's Nocturne, it is then.'

The Nocturne had been her favourite since she was a little girl and she used to sit at his feet and watch his big shiny shoes as they pressed the pedals. She'd thought his feet had magic in them.

'Boys like to be with their dads, don't they?' she said now and made an effort to sound reasonable. It wasn't fair to take it out on Grace. 'And since they've had…' When Brian's girlfriend had produced a son three months earlier, Isabel thought she would die with the pain. 'They're a family now. How can I compete?'

'It's not a competition,' Grace said. 'You'll always be Josh's mum.'

'That doesn't count for much at the moment.'

'It will. You'll see.'

'You bet it will.' Isabel stood up. 'I'm going to get my husband and son back, Grace. Whatever it takes. I'm going to get them back.'

When they arrived at the house, grief bit into Isabel. For minutes at a time, she'd been able to forget he was dead, but here, his mark was everywhere. The mosaic floor tiles in the hall that he thought would remind Mum of Italy. The old 78 records that he refused to throw away stacked in the corner of the dining room. His slippers by the front door drew her eyes towards them. He always wore the backs down and she used to buy him new ones every Christmas. He'd almost been due a pair.

Their mother was having a rest when they arrived and Grace went up to see her. Isabel pushed open the door to the dining room.

'Hi, Sis.'

'George! You made me jump.' Her brother was sitting at the table, their father's sheet music spread out in front of him. 'When did you get here?' Isabel stood in the doorway, unsure what to do. She felt she should put her arms round

George. But it was years since she'd had that sort of relationship with him, and, anyway, his mouth had its usual smile and his dark eyes studied her with their familiar quizzical gleam. If he was distressed by their father's death, he wasn't going to show it.

'About an hour ago,' he said now. 'Just in time to exchange the odd word with my dear brother.'

'Where is Rick?'

'Gone to the funeral directors.'

'Why didn't he wait so we could all go?'

George shrugged. 'Eldest son and all that.'

'But there's so much to decide.' Isabel tidied the sheets of music into a pile.

'Steady on, Sis. I'm going through those.' George scattered the pages across the table again.

Isabel tried not to look at them. Her father always kept his music in chronological order—it was one of the things she'd enjoyed helping him with. *He played the piano with me as well, don't forget*—The words she wasn't able to speak bounced around her head. 'Rick can't decide it all himself,' she said. 'We'll have to choose hymns. And what about readings?'

'You know our Ricky. Got to be in control.'

'But he hasn't even been to see Mum and Dad since Easter.'

'Too busy with his dot com company, I guess. Anyway, as soon as I was here to keep an eye on Eva, he pushed off.'

Isabel couldn't remember when George had started calling their mother by her first name, but he was the only one who could get away with it. She looked at the glass of wine in his hand. It was typical of him to sit here drinking and let Rick take over. He might be charming—their mother thought the sun shone out of his backside—but he was so irresponsible.

'Do you want a drink?' George asked. 'You look as if you could do with one.'

'It's the middle of the afternoon.'

'Your point is?'

'It's too early to start drinking.' Isabel wasn't going to tell George that if she had a drink now, she'd never stop.

'I thought you might need one when you hear the news.'

'What's happened? Is it Mum?' Isabel turned to the door, ready to rush upstairs.

George laughed. 'Nothing like that. But Eduardo's on his way. He phoned just after I got here.'

'Oh God! He's all we need.'

Isabel went into the kitchen. As always the fridge was full and she decided to make a meal for later. It would give her something to do. She took an onion from the vegetable rack and with one of her mother's beautifully sharp knives peeled and sliced it. Tears pricked her eyes.

From the room next door, came the sound of the piano, as George picked out the notes of the Moonlight Sonata. It was one of their father's favourites and the music filled her head. She held a tea cloth to her face, forcing the thick towelling material against her lips. Why couldn't her fingers tempt sounds of such exquisite melancholy as George's?

She went back to the dining room and stood at his side as he played. By rights neither he nor their father should have been a pianist. He was the only one of the children to have inherited their father's short stubby fingers and they were always comparing hands, matching palm to palm, arguing whose fingers were longer.

George stopped playing and swung round. He looked surprised to find her beside him.

'Dad loved this piano,' he said, his fingers lingering on the lid. She put her hand on his shoulder and he reached up and grasped it.

Isabel thought he might talk, drop the usual banter, but at that moment Grace appeared in the doorway.

'That was lovely. Mum said it was as if Dad was down here.'

'Grace!' George stood up and kissed Grace on each cheek. 'How's my sister?' He leant back and studied her face. 'Beautiful as ever.'

Grace pulled away. 'Not now,' she said. 'Play for us again.'

George sat down at the piano and flexed his fingers. 'You shall have your wish.'

Three

Rick drained the last of his coffee and stood up. The heavy drapes at the hotel window made the room dark apart from the glare of the desk light. He reached for the tasselled cord and the drapes swished back. Early morning sunshine slanted across the roofs opposite. Below him, the tree-lined street was quiet, apart from a group of four women gathered on the pavement outside the hotel entrance. Rick stared down at them until a taxi appeared, and they climbed in and drove away. He turned back to his laptop.

He'd been up since six and had already been out for his morning run. He was freshly showered and dressed—white cotton shirt and blue chinos. He adjusted the photo of Deanna and the girls, which he kept propped in front of him when he worked, until the light fell on it from the best angle. He turned back the cuff of his sleeve so that it measured exactly an inch and a half and twisted the signet ring on his little finger until the stone was straight. Deanna had given him the ring when they got married. Before the operation she'd run with him in the mornings, but the chemotherapy was leaving her exhausted. He pulled up the spreadsheet on the laptop.

'Honey, whatever are you doing?'

Hunched over the computer, Rick hadn't heard Deanna getting up. She stood behind him, her arms around his neck. He breathed in the warm smell of sleep and a lingering trace of her perfume. Her silk wrap stroked his cheek.

It had been one of her birthday presents last year. He'd chosen it because it was flimsy and when she wore it, he caught glimpses of her tawny skin and beautiful breasts, her jutting hip bones drawing his eyes down to her dark triangle. But now instead of turning to bury his face in her breasts, as he used to, Rick kept his gaze fixed on the spreadsheet on the screen. Since the operation he hadn't been able to bring himself to look at her naked body. He knew Deanna needed him to show he still desired her and he would. In time, he would.

'Sorry, darling,' he said. 'I won't be long.'

'Come on, baby. You can't work today of all days.' Her warmth pressed against his back.

'I must have these figures ready for—'

'It's your dad's funeral.'

He avoided her eyes in the mirror. 'I can't help it,' he said, more sharply than he'd intended. 'Why don't you have a lovely long bath and then meet the girls for coffee? You can have another go at convincing Alicia that yob is a waste of space.'

'Honey, his name's Gary—'

'I don't give a stuff what he's called. He's a mechanic.'

'Rick, she's nineteen.'

'She should have more sense then.'

Deanna moved her hands to his shoulders. 'You're so tense.' Her thumbs moved in circles, pushing into the hard knot at the top of his spine. Rick allowed himself to give in to the pleasure. He arched his back, easing the pain across his shoulder blades. She ran her fingers over his face and up around his eyes. He caught the scent of apricots, smelt summer, long hot afternoons. Champagne. She'd always loved champagne. They used to take a bottle to bed and he would lick golden drops from her breasts.

'That's better.' Deanna's voice caressed him. 'Easy now, easy.'

'Mum!' There was a thump at the door connecting to the girls' suite and Alicia's voice came through the thin wooden panel.

'Shit!' Rick slammed his fist on the table and the laptop jumped. The figures on the screen vanished.

'In a second, baby,' Deanna called. 'Give me a second.'

'Where's my black jacket, Mum?' Alicia persisted. 'You did pack it?'

Deanna didn't answer. She ran her hands over his belly and her fingers hovered between his legs.

'She can wait,' she whispered into his ear. Her lips were moist against his neck. He twisted round and pulled her closer. Her thighs were trapped between his. Her breast hung above his forehead, rounded and full. His palm tingled, longing to hold its smooth weight. He stretched upward, his mouth opening …

'Mum! I can't find my black jacket!' Alicia's voice came again.

Rick jumped up. Deanna was knocked off balance and stumbled against the table. She clutched his arm, steadying herself.

'Just go, Deanna. Sort her out.' He heard the coldness in his voice and hated himself. For a second their eyes met.

Rick had always loved his wife's blue eyes. They were the first thing he'd noticed about her. They seemed to change colour with her mood. They could be dark as midnight, or bright like a peacock's feather. But now he shrank from their stare. Deanna ran her finger down his arm. Even through the material of his shirt, he shivered at her touch.

She turned away towards the door. 'I'll be right out, honey.' She looked back at him. 'I'll take that bath.'

He sat down at the computer and pressed the mouse. The spreadsheet filled the screen again. He reworked the figures, but they still wouldn't add up. The take-over of a smaller company in Durham had strained him financially more than he'd expected, and it meant redundancies. He glanced at his watch. Time was getting on.

He started drafting an email: *As you all know, the recession has hit the IT industry as well as…* He stopped. Most of the staff meant nothing to him, but Jim Foster had been with him for ten years. He thought back over them, remembering the hard work, long hours, the highs and lows —Jim beside him every step. What price loyalty?

The door opened and Deanna peered round. 'How are you doing? The girls and I are ready for lunch.'

He didn't look up. 'You'll have to give me another half an hour.'

'Rick, you said twelve.' She came into the room and from the corner of his eye he glimpsed the black suit and the red and orange scarf wrapped in a turban round her head.

'Don't pressurise me, Deanna. The service isn't until two.'

'But we're going to your mom's first.'

'I want to go straight to the church. Make sure everything's going to plan.'

'I thought we were all leaving from the house together.'

He fixed his eyes on the screen. 'You can't trust people to get things right.'

'Eva might need you.'

'I doubt it. Isabel and Grace are there and George will fuss over her as usual.'

'Rick, darling, look at me.' Deanna moved to his side and cupped his face in both her hands. He was forced to meet her gaze. 'Don't you think, now with your father gone, it's time to ditch this thing with George?'

He didn't answer.

Deanna's hands dropped to her sides. 'We'll wait for you in reception,' she said.

'Yes.' He knew she wanted him to say more, but he couldn't.

'You won't be late?'

The nerve in his left temple began to jump. He pressed his finger against it. 'Have you ever known me be late?'

'No.'

'I won't be late for my own father's funeral, then, will I?'

*

He waited until the sound of their voices disappeared down the corridor. Pouring a glass of water from the bottle on his desk, he searched in the front pocket of his brief case for his tablets. He thrust two tablets into his mouth and flung back his head. His throat closed and he started to gag. He caught the edge of the desk, knocking over the photo of Deanna and the girls. Cursing, he repositioned it in exactly the same spot. He forced the tablets down and turned back to the computer. *As you all know, the recession has hit the IT industry…* He carried on the email where he'd left off, but a few sentences in and his concentration wandered.

It didn't matter how many times he explained to Deanna what growing up in his family had been like, she didn't understand. She was an only child brought up in Texas by wealthy parents who adored her. How could she appreciate the bewilderment, the anger he'd felt when he was seven and his mamma suddenly wasn't there any more? His grandmother had come to look after him and Isabel, and he'd hated her. Hated her thin spiteful nose, her big teeth that shifted when she spoke. She used to pinch him when he didn't say please and thank you, and she dragged the rough flannel across his face, not caring if he got soap in his eyes. Once he'd kicked her and she'd locked him in his bedroom without any tea.

Rick had never been sure how long Mamma was away, but by the time she came back, he'd moved up a class at junior school, and he was in the football team. Not that anyone cared. 'You must play the piano,' his mother told him, 'like your father and grandfather.' For years he endured piano lessons, but while his feet worked to order on the football field, his fingers refused to follow the simplest instruction.

Even worse than the piano was the new baby. It was bad enough competing with Isabel and Grace, but this was another boy. 'Here's George,' they said, 'a little brother for you to play with.' But what use to him was a baby in a lace shawl? And then, when he was still barely able to talk, baby George started to play the piano.

After that it was always George this and George that: *George, play the piano for us* and *Giorgio, carissimo, that's wonderful.* It didn't matter how well Rick did in exams, how many teams he captained, he couldn't compete.

Perhaps he should be grateful. If he hadn't been so jealous of his brother, he wouldn't have gone to America, and then he wouldn't have met Deanna. He'd got a job with IBM when he left university. The technology boom was beginning, and Rick turned all his frustration into a passion for computers. He was asked to go to Florida to work on IBM's new personal computer and it was in New York, at the party to launch the PC, that he met Deanna.

She was a model and had been hired by the company to create the right ambience. Rick's only sexual experience had been a drunken fumble at the end of Finals, so he could hardly believe it when this beautiful girl showed an interest in him.

'You're cute,' she pronounced, as she caught up two glasses of champagne from the tray that wafted by them. 'I'm Deanna. What do they call you?'

'They call me Richard.'

'Gee, that's so stuffy, but I just adore your accent.'

He'd been careful not to drink too much, but now he knocked back the champagne in one go.

'How about you take me to dinner when we get out of here?' She ran a red-tipped finger along his forearm. 'But only if I can call you Rick.'

The wedding in Texas a year later was a lavish affair and Deanna's parents couldn't have treated him better if he'd been their son. They were heartbroken when he brought Deanna back to England, but he needed to show his own family how well he'd done. When they first came back, he'd worked for IBM in Manchester, then set up his own company in Newcastle. Although Deanna wasn't happy at first, she blossomed when babies arrived. As the girls got older and his business flourished, life was good, and last year they'd moved to a Victorian property, in the village of Rothbury. He was longing to show it off to his parents. That was what his last call home had been about.

His father had answered the phone as he usually did. Eva said her English wasn't good enough and she got flustered if she couldn't understand.

'Dad, what are you and Mum doing for Christmas?' he asked as soon as he heard his father's voice.

'We thought we'd go to see George. You know he's set up this art school near Penzance.'

'Deanna and I want you to come to us this year. No arguments.'

'I'm not sure.' His father's voice was slow and measured, as always.

'There's plenty of room in the new house,' Rick told him, 'and Deanna's made a wonderful job of the decorating. We got in Vaughan Carlton from New York. Did you read the article about him in the paper last week?'

'Your mother wants to see George. You know how she worries about him.'

'He's a grown man!' Rick could see Deanna shaking her head at him from the other side of the room. 'You haven't been to see us for ages and the girls would love you to come.' It suddenly occurred to Rick that if her grandparents were staying, Alicia couldn't expect that mechanic to be invited for Christmas, something she'd been angling for.

'Don't you think it would be too much for Deanna, what with her treatment?' Henry asked.

'Deanna wants you to come. She hasn't got her own parents, has she? And she needs family at a time like this.'

'There's Isabel to consider as well. Rose and Josh are going to Brian this year, so she'll be on her own.'

'For Christ's sake, Dad! Are you sure Grace doesn't want you to fly over to Italy?'

'Don't be like that, lad.'

Rick gripped the receiver tighter, as if he could silence the voice on the other end. 'How come…' His heart bumped erratically in his chest. 'How is it that you consider every other fucking member of the family but not your eldest son?'

The figures blurred in front of Rick on the computer screen, as he remembered Deanna dragging the phone from him. He covered his face with his hands and found they were wet.

How pathetic! He was crying, for God's sake. He dragged his sleeve across his eyes. Saving the spreadsheet, he shut down the laptop. Deanna had laid out a fresh white shirt and his black tie on the bed. His dark suit was hanging on the wardrobe door. He stripped off his clothes and threw them on a chair. He yanked his suit trousers from the hanger and thrust his arms into the white shirt. He would go and find his girls. The sooner he told Deanna what he'd decided, the better.

He was an intelligent capable man and it was ridiculous that he'd never learnt to play the piano. Ridiculous that he'd let George lord it over him because he could. Ridiculous that he'd spent so much time craving his father's attention, when all it would have taken was a few plinkety plonks on the piano.

As Rick knotted his tie and pulled on his jacket, he felt more at peace than he had for a long time. The technology market would see another surge, Deanna's illness would soon be behind them, Alicia would stop all this talk about moving in with Gary and he, Rick, would learn to play the Moonlight fucking Sonata.

Four

Grace carried the tray of drinks carefully. It was hot and stuffy in the crowded room and she was light-headed from the glass of wine she'd drunk as soon as they arrived back from the crematorium. The noise in the sitting room grew: 'Yes, he was, thank you'... 'a lovely man'... 'thank you'... 'so sad'... 'a wonderful family'... 'a blessing really'... 'your poor mother'. She accepted the condolences, managed a few comments of her own, but was desperate for it to be over.

The funeral had gone well considering her mother, barely visible beneath her black mantilla, had wept all through it. There was one awful moment when the silence the priest had called for 'to remember the man who meant different things to each of us' was punctured by a wail from Eva. She stumbled from her place in the front pew and flung her arms around the coffin, crying 'Forgive me, Henry, forgive me,' the words echoing round the church.

At first no one moved, and then a laugh came from the back of the congregation. The sound broke the spell, and George and Uncle Eduardo rushed forward and led her back to the pew. In the car on the way to the crematorium, all she would say was 'I'm sorry. Henry would be so cross. He hated a fuss.' Rick had phoned ahead and the doctor was waiting at the house when they returned. He'd given her a sedative, and now she was asleep.

Grace made another tour of the room, collecting empty glasses. As she reached the door, a man standing in the corner on his own touched her arm.

'You must be Grace.' His voice was soft, but Grace detected a slight northern accent, similar to her father's. He was a short man with curly hair and sad-looking eyes, the colour of faded denim. 'I'm Archie Stansfield. I was a friend of Henry's.'

‘I’m glad to meet you.’ Grace shook his hand. ‘Thank you for coming. My father would have been pleased.’ She had repeated the phrases so many times that it took her a moment to realise what the man was saying:

‘I don’t think he would.’

‘Sorry, I must have misunderstood… I thought you said you were a friend.’ Grace was tired. The day had been a strain. Franco should be with her.

‘I was a friend of Henry’s,’ the man said again. ‘We went to school together, but…’ He shrugged.

‘Archie Stansfield?’ Grace said.

He nodded. ‘That’s me.’

‘I’m sure I’d remember if my father had mentioned you.’

‘We fell out. We hadn’t spoken for years.’

Grace stared at the man, not knowing what to say. ‘My father was the kindest of men,’ she managed at last. ‘I can’t imagine him falling out with an old friend.’

‘We had a fight.’

‘A fight?’ Grace’s arms ached from the tray of glasses. ‘An argument, you mean?’

‘No, we punched and kicked each other.’ The old man’s eyes no longer looked soft and faded. The blue blazed like the fiercest of skies. ‘My sister had just died, and I was angry.’

Angry? The hubbub of voices in the room fell away, and all Grace could hear was that word *angry*… Everyone seemed angry. She was angry herself, Franco was, Isabel, Rick, while her mother had always erupted in angry outbursts. It was her father who’d been the peacemaker, and now here was this man making accusations…

‘I blamed him, you see.’

‘What are you talking about?’

‘My sister died and it was his fault.’

‘I don’t know who on earth you are.’ Grace stopped. Words were trapped in her mouth. Heat rose up through her chest. She filled her lungs with air. ‘But today is my father's funeral, and you come here, souring his memory…' She put her hand to her head. It felt all swimmy, as if she might faint.

The man took the tray from her grasp and set it down on the coffee table. He straightened up. 'I'm sorry. I shouldn't have said anything'

She glared at the man. Who was he? None of it made any sense. 'You said you were at school with my father?'

'That's right. But after the fight… well… I saw him in the distance, a few times. That would have been when his parents were alive and he came up to visit them. But we didn't speak.' The man gave a small smile. 'I did see you once when you were a baby. He brought you with him when he came to the house. He wanted to try and be friends again. But I couldn't. I was still too angry.'

Grace noticed that people were starting to leave. Over near the window, Isabel was talking to Uncle Eduardo. She caught Grace's glance and Grace saw the frantic signals in her eyes: *Help*! *Rescue me*! Never mind Eduardo—he was nothing compared with this horrible Stansfield toad.

'I used to get letters from him every so often. Needed forgiveness, I reckon. But after your George was born…'

Oh no, he was still going on. She had to get rid of him. 'You said you hadn't spoken to my father for years.'

'That's right. Nigh on forty, I'd say.'

'Then how did you know? Who told you? About the funeral, I mean.'

'Eva.'

'My mother?'

'She phoned me the day after he died.'

'My mother doesn't even know you.'

The old man shook his head. 'Your dad must have told her about me.'

'Please go. I don't want to hear any more. Not today, of all days.'

She saw Archie Stansfield reach into his pocket. What now? Some new piece of evidence incriminating her father?

He held out a white business card. 'I'm truly sorry to upset you. But I'm staying in London for a few days. I've got a room at The Queen's Hotel in Highbury.' He pushed the card towards her.

'That's the telephone number,' he said. 'I'd like to see you again. Explain.'

It was early evening when the last mourners left the house. Rick and his family went back to their hotel, and Isabel and Rose left soon after Brian appeared to collect Josh.

Grace went upstairs to check on Eva. Uncle Eduardo had wanted to sit with her, but Grace had eventually persuaded him it would be better to let her sleep. Grace tiptoed into the room and gazed down at her mother in the gentle light of the bedside lamp. She looked peaceful, but what secrets did that head hold? What did she know about Archie Stansfield? Her hair, which she had worn in a bun for the funeral, had worked loose and now lay in untidy straggles across the pillow. It was the first time Grace had known her go to bed without her hair neatly drawn into its thick plait.

Downstairs in the dining room, George was sitting at the table with a bottle of wine and two glasses.

'Thank goodness,' he said as Grace pushed open the door. 'I thought I might have to drink myself into oblivion on my own.'

Grace sat at the table opposite him and for a moment their eyes met. They both had the same chocolate-coloured eyes, olive skin, full lips. Their mother's face.

George raised his glass to the portrait of Henry that hung over the fireplace. Since he left school, George had only worked when his father refused to subsidise him, preferring to paint and travel. But last year, he'd set up an art school in Cornwall. None of the family thought it could work. George had never managed to sustain a relationship or a job for long, so how would he find the dedication needed to run a business? Henry had gone down to check on him.

He didn't say much when he came back except, 'It's a good set up he's got there. We've got to give the lad a chance.' And he'd produced the portrait George had done of him, insisting it hung in pride of place. It was a painting full of gaudy colour and awkward lines. When they sat at the table to eat, everyone said it made them feel uncomfortable, but as Grace stared up at the portrait now, it was her father's eyes which sought hers.

George followed her gaze. 'What do you think?'

'I like it.'

'You're not just saying that? You know what a sweetie you are.'

'Honestly. I was thinking that minute how like Dad it is.'

George poured them both another glass of wine. 'I'm going to miss the old man so much, you know. He's the only one who always believed in me.'

'How can you say that? Mum's besotted with you. Always has been.'

'I know… oh, don't get me wrong,' he said quickly as Grace started to protest. 'Mum's great, but it was Dad you could rely on to be there for you.' He moved across to the piano and opened the lid. 'It's the music I'll miss him for most of all,' he said. 'I loved it when we played together. In fact, Grace, my darling…' his fingers wandered up and down the keys '…I made a decision during the service in church today.'

'Did you?' Grace asked warily. 'What did you decide?'

George sat down on the piano stool. He stretched his arms and paused, his fingers poised over the keys: the thrilling opening notes of Beethoven's Fifth filled the room.

'Ssh,' Grace said. 'You'll wake Mum.'

George stopped playing as abruptly as he'd begun. 'I'm the only one who ever plays it, so I'm going to take Dad's piano down to Cornwall.'

Grace left George finishing the bottle and went to her room. She needed to speak to Franco. When they met, he'd been working at his parents' pizzeria, and she'd been teaching English in Naples. Franco was one of her students. When the course came to an end, he arrived one evening at the marble-floored palazzo she shared with other teachers, on the hill high above Naples. He stood in the courtyard below her window and called up to her. She leaned out and laughed when she saw him by the fountain, his arms stretched high above his head, an earthenware pot balanced precariously in his hands.

'I have the bolognese, Signorina,' he cried. 'Can you cook the spaghetti?'

A month later, he asked her to marry him.

Grace had planned to go to South America after Naples. But caught up in the excitement, and wanting to make her father happy—'How romantic! Like your mother and me, but in reverse!' Henry had said—she'd accepted Franco's proposal. After their marriage, her in-laws had bought them their own restaurant on an island off the Neapolitan coast. 'You're so lucky!' everyone told her.

Now she dialled the number of the *ristorante*. It would be midnight in Italy,. time for the staff to wind down. At this time of year only the regulars would still be there, chairs gathered round one of the tables, circles of smoke rising as they argued about last Saturday's football results. Franco liked to join them for a nightcap. She pictured the reception area where the phone would be ringing out. It rang and rang, but there was no answer.

She lay down on the narrow bed. She was sleeping in the bedroom at the back of the house that she'd shared with Isabel until Isabel got married. She'd missed her big sister at first, but soon began to enjoy the extra space. Her collection of teddy bears still filled the windowsill. An enlargement of her first communion photo stood on the bedside cabinet. She remembered being so excited about her white dress and new patent shoes. Her parents stood on each side of her in the photo. Her mother wore a smart red suit, scarlet pointed shoes, a lace mantilla covering her dark hair. She was always far more glamorous than the other mothers. Her father was dressed in his blue blazer with its silver buttons. Grace only came up to his waist in those days and she used to stand on tiptoe to peer into the buttons, making faces at her distorted reflection.

Grace thought back to the night her father died. She and Franco had argued earlier on that day.

'Let's have a baby,' he'd said.

'Not that again.' Grace had been irritable. 'Look, I want to go through these new menus with you.'

'Why do you always change the subject?'

'Because I'm not ready to have a baby.'

'But we've been married for three years.'

'That's nothing. Is it so wrong to want you to myself for a bit longer?'

She shut the door of the office. She wound her arms round his neck. The last stragglers from lunch had left the restaurant and the street outside was quiet as the afternoon heat settled over it. 'Why don't we go upstairs?' she said. She pushed her body against his. She felt him grow hard and she smiled. 'See.' She moved her hand to caress him. 'You know you want to.'

Franco's brown eyes swivelled away from hers. 'Mamma's started to ask questions.'

Grace laughed. 'What's it got to do with her?'

'You don't understand.' Franco clasped her wrists, pulling her arms from behind his neck.

'Have you been discussing me with your mother?'

'You're not getting any younger.'

'Franco, what's going on?' Grace took his hands but he shrugged her off.

'The older you get, the more likely complications are.'

Grace had never noticed before how his chin jutted in the air when he didn't get his own way. 'I suppose Mamma told you that?' She couldn't keep the sneer out of her voice. Then she saw Franco's face. 'I didn't mean it,' she said quickly. 'It came out the wrong way.'

She reached for his hands again, but he pushed her away. She stumbled against the computer. The corner of the screen jabbed her in the small of her back. She closed her eyes against the pain.

The phone rang, the sound jerking her eyes open. As she picked up the receiver, Franco slammed out of the door. '*Pronto*.' Her back throbbed.

'Grace, I thought you'd never answer.'

'Isabel?' Her sister hardly ever phoned—why now when she wanted to chase after Franco?

'It's Dad. He's in hospital.'

'What? When? What's wrong?'

'We've only just got here, but they think it's a heart attack.'

'I'm on my way.

Grace rushed to tell Franco. If they could get cover, he'd be able to come to England with her. Forget about the quarrel for now. But by the time she arrived in the restaurant, the revving of Franco's car engine had shattered the silence of the street outside. He'd gone.

Alfonso, the waiter, was standing on the pavement staring after Franco. He must have heard their raised voices. She kept her tone business-like. 'How many are in tonight?' If it was quiet, the staff could cope on their own. She glanced at her watch. She might still make the eight o'clock flight.

'A big party from one of the hotels booked in this afternoon. We're full, Signora.'

Five

Rick parked the car at the end of the road and walked the remaining distance to his parents' house. If he could keep his visit secret, so much the better. He got to the gate and reached out to push it. The wood was smooth under his palm, with a slight hollow worn by countless hands.

In an instant, he was back. School blazer hanging from one shoulder, cap stuffed in his bag, homework weighing down his steps. In his pocket lay the golden message—centre half in Saturday's game. The sports master posted the names for the match in envelopes on the notice board. One of the highlights of the week was crowding round the board on Thursdays, pushing and shoving to the front to find that little piece of magic pinned to the board. 'You're in, you jammy sod!' For a second, he felt the sputter of joy, all over again. Then he opened the gate.

A glimmer of light shone through a gap in the curtains from the right hand window. Damn. Someone was still up. No doubt George was knocking back Dad's whisky. Chances were Isabel would be there as well. She thought the sky would fall if she left their mother's side. Grace was the only one of his siblings he could stomach. At least she'd made something of herself, getting away from home, running that business in Italy. Not that Italy appealed to him. Christ, he'd had it up to here with Italy. When Mum and Eduardo got together, the yap, yap, yap was interminable.

He leant back and studied the upstairs windows. They were all in darkness, apart from a glint right at the top of the house—the attic that had been converted for George, because he was too important to have a bedroom on the same floor as the rest of them. What was it his mother used to say? 'Closer to the angels, *mio tesoro*.' Rick used to fantasise about cutting down the funny little ladder that you had to climb to get up to the attic and leaving 'mio tesoro' to starve up there. Not that it would have made any difference. His father would have sawn the house in half to rescue George.

He reached under the mat for the key and fitted it in the lock. Slipping into the hall, he eased the front door shut and leaned back against it. Listening. The odd bump and clink of central heating pipes cooling down, but otherwise, nothing. He thought he heard the distant sound of a sneeze, but then, nothing. Gradually his eyes adjusted to the darkness, lit only by the glow filtering through the fanlight from the street. He moved towards the dining room and put his ear to it. Nothing. The light shining through the curtain on to the front garden must have been a false clue. The idiots had gone to bed and left it on. Okay for them—they weren't paying the electricity bill. He presumed his father had left his affairs in order—he'd spent long enough hunched over his accounts—but if not, Rick knew precisely who'd be expected to foot the bill. And it wouldn't have Georgie boy's name on it.

He turned the knob of the dining room door and pushed. No one there. Despite the silence, he hadn't been able to dispel the fear that the entire family would be inside, waiting to shout 'Surprise!' Or something equally moronic. His eyes took in the table, the empty wine bottle, the two glasses, one still half-full. That wouldn't be George's for sure. He picked the glass up and drank the remains of the wine in one go. Ugh. It was warm and slightly sweet. He thought at least the old man had better taste than that.

His gaze shifted to the painting hanging over the fireplace. He'd never seen anything so ridiculous, but to hear his parents cooing over it, you'd have thought it was Picasso or Gauguin at the very least. Georgie boy might be able to play the piano, but he sure as hell couldn't paint.

Rick turned away, but as he did so, the back of his hand caught on the corner of the piano. Damn, that hurt. He cradled his knuckles in the palm of the other hand. They felt bruised, as if he'd aimed a punch at someone. It seemed out of all proportion to the glancing blow. He leant against the piano waiting for the pain to subside.

The wood of the piano was a mellow honey colour with an exquisite texture and even grain. It was a handsome piece of furniture and it would look perfect between the big bay windows in his drawing room. The lid of the piano was raised. No doubt George had been demonstrating his virtuosity yet again. Rick reached out and lowered it. It landed with a satisfying thud.

The lounge was opposite the dining room. Rick took a pace and fastened his hand round the doorknob. As he twisted it, pain pricked his knuckles. The door slid a couple of metres ajar and he squeezed through. His mother was in the room above and his plan would be scuppered if she woke up. The darkness in the room was thick and dense—it filled his nose and throat. He breathed deeply, screwing up his face at the aroma of stale alcohol.

He bent forward to feel for the lamp on the coffee table and blinked as the light hit his eyes. He glanced round. The chairs had been straightened and the cushions plumped up—all sign erased of the people who had crowded into the small space for the wake. Rick hadn't recognised half of them. People of all ages and types. Who would have thought there were so many who wanted to mourn the old bastard?

He moved across to the bureau set in the alcove to the left of the fireplace. This was what he'd come for. It was his father's, and from when they were children, they'd been forbidden to touch it. A small, brass key stood in the lock and Rick had often put his fingers to the key, imagining what it would be like to turn it, to open the lid and… And what? What the hell he was expecting to find in there, he didn't know. Papers, documents—he'd watched his father sorting through them often enough—but what about other things? Those things he'd needed to be alone for—when he'd say, 'Run off and play, there's a good lad,' and Rick would have to leave the room while his father presided over the bureau like Midas over his gold. There must be secrets in there.

Rick began with the drawers. They weren't locked, so it would be routine stuff. He searched through the piles of letters, cards, packets of photos, bills, his father's account books, each with the relevant year blocked on the front. He hesitated over the letters with his grandmother's elaborate writing on the envelopes. Perhaps they held some clue. Stupid idea. Why would his father confide in that bitch? At the back of the bottom drawer, he found an old black and white photo. Interesting that it wasn't in a packet like the others. He studied it: a woman and two men, all arm in arm. He turned the photo over. Across the top were the names, Henry, Dottie, Archie, with a date 23rd August 1948, and underneath the words: *For Henry, In memory of a wonderful day, All my love, Dottie.* He threw the photo back into the drawer and began piling everything carefully into its place. If anything, the drawers were tidier than before—no one would guess they'd had the once over.

He touched the key, his entry to the secret top section of the bureau. His mouth was dry and he had to keep swallowing. The little key turned smoothly. He drew the lid down, rubbing his hand over the leather inside. It wasn't tidy like the drawers, but a jumble of papers, strewn haphazardly, like a scene in a television drama after a burglary. Rick felt himself smiling—this was it, he was sure. Somewhere in here was the answer he wanted.

He began to search the papers one by one, piling them on the floor when he'd finished. Every so often he put his hands to his waist and stretched: Christ, this was a backbreaking chore. He checked his watch: 3 a.m. It was taking too long. He needed to be out of here. Returning to the papers, he almost ripped one in his hurry. The trouble was he didn't know what he was looking for. Some pages were full of lines of poetry, all in his father's copperplate writing. But were they his own work, or lines he'd copied from some book? Rick scanned a few, but they were all about hills and trees, and rivers and birds… and music—there was no escape from the damned music. Crescendo… lento… forte… pianissimo… Looked as if his father could only see life in terms of music. Rick remembered once asking him to explain what the terms meant. It still made him laugh when he thought of 'rococo'—excessive, ornamental, trivial—summed George up exactly.

Another few minutes and he'd found it. He punched the air and waved the envelope above his head, as if he'd won a six-figure deal. He ran his finger over George's name on the front of the envelope. It had to be what he was looking for. The envelope was sealed, but Rick could imagine the words his father would have used: *You're bound to be upset, lad… you love that piano… as my eldest son, Rick deserves… I admire Rick enormously… his talents…* Oh yes, Rick could see it clearly. In fact, thinking about it, wasn't it better that the letter was for George, that his father had intended George to see how much he'd loved his first son?

Rick bundled the remaining papers back into the bureau. He didn't care any more if they looked as if they'd been disturbed. He closed the lid and turned the key, the letter still clutched in his hand. He hesitated, his eyes on George's name, but then turned it over and ripped the envelope open. *My dear George, As you know, you and I have shared the closest friendship possible between father and son…* The opening words made Rick blink. His father had been famously undemonstrative, rarely giving hugs or kisses, even when they were growing up. Occasionally he'd called their mother *sweetheart.* So, it hurt to read the affectionate address to George, but it made sense to sugar the pill he was about to administer.

Rick skimmed the rest of the page: *bond... music... piano... bond... piano... music...* Christ, how much more of this crap was there going to be? Cut to the chase, Dad. He turned the sheet of paper over—only half a side to go. His eyes moved to the last paragraph: *And so, lad, I want you to know that when I go, the piano is yours. It's possible Rick will claim it, but he's never played it, nor wanted to, so it's my wish that you should have it. Much love, Dad*

Rick tightened his fist round the sheet of paper. The bastard. He felt the paper crinkle and collapse in his grasp. His nails dug into the flesh of his palm. The fucking bastard. He closed his eyes against the rage that churned the air around him. But the blackness was worse.

He dragged his sweatshirt away from his throat. It was choking him. Water. He had to get water. Stuffing the letter into the pocket in his joggers he reached for the doorknob. He made it to the kitchen before the nausea hit him. He flicked the light switch and staggered to the sink. The vomit catapulted into the bowl. His throat felt raw, and he hung over the draining board, hot and shaking. He ran the cold tap and scooped up water to his face, before swilling the sink clear of vomit. Straightening up, he rubbed his hand over his damp face. He was tired. His bones felt as if they might melt. He had to get back to the hotel before Deanna woke and wondered where he was.

He swung round, ready to leave, when the clock caught his eye. That fucking station clock. His father's pride and joy. The nightly ritual of the winding. No one else allowed to lay a finger on it. Christ, the man was a tyrant. He reached up and wrenched the clock from the wall. It was heavier than he'd expected, but he put both hands to it and raised it in the air. One, two, three... when he reached ten, he hurled it across the room. It smashed against the wall opposite and bounced off.

Rick stared at the shattered pieces: springs, coils and shards of glass littered the floor. What had he done? What the fuck had he done? His mother would never forgive him. Above his head, he heard the creak of floorboards, footsteps. He had to get out. If he made a quick escape, no one need see him. There was no reason for anyone to know he'd even been here. He looked back at the clock face, upturned on the floor. Would you believe it? Five to four. He had to stop himself laughing out loud. Both clock and old man had well and truly had it and both at five to four. He turned off the kitchen light and made a dive for the front door. He could hear voices on the landing. They were coming to check. He was out of here.

Six

Two days after the funeral, the temperature plunged overnight. When Isabel got up, frost sparkled on the grass in early morning sunshine, but the sky was an unbroken blue.

She rushed round the kitchen tidying up. She tucked the cornflakes packet in the cupboard and swept crumbs from the table into her palm. They would be here soon and she still had to change. She hadn't been going to bother. Since Brian left she'd got used to slopping around in old jeans and a baggy sweater, but Rose's comment the other day: 'Those jeans make you look fat, Mum' had stung.

Samson was asleep on the bed. That was something Isabel would never have allowed in the old days. She'd always been so particular. 'Neurotically tidy,' Brian said. Some of their worst rows had been about his slovenliness. But now a pile of clothes cluttered the chair, and books and magazines were stacked next to the bed. She pulled on a pair of black trousers and studied herself in the mirror. They were tight, especially at the back, but if she wore a white shirt and her new purple jacket, she should get away with it.

When Grace got out of the taxi looking elegant in a dark green trouser suit and cream polo neck, Isabel was glad she'd made the effort. At the same moment Brian's car pulled up at the gate and he and Josh came up the path. Brian and Grace each aimed a polite kiss at the cheek of the other.

'How are you, Brian?'

He shrugged. 'Still grafting away. Sorry about your dad.'

Grace inclined her head, her dark hair falling forward across her cheek.

'I had a lot of time for Henry. He was a good man.'

Grace caught Isabel's eye. 'We thought so.'

Brian looked past Grace at what was clearly empty space. 'Franco not with you then?'

'He couldn't leave the restaurant.'

'I thought you'd have staff.' Brian winked at Isabel.

A shadow passed over Grace's face. 'Did *you* actually put in an appearance, Brian?'

He looked down at his feet. 'Bit of emergency at the last minute. Washing machine flood.'

'Oh, right. Obviously more important.'

Isabel stared at Grace. How did she do it? Two minutes in Brian's company and she'd got the better of him.

Grace moved forward, almost pushing Brian to one side as she swept Josh up in a hug. 'How's my favourite nephew?'

Isabel winced. Since he'd gone to live with Brian and Anita, Josh had rejected any show of affection. When she went to give him a goodbye kiss, he always managed to avert his face so that she was left kissing air. But now he was smiling, enjoying the hug.

'I'm your only nephew,' he protested and Grace laughed.

'Come and see what I've got for you,' she said, taking him by the hand.

'Have a good time, mate,' Brian called after him, and Josh turned and gave his father the thumbs-up sign.

Isabel was left in the narrow hallway with Brian. He was wearing the checked woollen shirt and brown corduroys she had once put out for jumble. His hair was curling over his collar. She'd always had to remind him to get a haircut.

'That coffee smells good,' he said. She didn't reply. She certainly wasn't going to invite him to stay if that was what he was hinting at. He was a big man and seemed to fill the hall. He leaned towards her. Their faces were so close; she could feel his breath on her cheek. It smelt sour as it used to when he wasn't well.

'You look tired, Bel,' he said.

Isabel's heart lurched at the nickname. She shrugged. 'I haven't been sleeping very well.'

'I can't seem to sleep either. I was watching a film at three o'clock this morning.'

'I expect you've a lot of disturbed nights with a baby in the house.'

Brian looked at her sharply, but she made sure her face gave nothing away.

'Where's Rose?' he asked.

'She's gone out.'

'Avoiding me, I suppose.'

'No, Brian, she's gone to school. I doubt you feature in her plans.' She'd had enough of this conversation and wanted to get back to Grace and Josh. The three of them were going for a trip on the London Eye, and Josh was having the day off specially. Isabel didn't want to miss a second with him.

'I was hoping Rose would come for tea one evening.'

'I've told you—she doesn't want to see you.'

'I want her to meet Anita and the little'un.'

'Well, she obviously doesn't want to meet them.'

'You could persuade her.'

'Like you do for me with Josh?'

'He's here today, isn't he?'

'Only because Grace invited him. Nothing to do with you.'

'He came to your dad's funeral.'

'For God's sake Brian, Henry was his grandfather.'

'I try,' he protested. 'He's going through a bad phase.'

'And whose fault is that?'

His face puckered up in a scowl. 'Don't start, Bel.'

He moved towards the front door, but then turned back. His eyes were fixed on her. 'Will Rose be out tonight?'

'Why?'

'You know why.' His frown vanished. 'I could get away about nine.'

Isabel managed to meet his gaze. She felt her nipples pushing against the flimsy material of her white shirt. 'Now's not the time,' she muttered.

'When?'

'Brian, leave it. Pick Josh up at six. I'm spending the evening with Grace.'

He gripped her upper arm, his fingers digging into the flesh through her shirt. 'Don't be like that, Bel. I'll pick Josh up and be back here by nine.'

Her eyes darted towards the kitchen where Grace and Josh's voices rose and fell. 'I told you last time it wasn't going to happen again.'

'Come on. You know you want to.' His voice had that teasing note she'd never been able to resist. She pulled her arm free of his clasp.

'Make it nine-thirty,' she said.

In the kitchen Grace had set out the small white coffee cups and the cafetière. Josh was sitting in the rocking chair, his fingers flashing across the Nintendo Grace had given him. A smell of coffee mingled with the sweetness of the croissants that curled against each other in a basket on the table. Grace had brought some dahlias and their red was a splash of colour on the windowsill. The kitchen was homely and welcoming and Isabel felt a pang. There was no sense of home in her new life.

She crossed to Josh and stood by the chair. His hair was different. It had been cut really short apart from a tuft sticking up in front like a cockscomb. Isabel put her hand on her son's head. It was thick with gel. He pulled away. 'Get off.'

'Your hair's different,' she said.

'So?'

'So nothing, Josh. I was just saying. Are you sure you're all right?'

'Yeah. Why wouldn't I be?'

'I thought you might be upset about Granddad.'

Josh didn't reply. His fingers moved faster than ever across the keys of the game.

Isabel crossed to the fridge. 'I'll get you some juice.'

'Can I have tea?'

'You don't like tea.'

'Yes, I do.'

'But…' Isabel saw Grace raise her eyebrows and bit back any protest. She boiled the kettle and dropped a tea bag into the cup. 'Do you take sugar?'

'Two, please.' Josh blew on the surface of the tea. It used to irritate her when Brian did that.

'How's Anita and the baby?' she asked.

'Okay.'

'I expect the baby's smiling by now.'

Josh's gaze remained fixed on his game.

'Don't shut me out, Josh.' Isabel cursed herself for the wheedling note in her voice. 'I want to make sure everything's all right.'

Josh stood up and the rocking chair banged against the kitchen unit. 'I'm going to watch telly for a bit,' he said.

Grace covered Isabel's hand with hers. 'Give him time, Bel. He'll come round.'

'Why is he so angry with me? It wasn't me who broke up the family.'

'He can't blame Brian. He needs his dad.'

Isabel sipped her coffee. It was bitter. 'But it was always me he came to when he was upset.'

'He will again. I remember Mum and Rick having terrible rows.'

'They're not exactly bosom pals now.'

'He paid for Mum and Dad's holidays in Italy.'

'With all his money that's the least he can do.'

Isabel felt her sister's eyes on her. Grace didn't say anything, but Isabel could sense the reproach. She knew she sounded hostile, but it was all right for Grace shut away on her romantic island. Isabel had been the one of the four of them to look after their parents in recent years. She hadn't minded—she'd enjoyed being needed—but that was before…

'Grace,' she began in a rush, 'the morning after Dad died…' She waited hoping Grace would say something, but instead Grace stood up and moved to the window, and Isabel was left staring at her back. It made it difficult to go on, but their mother's revelation was eating at her. She'd burst if she had to keep it secret much longer. 'When we got back from the hospital, I sat with Mum while she went off to sleep… she said something really strange…'

Isabel hesitated. Grace would surely quiz her now. But, no, nothing. Isabel wanted to shake her—*say something, for God's sake … anything*—'

'I miss England at this time of year.' Grace was staring out of the window. 'Look at that Virginia creeper on the fence.' She pointed to the other side of the garden. 'You said the flat was poky, but you've got a lovely view.'

'Did you hear me?' Isabel asked. 'After Dad died—'

Grace's head whipped round. 'I don't want to talk about that time, Bel!'

Isabel put her hand to her cheek—she felt as if she'd been slapped. What was going on? She'd always got on well with Grace. Cool and beautiful, that's how she'd thought of her sister. 'What's wrong, Grace?'

Grace swung round from the window. 'Why? Why should there be anything wrong?'

Isabel shrugged, uncertain now that Grace's eyes had fixed on her in a fierce stare.

'You seem on edge.'

'Do you think Brian is happy?' Grace asked.

'Why?' Isabel felt the blush across her cheeks. 'Don't you think he is?'

'He seemed kind of sad.'

Isabel moved round the kitchen, collecting coffee cups and putting the biscuits away. If Grace could avoid the subject, then so could she.

That night, Isabel's sleep was fitful. She watched the minutes come and go: 3 a.m. 3.30, 4. The bed grew hot and uncomfortable as she twisted from side to side. The day out —laughing with Josh on the London Eye, feeling his hand in hers as she pointed out Buckingham Palace, Big Ben, Hampstead Heath where they used to fly the kite—had been wonderful. It made the moment Brian came to collect him even worse.

The night wore on. The digits on the clock changed from 05.29 to 05.30.

She could still get a few hours' sleep—Rose was staying with a friend overnight and would go straight to school from there. But her eyes refused to close. Instead they searched the shadowy room for familiar shapes, the outline of the wardrobe, the curve of the mirror. She pushed Josh and thoughts of her father from her mind, but then her mother's secret appeared, like earth falling into a newly-dug hole.

She had tried to broach the subject several times, but her mother seemed determined to avoid her. One morning, Isabel had arrived at the house early. Grace and George weren't up yet, so Isabel took Eva her cup of coffee.

'Mum, you know what you told me after Dad died.'

Eva was sitting on the stool in front of the dressing table unplaiting her hair. She didn't look round.

'You might feel comfortable with a secret like that, but I feel as if I've got *liar* branded on my forehead.'

'Forget about it, Isabel. There's a good girl.'

'I can't. You shouldn't have told me if you didn't want me to know.'

'You made me tell you.'

'I did no such thing!'

Eva picked up the cup and drank the coffee in one go. 'I thought I could trust you,' she said, her voice cold. 'My darling Henry was gone. I didn't know what I was saying.'

Isabel had stood behind her mother, looking into the mirror. Eva's reflection, closed and hard, had stared back at her.

Seven

Grace leant back in her chair and took in the room. The chandelier above their table highlighted the patterns on the damask tablecloth. Floral curtains framed the windows with elaborate drapes and frills. The dining room might have been in a stately home rather than the exclusive hotel in West Hampstead, where Rick and his family were staying. 'Bragging again,' Isabel had said when she heard he'd invited them all for dinner, but Grace thought it was generous of Rick. And at least tonight they had avoided any rows.

She gazed round the circular table at her family. Her mother had been unusually silent. Normally she loved these occasions. The silver bangles she wore on each arm would dance and jangle as her hands took over when her English faltered. But this evening, without Henry at her side, she disappeared. She had insisted her sons sit next to her: Rick on her right, smart in his dark suit, George on the other side, a jumper flung around his shoulders. Isabel was next to George. She was less edgy than the day before, at the London Eye with Josh. She had made an effort and looked almost her old self in a long black velvet skirt and matching jacket.

But they were all eclipsed by Deanna, Rick's wife. Grace remembered their wedding and how gorgeous Deanna had looked. In their three-quarter length off-white tulle dresses, she and Isabel were positively plain in comparison. And the years hadn't dented her beauty and glamour. Grace would never have dared to wear the multi-coloured turban that was wound in an elaborate twist. But on Deanna it worked. Even more beautiful than their mother were 'the three princesses' as Rick called them, Alicia, Flavia and Camilla. Nineteen, eighteen and fourteen, each was more glorious and golden than the last, with their endless legs and long blonde hair.

Alicia and Flavia had gone to the cloakroom some minutes before and now Grace followed them. As she pushed open the heavy oak door, she knew something was wrong. Flavia was leaning over the marble surround of the washbasin, her head cradled in her arms. She jerked round when she heard Grace come in. Her skin had an unnatural pallor and her blue eyes glittered.

'Where's Alicia?' Grace asked. The reply was a series of loud sniffs from one of the cubicles. The loo flushed and Alicia emerged, even more ghost-like than her sister, apart from the two spots of colour raging on her cheeks.

'What's going on?' Grace heard the hollowness of her question.

'Come on, Auntie Grace.' Alicia crossed to the basin and turned both taps on full. Water gushed out, splattering Grace's skirt. 'Surely you're not such an innocent.' Alicia met Grace's eyes in the mirror. Flavia hovered behind her sister.

'No, but you obviously are, letting yourself get involved in drugs. And dragging Flavia into it as well.'

Alicia had finished washing her hands and began drying them on one of the thick white towels. She lifted the lid of the wicker basket in the corner and flicked the towel in. It was clear she wasn't going to beg forgiveness.

Grace turned to Flavia. 'What would your parents say?'

Flavia's huge eyes filled with tears. She reached out for Grace's hand. Grace felt the clamminess of her skin and could see sweat moistening her top lip.

'You won't tell them, will you?' Flavia implored. 'Especially not with Mom so sick. Dad would kill me.'

Alicia was at the door, holding it open. She had smoothed her hair and touched up her make up. Only a close observer would notice the change in her eyes as they flitted around the room. 'You can stay for the lecture, Vee, I'm off.'

'Not so fast, young lady.' Grace made her voice as stern as she could. It looked as if Alicia was going to ignore her, but at last she let go of the door. She stood in front of Grace, her arms folded. 'Well?'

'I've got a fair idea what's been going on here…' Grace paused. 'And I notice neither of you denied it when I mentioned drugs.'

'We're sorry, Auntie Grace…' Flavia's voice trailed off at a glare from Alicia. 'We didn't mean…'

'Shut up, Vee. I told you—'

'Never mind what you told Flavia. I'm telling you both that if I ever get a hint of anything like this again, I'll go straight to your parents.' Grace looked from Alicia to Flavia. 'Do you understand?'

'Yeah, yeah, we hear you. We've been naughty girls and it won't happen again.' Alicia turned away and the door shut behind her with a dull thud. Flavia, with a last 'Thanks for not telling,' followed.

Isabel volunteered to drive Eva home and Grace travelled with George. As she settled herself in the front seat of the car, she debated telling him what she'd seen in the cloakroom. As the two youngest, she and George had always been close and they were the only ones, apart from Eva, who spoke Italian fluently. But George led a rakish kind of life. He probably dabbled himself and would only laugh at her fears.

George eased the car away from the traffic lights. 'That was some outfit Deanna was wearing!' he exclaimed. 'I kept looking at the head-gear. Couldn't see how it worked. I suppose she didn't have time for her usual highlights and couldn't bear us to find out she's gone grey.' He laughed. 'There's a thought.'

'I expect she's losing her hair. The chemotherapy does that,' Grace said.

'What the hell are you talking about?'

'You mean you don't know?'

'For Christ's sake, know what?'

'Deanna has breast cancer. She's had a mastectomy.'

George let out a long low whistle. He banged his hand on the steering wheel. 'Why the fuck didn't anyone tell me?'

'I presumed Rick had told people.'

George snorted. 'He wouldn't let me know there was anything wrong with the perfect family, would he?'

The next morning Grace was awake early. She let her eyes adjust to the shadowy light beginning to slip below the curtains. It was a surprise to find herself in her old bedroom and not in the room she shared with Franco on Ischia. Franco. Why hadn't he phoned? She'd called the *ristorante*, but he was always somewhere else: 'He's gone to the market, *signora*,' Maria told her. 'He's driven into Ischia Porto,' Alfonso said. 'He's just left for Napoli.' All perfectly reasonable excuses. All places she would have expected him to go. She'd left him messages. It was starting to be embarrassing—she heard the hesitation in the voices of the staff when they knew it was her. They didn't want to have to say yet again that he wasn't there. In the end, she'd sent him a text about her father. But he still hadn't phoned back.

She turned on the bedside light and picked up the small photo of Franco she carried with her. She lay back on the pillow and studied the face she'd fallen in love with. Had it been love? The sex had certainly been crazy at first. That night—*bolognese night*, she called it—she couldn't resist his bronzed skin, his dark eyes locked on hers, his hardness as he slipped inside her. It was like a never-ending erotic dream those first few months. It was only when a baby didn't appear that he started to sulk.

But now, she was the aggrieved one. He'd walked out on her when she most needed him, and it was because of him she hadn't been there when her father died. He was to blame, and he hadn't even phoned.

She switched on her mobile and thought about her remaining time in England. Only today and tomorrow to go. Her family were driving her mad: Rick and George sniping at each other all the time, her mother playing the grief-stricken widow to perfection and Isabel whinging about Brian. She loved her sister, but she lived in some fantasy world—Brian was a boorish idiot and she was better off without him.

It made Grace's life in Italy seem idyllic. In Ischia she had places to escape to. However busy she was, there were moments when she could sit by the sea, wander the *castello*, drink sweet, strong coffee and think. That was what she wanted. She craved time and space to think about her dad. She was never going to see him again, and she had to adjust.

Her mobile bleeped. A voicemail from Franco must have arrived while she was asleep. At last. Whatever he had to say had better be good. She clicked to hear it and Franco's warm voice filled her ear: *carissima, I miss you so much. I am sorry about your papa. Come home soon, so I can kiss you better.* A pause. Then *Is busy in ristorante.* Grace kept the phone to her ear. Was that it? No apology. No explanation.

She swung her legs round and sat up. She checked her watch on the bedside cabinet: ten past eight. She supposed she'd have to go and see her mother.

Grace caught the bus to Highbury Corner. When she was at school, one of her friends used to live in Highbury, but it was a long time since she'd been there, especially on the bus. She gazed out of the window at the places that formed the fabric of her youth. The bus approached Hornsey Lane Bridge, and as they passed underneath, she remembered the man she'd seen jump. She was about fifteen and on her way home from a hockey match, when the school bus slammed into an emergency stop. Grace had pressed her face against the cold glass of the window. While sirens screamed, and ambulance men and police swirled round him, the man's body had lain, limbs broken like matchsticks. When her mother heard what had happened she became hysterical. *He could have killed you. You could be dead.* The words had resounded in Grace's head until it was as if the man's purpose had been to aim for a bus of teenage schoolgirls. It had been Isabel who'd held her hand across the narrow gap between their beds and talked to her, until she fell asleep that night.

The bus pulled up just before the Archway. Her first boyfriend had lived round the corner. She used to get off the bus here, heart racing at the thought of kisses and wandering hands—it was getting harder to say no. He'd sent her a message recently, wanting to be friends on Facebook, but she'd deleted the request immediately.

They drove down the hill towards Holloway. Grace had been terrified of the prison when she was a child. Prisons in storybooks meant dungeons and torture and violent men with matted hair. She imagined an escape and a prisoner on the run climbing through the window into her bedroom. It didn't matter that she'd been told it was a prison for 'naughty ladies'. *Her* prisoner was always a giant like the one in Jack and the Beanstalk.

Grace got off the bus at Highbury Corner. She fished in her bag for the directions to the hotel she'd got from the website. The Queen's was a ten-minute walk.

Archie Stansfield was waiting in the lounge. He held out his hand. 'Grace, it's good to see you.' There it was again—the soft burr that reminded her of her father's voice. 'I didn't expect to… you know… after the funeral.'

Grace hesitated and then shook his hand. The skin felt dry and papery. 'No,' she said, 'I'm surprised myself that I'm here.'

'I'll get them to bring us some tea… or coffee, perhaps?'

'Tea will be fine.'

He shuffled off to the reception desk, and Grace sat down in one of the leather armchairs in the big bay window, overlooking the hotel garden. A huge cedar tree, menacing against the metallic sky, dominated the view from the window.

Phoning The Queen's this morning and arranging to meet Archie Stansfield had been an impulse. She'd helped her mother have a bath, and Eva was being particularly complaining and difficult: 'Henry always got the temperature of the water exactly right'… 'Henry always warmed the towel'… 'Henry liked to scrub my back'… Grace had held back her words—*Henry was nothing short of a saint*!

Then Uncle Eduardo had arrived to take Eva out for lunch. He cornered Grace in the kitchen to tell her—for the millionth time—that she was *la piu bella del mondo.* Just like her mamma. When Rick turned up to check on the final details for scattering the ashes tomorrow, sending Eva into extravagant sobs, Grace had escaped to her room. Seeing the card for the Queen's Hotel on her bedside cabinet had prodded her nagging feelings about Archie Stansfield. She didn't believe what he'd told her at the funeral for one minute, but there must have been something, or why—

'Sorry about the delay. The tea's on its way.' Archie Stansfield sat down opposite Grace.

She was struck as before by his sad blue eyes. They watered constantly and he dabbed at them with a handkerchief. His face was cracked with wrinkles. He looked so old, yet he must be the same age as her father.

Had he looked as old as this? If he had, Grace hadn't noticed.

When the tea arrived, Archie Stansfield motioned to Grace to serve.

She handed him a cup. 'I'm sorry if I was rude to you at the funeral, Mr Stansfield.'

'It was my fault,' he said. 'I shouldn't have told you what I did. And call me Archie, please.'

Grace glanced across at the old man. She couldn't imagine calling him Archie. 'You said you were a friend of my father's.'

'Aye, we lived a few streets from each other. We used to go fishing together.' His eyes watered more than ever. 'Till we fell out, of course.' His hands circled the teacup. A ridge of knotted veins ran along the thin skin on the back of his hand. His fingernails were long and didn't look very clean.

'When did you last see him?'

'Ooh, let me see.' Archie gazed up at the ceiling as if the answer was imprinted there. 'I saw him at his dad's funeral, but we didn't speak. I didn't go back to the house—it would have been embarrassing.'

Grace was still sceptical, but if this man was making it all up, he was a good liar. 'Was my mother with him? At the funeral, I mean.'

Archie shook his head. 'That would have been when they'd split up.'

Shock shivered through Grace. 'Split up? My parents didn't split up.'

'Sorry, lass. I shouldn't have put it like that. Your mam went back to Italy and left the wee ones with your dad.'

'Her mother was dying,' Grace protested. 'She took me with her.' She'd heard the story often enough—how she'd only spoken Italian until she was four; how she'd cried every night for months after she and her mother had come back to England.

Archie Stansfield smiled. 'Happen so, lass. But Henry told his mam Eva had left him. Wrote as much to me in a letter, an all. Heartbroken he was. I thought it was no more than he deserved… after what he'd done.'

Grace decided to cut short the topic. He'd spouted enough rubbish on her parents. 'You and my father had a fight?' she said.

He seemed unperturbed by her change of direction. 'Aye. I was proud of myself. Gave him a right shiner.' He tore open a sachet and stirred sugar into the tea, the spoon grating on the bottom of the cup. He opened a second sachet and began the process again. He looked as if he might stir the tea forever.

This was hopeless. If there was any secret to reveal, Grace couldn't imagine it coming out of this man's mouth.

He stopped stirring at last. 'Your dad and my sister were sweethearts.'

'Sweethearts? When they were children, you mean?'

'Nay. They knew each other, of course, but our Dottie was about seventeen when they started courting.' He hesitated. 'And she would have been twenty the day after it finished. I remember that birthday clearer than yesterday.'

Grace had never heard about any early girlfriends. As far as she knew, Eva was her father's first and only love.

'Why did it finish?'

Archie leant forward. It was warm in the hotel lounge, but he was wearing a thick tweed suit. Beads of perspiration pricked his forehead. He'd probably brought his best clothes with him to London. His faded eyes met Grace's.

'Dottie was a year older than me and Henry,' he began. 'She was a clever girl.' He smiled. 'She came first and I reckon as she got all the brains! She wanted to stay on at school, but there wasn't the money in those days. She got a job in the mill, but then she went to night school. "I'm going to do something with my life," she used to say.' He took out the handkerchief and dabbed at his head. 'She and Henry started courting. Me mam was dead chuffed—our Dottie with a boyfriend from the posh side of town. He taught her to play the piano. Course we couldn't afford one, so she used to go to his house to practise.'

'What happened then?'

'Dottie fell pregnant.'

Eight

Isabel sat down at the piano and opened the lid. The black and white keys stared back at her. She could hear her father's voice: 'Take it slowly. You always want to rush this bit.' His fingers appeared on the keyboard beside hers and the sounds of a duet echoed in her head. She slammed the lid down.

She had to start playing—the income from the lessons she gave bumped up the allowance from Brian, and several of her students were about to sit exams. But each day so far, she'd found a reason not to practise.

She avoided the living room where the piano stood, preferring the kitchen or her bedroom. She'd brought very little furniture from the family home, but several favourites hadn't gone to the auction rooms with the rest. The chaise longue covered in rich cream brocade had been her pride and joy, and the Victorian nursing chair was the first antique she'd bought. They'd looked beautiful in her old sitting room, but in the flat's twelve-foot square box they were stripped of their glory, and the room was like an over-full junkshop.

She ran her hand over the smooth wood of the piano. It was nowhere near as splendid as her father's. His father had bought that for him when he won his scholarship to the Royal College of Music and Grandpa always liked to say that Elgar had played on it at one time. Isabel's had never sounded as sweet and it was covered in scratches where Samson had climbed on it as a kitten. But as soon as her fingers touched the keys, she knew her father's death would become real. Tomorrow, they were scattering the ashes. Perhaps she'd manage to play after that.

Isabel was still sitting at the piano when Rose came in. She rushed straight to her bedroom and the door banged shut.

Isabel went into the hall. 'Rose?' she called. 'Are you all right?'

'Go away.' Rose's voice was muffled.

By the time she emerged, Isabel was in bed reading. Samson was in his favourite position across her feet.

Rose hesitated in the doorway. 'Can we talk?'

Isabel patted a space beside her, and Rose came and lay spread along the length of the bed as she used to when she was younger. Her face was red and blotchy and her eyes were puffy.

'What's happened?'

'I feel stupid! I wish I'd never sent the text.'

'Which text?'

'There's this lad…' Rose had been difficult since Brian left, sullen and argumentative, and Isabel gripped her book, afraid to say anything in case she put her off. 'I've liked him for ages.' Rose ran her palm down Samson's back, and he got up and stalked off. 'I told Sarah I liked him. I thought I could trust her, but she told Abigail, and she told that idiot Fallon and once she knew…'

'What happened?'

'Andy—that's this lad's mate—said to ask him to the pub at lunchtime.'

The pub? Isabel forced herself not to comment.

'I thought if Andy said that, it must mean he liked me. So I texted him.'

'And? What did he say?'

'No ta.'

'What do you mean—no ta? What did he actually say?'

'That was what he said. No ta. Why did he have to be so cruel?'

Isabel stroked Rose's hair. Poor love. *Why did he have to be so cruel?* The kind of question for which there was no answer. Rose's breathing slowed and her eyes closed. It was as if she was a little girl again. Her limbs twitched and Isabel thought she'd fallen asleep.

'Mum, I'm hungry.'

'At this hour? What do you fancy?'

'Comfort food. Like you used to make me.'

Isabel kept tins of spaghetti hoops in the cupboard for when Josh came and she warmed some now and piled them on toast. She leaned back against the sink unit and watched Rose gulping them down. The glare of the overhead light drained Rose of colour, but the tension in her face had softened. Isabel smiled. Perhaps they'd turned a corner and she would be that sweet girl again, like she used to be.

Rose sucked in the last spaghetti hoop and scraped her knife across the plate. 'I'd like to see Dad.'

Isabel felt the smile stitch itself to her face. Rose had previously refused to see her father. It was Isabel's only weapon in the war with him. He'd won on all other fronts. He had Josh, he had that woman and he had the new baby. Everything he wanted.

But was it? For weeks now, whenever Brian dropped Josh off, he'd find a way of getting Isabel alone. 'You know I want you, Bel,' he'd wheedle. 'Get lost!' she said on the first few occasions, but gradually he wore her down. She could hardly bear to admit to herself what was happening, but…

'Mum, did you hear what I said?'

'Yes.'

'You wouldn't mind, would you?'

'Why should I? It's up to you.'

Isabel had been dreading it, but scattering her father's ashes was nothing like the day he died. She felt detached, as if she was hovering above the scene, looking down at the ill-assorted procession wandering around, searching for the best place to lay the ashes. Every so often, the man from the crematorium would stop and look at them questioningly. Here, in the shade below the beech tree?

Here, in the washed-out sunshine? At each stop, they surveyed the area, as if they were looking for the ideal picnic spot.

Rick was in front, carrying the container with the ashes. It looked like an old-fashioned sweetie jar, Isabel thought. Deanna clutched his arm. Eva, leaning heavily on Uncle Eduardo, tottered behind in the most inappropriate heels. Grace and George were next, and somehow Isabel found herself at the back, on her own. She didn't mind. It felt easier to be apart from the others

They arrived at a dark corner below a line of yew trees.

'This is it,' Rick said. Isabel shivered. The trees blocked out any hint of sunlight, and she didn't want to leave her father here. But if Rick had made his mind up, then this is where it would be. When it was her turn, she dipped her hand into the jar and felt the soft powder clinging to her skin.

Afterwards they went back to the house for tea. Nobody said much. Eva needed to lie down, and Isabel sat with her until she fell asleep. When she went downstairs, Grace was in the dining room on her own. George was in the kitchen talking on his mobile, and Rick had driven Deanna to their hotel.

'He's coming back once he's got Deanna and the girls settled.'

'You don't mean Mr High and Mighty actually wants to spend time with us?'

'Even Rick might need his brother and sisters more now,' Grace said.

Isabel sat down at the table. She rested her chin in her hands and looked across at Grace. Perhaps this was the chance to recover some of the closeness they'd shared. 'I still can't believe Dad's gone.'

'I can't get a picture of his face.' Grace glanced up at the portrait above the mantelpiece. 'Despite George's efforts.'

'I keep expecting him to walk in,' Isabel said. 'That it's all been a mistake.'

'I hadn't seen him since the summer. Their visit to Ischia seems such an age ago.' Grace looked wistful. 'I thought there would be lots more holidays.'

Guilt pricked Isabel: she'd spent a lot of time with their father since she'd been on her own. He'd helped her move into the flat; got rid of furniture, consoled her when she was upset. She'd seen him every day, whereas…

'I always thought I'd have time to get to know him.' Grace was picking at some candle wax on the table. 'Find out what made him tick.'

'He was a private man. He had Mum, I suppose.' This was safer territory. Isabel didn't feel as if her words would explode in her face. 'I read in some magazine that children can feel left out when their parents have a great love affair.'

'Only two of the children in our case.'

It was Isabel's turn to tense. 'Two? You're not on this middle child thing—'

'Rick and me—we were the ones left out.'

'Don't be ridiculous.'

Grace swept the slivers of wax into a pile. 'I can't recall Dad ever saying he loved me.'

'But somehow you knew he did.' As the words slid from her mouth, Isabel heard how complacent they sounded. As if she and their father had shared some bond that didn't need voicing. 'What I meant—'

'Do you remember the day of the funeral?'

What was this now? She'd never known her sister analyse things so much. 'How could I forget? The sight of Mum…'

Grace shook her head. 'I wasn't thinking of the ceremony.'

'What, then?'

'Afterwards, back here. There was a man on his own. Archie—'

'Anyone fancy a drink?' The door opened and George came in, brandishing a bottle of champagne.

'Do you think that's a good idea?' Isabel said. 'Supposing Mum comes down? She won't want to see us all celebrating.'

'Why not?' George eased the cork from the bottle. 'We're celebrating the best old man anyone could have wished for.'

The cork shot across the table. It struck George's painting of Henry full on and bounced back hitting Grace on the side of her head. She gasped and her mouth dropped open. She looked so different from her usual self that Isabel started to laugh. It felt wrong and she pursed her lips trying to smother the bubble rising inside. But the more she tried, the worse it got. She glanced at the others: George's eyes were screwed shut and Grace had clamped her hand across her mouth. Isabel laughed in uncontrollable gulps of noise that burst from her throat.

George managed to stop first. He poured out the champagne and held up his glass. 'Cheers, Dad.' Isabel felt a surge of love for her sister and brother as she sipped. She'd been so preoccupied with her own problems since Brian left that her family had taken second place. Now as she looked from one to the other—and it was like looking at twins—she realised how important they were to her. George could be thoughtless at times, but he meant well.

George crouched down, sorting through the pile of 78s stacked beside the piano. 'Beethoven, Brahms, Mozart, Elgar,' he listed. 'Walton, Wagner, Mahler.' He let out a low whistle as he flicked through the records. 'The old bugger. It's some collection Dad's got here.'

'He did love his music,' Grace said. 'It got more difficult each year to find something he didn't already have.'

'He was only just coming round to CDs though,' George said, refilling their glasses.

'It would be nice to hear some music,' Grace said. 'Why don't you play for us, George?'

He settled himself on the piano stool. 'What do you fancy?'

As he spread his fingers above the keys, Isabel felt the familiar knot in her stomach. Why was she never the one asked to play? She closed her eyes and soon the power of the music overwhelmed her negative thoughts.

Images trickled through her mind: a meadow, green and lush, an expanse of water, fringed with stooping trees, a sky of cerulean blue, across which kites dipped and soared. Brian appeared beside her, a smiling, handsome Brian. In their first years together they'd often walked on Hampstead Heath. When Rose was born, Isabel carried her in a papoose, slung across her front. Her little body was warm and reassuring. She remembered Brian kissing the baby, and then his lips on hers.

The sound of the music died away. Isabel kept her eyes closed. It was the most peaceful she'd felt since Brian left. When she opened them again, Grace was staring straight ahead, tears streaming down her cheeks. George's elbows were on the piano, his head in his hands.

She sensed a movement behind her and looked round. Rick was standing in the doorway. His eyes took in the almost-empty champagne bottle and the glasses on the table. Isabel waited for the explosion. He wouldn't approve. Instead a smile spread across his face. He pulled out a chair from the table and sat down, drawing the champagne bottle towards him. 'I could do with a glass myself.'

George swung round on the piano stool. 'Let's open another. I put some in the fridge specially.'

Isabel avoided George's eyes. She couldn't gauge Rick's mood and didn't want to say the wrong thing. Grace didn't answer either.

'Good idea.' Rick nodded at George.

Isabel breathed out. Perhaps it was going to be all right.

George went into the kitchen and came back with a couple of bottles.

'Two?' Rick's voice was sharp.

'One will be gone in the first round.' George poured them all a generous glass.

Isabel hadn't eaten much all day and the champagne was going to her head.

'Bad luck about Deanna, Rick,' George said. 'I had no idea until Grace told me.' He took Grace's hand and made an elaborate show of kissing each of her fingers.

'Sorry about that, Rick.' Grace looked uncomfortable. 'I assumed he knew.'

Rick shrugged. 'No problem. We didn't want to make a big thing of it.'

'How is Deanna? How's the treatment going?' Grace asked.

'She's good. One more month of chemo and then we should get the all-clear.'

'An excellent reason for another round.' George started filling up the glasses again.

Isabel noticed Rick covering his with his hand, but George pushed it away. 'Don't pussy foot around. Let's give the old man a send-off he'd enjoy instead of all that stuffy church crap we had at the funeral.'

Isabel glanced from George to Rick. Rick was looking down at his hands. He pulled at the cuff of his shirt until it was just below the sleeve of his jacket. She watched him adjusting it until it seemed to satisfy him and he began the same process with the other one. She stared, mesmerised, at the sprinkling of hairs on his fingers.

'I don't suppose it was quite Dad's thing,' he said eventually. 'But it was what Mum wanted.'

Grace caught Isabel's eye and they managed a quick smile at each other. Could this be a truce?

'Since we're all here together,' Rick was saying now, 'there's something I want to tell you.'

'That's funny.' George poured himself another glass of champagne. Isabel watched the bubbles forming on the surface. 'I've got an announcement as well. But age before beauty.'

All at once sweat prickled in Isabel's armpits, and the room felt hot and cramped.

'Okay.' Rick placed his hands on the table. 'As soon as I get home, I'm going to make arrangements to have the piano moved to Northumberland.'

'What piano?' George asked.

'Dad's, of course.'

'What for?'

'Mum won't have room for it once she moves.'

'Hang on.' Isabel jumped in before she'd had time to think. 'Who said anything about Mum moving?'

'Stands to reason.' Rick glared at her. 'This place is too big for her. She won't want to stay here without Dad.'

'It was me who shared Dad's love of music,' George said. 'And I decided at the funeral. I'm going to have the piano. I told you that evening, didn't I, Grace?'

Grace chewed her bottom lip. Her hand moved across the table towards Isabel. George was sitting on the piano stool. He had pulled it up to the table, but now he turned back to the piano and deliberately and slowly picked out a few notes.

Rick stood up. 'As Dad's eldest son, that piano belongs to me.'

George bent over the keyboard, his fingers moving faster. There was no sign that he had heard. Rick looked back at Isabel and Grace, his mouth set in a tight line. 'The piano belongs to me,' he repeated.

George turned round, his lips curved in that lop-sided smirk of his. 'But you can't even play the damn thing! It's not like tapping the keys on a computer, you know.'

'I'm going to learn.'

'You're going to learn? You never managed it while Dad was alive. What makes you think you can do it now?'

'I didn't choose to then. I was busy making a success of my career. A concept you've never grasped!' Rick snatched up the second bottle. He sloshed champagne into his glass, knocking it back in one go.

George laughed but his eyes had that hooded look which had always meant a tantrum when he was a child. 'You're a fucking arrogant bastard, aren't you?'

'If being proud of what I've achieved makes me arrogant, then, yes, I am.' Rick stared at George over his glass. 'I run a successful company; I've got a wonderful wife and daughters, a beautiful home. What have you got to show for your thirty-five years?'

'I can play the piano and I got on with Dad, which is something you never managed.'

'Leave Dad out of this!' Rick's eyes blazed.

'Face it, Ricky. You can't stomach it because Dad and I were closer than you and he ever were.'

Rick stepped towards George. He grasped his shoulders and yanked him from the piano stool. The shock on George's face passed in a second and his hands came up, knocking Rick's arms away from him.

'Don't you fucking touch me like that ever again!'

'Get away from that piano, then. It's mine now.' A blue vein bulged and throbbed at each of Rick's temples.

From the hallway, came the creak of the stairs. They'd always hated the fourth step from the bottom when they were young. If you were trying to creep to the kitchen for another packet of crisps or to the front door to slip out unnoticed, you'd get to that one and the sitting room door would fly open and their father would be standing there. That night, though, it gave them vital seconds to pull themselves together. When Eva appeared in the doorway, they were all sitting round the table as if nothing had happened.

‘Sorry, Mum, did we wake you?’ Rick asked. His voice was calm, but his face was still stained red.

‘I heard the piano.’

‘Was it too loud?’

‘No. I love it. It reminds me of Henry.’ She rested her hand on the piano lid. ‘I’ll never get rid of it.’

Nine

Grace was pre-occupied on the way to the airport. She searched her handbag and checked her mobile. Isabel tried to talk, but felt driven to silence in the end. She wished she'd let Grace get a taxi, as she'd wanted to. But it seemed heartless to let her go on her own.

Isabel had always been in awe of her little sister. She was taller and slimmer, wore the right thing, said the right thing, and even when they were young, Isabel had known her sister was the pretty one—and the nicer one. Although Grace had their mother's stunning looks, it was their father's personality, sunny and calm, that she displayed. Isabel used to resent the unfairness. She'd inherited the short wide-hipped stature of Henry's family and seemed to have got the worst of her mother's sensitivity. That's what Brian always said anyway.

But this time, although Grace was as beautiful as ever, she'd been edgy and distant. There was the day in London with Josh when she'd seemed her old self, but otherwise it was a miracle they hadn't ended up in a row. Some of Rick and George's bad blood must have rubbed off.

Isabel was bursting to talk about Eva's secret, but Grace's closed expression made it impossible to broach. They waited in silence for the flight to be called. When the boarding sign for Air Italia to Naples flashed on the screen, Grace leapt from her seat. She still had to go through passport control into departures, saying she preferred to wait here until the last moment. Now, as Isabel stood up to say goodbye, she saw the tears in her sister's eyes.

'Come over, Bel.' Grace hugged Isabel tight. 'I get lonely.'

Isabel hugged her back. 'I'll try. I'd love to see Ischia. Dad never stopped talking about their holiday.'

Grace picked up her bag and strode off. Isabel waited for her to turn and wave, but she didn't look back.

On the way home, Isabel called at her mother's. Rick and George had left that morning, and Uncle Eduardo had flown back to Italy after the scattering of the ashes, saying he had *questioni di business.*

Eva was sitting at the kitchen table. It was early afternoon, but her hair was loose and she was still in her dressing gown. The bits and pieces from Henry's shattered clock littered the table in front of her.

'Mum, whatever are you doing?' Isabel pulled a chair next to her.

Her mother held up a coil spring. 'Look at it.' She waved her hands at the other bits of the clock's mechanism. 'It's a good job your father's not here to see this.'

'It probably wouldn't have happened. He'd have noticed the screws were coming loose.'

When Isabel had arrived at the house the morning after the funeral, her mother had been in her bedroom shouting and crying. Isabel heard her as soon as she opened the front door. She went to rush up the stairs, but Grace appeared from the kitchen: 'Leave it.' She beckoned Isabel towards her. 'George is with her.'

'What's happened? She seemed okay when I left yesterday.'

'There's been a bit of drama.'

'What? Tell me.'

'I was asleep last night, and this crashing noise woke me up. It seemed to go right through the house. I thought it was someone smashing a window.' Grace broke off and listened. 'Thank God for that! She's stopped.'

'Come on,' Isabel urged. 'Don't keep me in suspense.'

'I rushed downstairs—'

'What? Into the arms of a burglar?'

'Don't be stupid. George had got down here before me.'

'And? What was it?'

'The floor was covered...' Grace spread her hands wide '... and I mean *covered* in broken glass and bits of spring and—'

'Oh no!' Isabel's eyes darted across to the wall. 'Grandpa's clock.'

'Yep. It must have fallen off. The screws looked as if they'd worked loose.'

'Did Mum come down?'

'No, she slept through. She'd had another sleeping tablet. But when she saw the mess this morning...'

'Where is it now?'

'I've shoved it all in the broom cupboard.'

Isabel took the spring from her mother's hand. 'Why don't you go and get dressed? I'll put all this stuff in a box, and we'll decide what to do about the clock when you're feeling stronger.'

Her mother drew her hair back from her face and piled it into a bun. Her bracelets jangled as they slid up her arm. Despite the dressing gown and unkempt hair, she'd coated her lashes in mascara and lipstick had smudged on to her teeth. 'Your father would be *desolato*. It was his father's.'

'We might be able to get it repaired.'

Her mother shook her head. 'No, it was an omen. It fell down at five to four.'

'Go on, Mum. Get dressed and I'll make some coffee.'

Isabel carried the tray of coffee and biscuits into the dining room. It faced south-east and was usually filled with light in the mornings. She remembered her father reading the paper in there when he came back from his walk. She set out the cups on the table and poured the coffee. It was very strong and sweet, as Mum liked.

As Isabel looked up, she caught Henry staring down at her from his portrait. She'd hated it when she first saw it. It seemed full of harsh lines and shadows, and she thought it made him look old and cruel. She was surprised he liked it himself and decided he was only pretending for George's sake. But now, she felt a shiver of recognition, as Henry's eyes met hers.

When her mother came downstairs again, she seemed calmer. Her hair was drawn back in its customary plait, and she'd reapplied her lipstick. She was dressed in a black cashmere jumper and dark grey trousers. Henry had always insisted on buying expensive clothes for her. She sat down at the table and sipped her coffee.

'Have you heard from Uncle Eduardo?' Isabel asked.

'He phoned this morning.' Her mother nibbled at a biscuit. 'He wants me to go home.'

'Home? This is your home.'

Eva stroked Isabel's cheek with the back of her hand. 'I know, but Eduardo's old and lonely like me.'

'Tough! He should have thought of that when he was the big *I am*, swanning all over the world. You belong here, with us.'

Her mother reached forward and took another biscuit. She didn't answer.

'You're not thinking of going, are you?'

'I don't know. I still miss Italy.'

Eva was the youngest of a large family from Cassino, a small town north-east of Naples, and Eduardo, her cousin, was her only surviving relative. He had visited England several times over the years and always brought expensive presents. '*Mafioso*,' Rick used to mutter whenever he arrived. He had a shock of jet-black hair and a pencil thin moustache. He talked in a constant stream of loud Italian to Eva, and she became even more excitable in his presence. He was the one that Henry and Eva had stayed with on their annual visits to Italy.

'What was it like for you when you first came to England?' Isabel asked her mother now. Neither of her parents had talked much about their lives before the family arrived. Isabel only knew Eva had come to London to work as a nanny for her Aunt Rosa who was married to an Englishman.

'Cold,' Eva remembered now. 'So cold. I arrived in London on 20th November 1954. It was foggy. When you breathed in, it made black marks under your nose.'

'Could you speak English?'

'Not much. Aunt Rosa used to send me to the shops every day so that I had to speak it. The first thing I asked for was a bag of flour.'

'How did you meet Dad?'

'His father knew Uncle Dennis, Rosa's husband, and he asked if Henry could lodge with them when he came to London to go to Music College. Aunt Rosa had a photo of the family on the sideboard and your father told her I had beautiful eyes.'

Isabel laughed. 'So, he fancied you even in the photo?'

Eva smacked Isabel's hand. 'Fancied! What would I have known about such things?'

'Come off it, Mum. You were nineteen!'

'But I was innocent.'

'What made you come to England?'

Eva shrugged. 'Oh… you know…'

'Come on,' Isabel said. 'We've never talked about this before.'

'It's difficult for me. I had no choice. Papa died during the war. The bombing… it was so bad in Monte Cassino. We even had to run to the church for his funeral.'

'Really?'

'After he died, the farm was neglected. My brothers said I would have a better life in England with Aunt Rosa.' Eva sighed.

'You didn't want to come?'

‘I wanted to stay with my mamma. But lots of Italians came to England in the fifties and sixties and my brothers made me.’

‘What about when you met Dad?’ Isabel asked. ‘Was it love at first sight?’

‘Poof! I was too homesick. I cried every night.’

‘How long did it take to settle down?’ It was helping her mother to talk about the past, but Isabel hadn’t got any closer to the question she was desperate to ask.

‘I felt better when Rick was born. My little Ricardo, I called him. And then I had you. But Mamma got ill. She needed me.’

‘What about your sisters?’

‘Mamma needed *me*,’ Eva insisted. ‘I couldn’t eat. I went down to seven stone and Henry—he was so kind—he said I must go home. I took my little Grace.’

‘And you left us.’

‘*Cara mia*, Rick was at school and you’d started nursery, or I would have taken you all with me.’

‘I wish you had.’

‘It broke my heart to leave you,’ Eva said. ‘Henry’s mother came to look after you. I had three months with Mamma before she died. I nursed her day and night.’

Isabel poured some more coffee. ‘But you were away longer than that. Grandma seemed to live with us forever.’ She thought of her father’s mother—a big, harsh woman, who rapped you over the knuckles with a spoon if you came to the table without washing your hands.

‘Once I was there, I couldn’t bear to leave. I missed my *bambini*, but it was wonderful to be with my family, not having to speak English. After Mamma died, I just stayed on.’

‘Didn’t Dad mind?’ Isabel tried to keep the question neutral. What she wanted to say was *how the hell could you abandon your husband and children*, but she was terrified her mother would clam up.

'Of course. He kept writing, asking when I was coming back. He missed little Grace as well. She'd only been a baby when we left.' Eva stood up and started rinsing the coffee cups at the sink.

Isabel stared at her back. You're telling *me* that? she wanted to shout. She'd cried herself to sleep every night when her mamma and little sister disappeared. Grandma had got fed up with her: 'It's no good fretting, child,' she'd shouted. 'You'd better think of them as dead.'

Eva dried the cups. She seemed to take forever to twist the tea cloth inside each one. 'Henry came to fetch me in the end. I talked to my sisters and they persuaded me to come back.'

'And then you had George.' Isabel was sure her mother must be able to hear her heart thumping. This was getting closer to the secret she'd blurted out.

'Yes. My little Giorgio.'

'When? How soon after you got back?'

'Questions, Isabel, so many questions! You know I'm no good with dates. Your father saw to everything like that.' She threw the teacloth onto the draining board.

'Mum.' Isabel kept her eyes fixed on the jug of milk in the middle of the table. It was black with a gold line running round the lip. 'What you told me that morning… you know… after Dad died.'

'What was that?' Eva was smiling to herself as if she'd retreated into her memories again.

'You know… you said about George and Dad.'

Eva turned away. 'I was upset. I probably said a lot of things.'

'Is it true or not?' Isabel wasn't going to let her off the hook so easily this time.

At first she just stood there gazing out of the window. But finally she nodded; a small, almost imperceptible movement.

Isabel stared hard at the milk jug. The gold line seemed to waver. 'Does George know?'

'No.'

'Does anyone know?'

'Leave it, Isabel. Forget I ever told you.'

'Did Dad know the truth?'

'Of course he knew. We told each other everything.'

'So, if it wasn't Dad, who was George's father?'

Eva swung round from the window. 'Your father made me promise never to tell anyone.'

'Why?' Isabel asked. 'Surely George had a right to know.'

Eva shrugged. 'Leave it alone, Isabel. Do as your father wanted.'

Isabel stopped off at the supermarket on her way home. When she got to the flat, a light was shining from under the kitchen door, but Rose had said she would be late back. The kitchen was so small most of the room was obscured by the door until you were inside. Isabel was prattling brightly about not expecting to see Rose for hours, when she stopped. It wasn't Rose sitting at the table. It was Brian.

'What are you doing here?'

'I came to see Rose. She rang me.' He stood up and teased the plastic carrier from her fingers. It seemed such an intimate gesture. She turned away and started unpacking the shopping.

'I thought Rose was going out tonight.' Isabel couldn't bear to be wrong-footed by him. She was the one who was supposed to know what Rose was doing. A tin of baked beans slipped from her grasp and banged on to the worktop.

'She has,' he said. 'She left about an hour ago. I said I'd wait for you.'

Isabel could feel him standing behind her but she was determined not to turn round. The shopping bag was empty, and she was hemmed in between Brian and the worktop.

'I don't want you in my house when I'm not here.'

'Bel.' He put his hands on her shoulders. They felt warm and heavy and she clenched her teeth. Heat spread across her belly and down into her thighs. 'Rose said it would be all right.' His voice was barely a whisper. Isabel felt his breath on the back of her neck, and his lips fluttered over her skin.

At last she found the strength to swing round. 'I'd like you to go.'

His face was close. His cheeks were rough and reddened as if he had been out in a harsh wind. Lines of blood scarred the whites of his eyes. He pushed himself against her. Perspiration sprouted on his top lip. She felt his hardness.

'You know you want it as much as I do, Bel.' He slurred the words and she realised he'd been drinking. 'Let's go to bed.' This time he seemed to fall against her.

'I've told you.' Isabel raised her hands against his chest. 'Go home.'

'You don't mean that.'

'What about Anita? She'll be waiting for you.'

'I'll make it good for you. Who'll be any the wiser?' He cupped her breasts in his hands. 'You've got lovely tits. Did I ever tell you that?' He leered into her face, his breath foul-smelling.

'You're too late, Brian.'

'What do you mean?'

'I've met someone else.'

Ten

When Grace woke, the shutters were ajar and a sliver of light slanted across the room. She stretched, easing her limbs into the cool reaches of the bed. There was no sign of Franco.

She turned on her back and listened. The *ristorante* was gearing up for another day. The familiar sounds calmed her, like waves breaking on shingle. It was the end of the season and a lot of the hotels were closed, but the *ristorante* had a regular clientele, especially at weekends when Neapolitans arrived on their fast boats. Franco's parents' pizzeria in Naples was famous, and people came to see what *il figlio* was up to.

From outside came a harsh grating noise as the door of a van slid back. A man's voice called '*Giorno! Giorno! Permesso! Permesso*!' and Grace recognised Giuseppe, who delivered the fish Franco selected from the morning's catch. The bedroom was above the kitchen and she heard the clatter of pans, the sound of Maria's high-pitched singing.

Grace would usually be busy preparing the restaurant at this hour. She liked the feel of the crisp white tablecloths and the scent of the nosegays adorning each table. In winter the glass doors were shut against the winds that blew off the sea, but for much of the year, they were folded back and tables were set out on the terrace which overhung the Bay of Cartaromana. She'd persuaded Franco to redecorate in pale cream with dark green floor tiles. A richly quilted canopy in a darker shade of cream hung across the ceiling. The wood-burning stove was a new addition for cool evenings.

She slipped from the bed and crossed to the window. She pulled back one of the shutters. The sun was shining and the light glinting off the sea was sharp and clear. It was a shock after the leaden skies of England. She drew a cardigan over her flimsy nightdress and stepped out onto the balcony.

Her eyes sought Sant'Anna's rocks, sturdy tuffs rising steeply out of the sea. On summer mornings, while it was still quiet, she liked to scramble down the steep path to the beach and swim across to the rocks. Franco had attached a rope to one of them so that she could haul herself up. She'd found a spot, where the sea had washed the rock smooth. She could sit in it, almost like an armchair.

She lifted her gaze from the rocks to the *castello*, her favourite place on the whole island. Like something from a fairytale, it stood on its cone of volcanic lava, mysterious and compelling. Grace had lost count of the number of times she had crossed the bridge and climbed up to the remains of the castle cathedral, where in the sixteenth century the poet Vittoria Colonna's wedding was celebrated. She always took her copy of Vittoria's poetry with her and read in the shadows of the high vaulted arches. To her it was the most romantic place in the world, but Franco scoffed at her obsession with *that old ruin*.

It was chilly standing out on the balcony in her nightclothes. She stepped inside and drew back the sliding door which hid their kitchen. She boiled water for coffee. In the summer she was so busy, she scarcely noticed their cramped living conditions, but as the winter drew on, she resented being cooped up in one room. They usually ate downstairs in the restaurant, either in the late afternoon, or when they'd finished serving at midnight, but this was always a public occasion shared with Vincenzo and Alfonso who waited at table, and any of the locals who were there that evening. It seemed a long time since Grace had made supper for the two of them, as she used to before they married.

She got dressed and went downstairs to the kitchen. '*Buongiorno*, Maria!'

Maria was at the sink washing vegetables. She turned at Grace's voice. '*Signora! Bella! Bella*!' A string of impenetrable Italian followed. Maria's Sicilian dialect was sometimes too much for Grace. Maria flung her arms around Grace, squashing her against her breasts.

Grace went into the restaurant. A young girl she hadn't seen before was spreading cloths on the tables. She smiled shyly. '*Buongiorno, Signora*.'

Franco emerged from the reception area. He looked bright and energetic, his eyes shining and his black hair combed back from his forehead. '*Carissima*, you're up.' He was dressed in black trousers and a white linen shirt worn loose. 'I left you to sleep.' He put his finger under her chin and scrutinised her face. 'You look tired.'

'I am. I'll be better now I'm back.' She saw the question in his eyes and felt her face flush. She leant forward and touched his lips with hers. Without warning he slipped his tongue into her mouth. She tasted the bitterness of his cigars and steeled herself not to pull away.

They had made love yesterday after they got back from the airport. He had been gentle and tender. When they first met, she'd teased him, wondering how a good Catholic boy had become such an expert lover. But last night his kisses didn't send her heartbeat racing. As his tongue caressed her body with tiny darting movements, she'd felt wooden.

She scanned his face now, but it was impossible to detect if he suspected.

'Shall we have lunch together?' he asked. 'There aren't many bookings.'

They sat at Grace's favourite table next to the window. Only four of the other tables were occupied.

Alfonso came to serve them.

'I'll have the *pollo*,' Grace said.

'The squid, he is good today.'

'Chicken is fine, thank you.'

'It's good to have you back, *Signora.*' Alfonso poured prosecco into her glass. The sparkling wine had been her favourite drink since her first visit to Venice when she was seventeen. She smiled up at Alfonso's eager face. 'It's nice to be back.'

Franco took her hand across the table. 'You look so sad,' he said, dropping little kisses into her palm. 'Do you miss your papa very much?'

'It's hard,' she said. 'I'm not sure how I feel at the moment.'

'Grace…'

She looked across at him expectantly, but he was taking a gulp of wine, his head thrown back as he drained the glass. She was surprised. He didn't usually drink at lunchtime. He put the glass down and wiped his mouth on the white napkin.

'What is it?'

'That night… when you heard about your papa—'

'Don't,' Grace said. 'I don't want to think about it.'

'I wanted to say… I'm sorry.' He managed to meet her eyes at last. 'Sorry I wasn't with you when you got the news.'

When Franco had stormed off that afternoon, Grace had expected him to be back in a couple of hours. There was dinner to deal with, for a start. But he didn't return. Grace and Maria did the cooking between them, and Vincenzo and Alfonso waited at the tables. Grace caught them all looking at her inquisitively, but none of them said a word. All through the long evening, her mind wandered to hospital wards, doctors, her father in bed, striped pyjamas too small for his long arms. When Isabel phoned again to say he seemed worse, she swayed as she clutched the receiver to her ear. She had to see him again. She had to feel his smile on her one last time. Then she'd know.

Her mobile rang in the early hours with the news her father had died. She turned to Franco for comfort, but his side of the bed was still empty. He hadn't returned in the morning when she left to catch the ferry to Naples.

'Where did you go?' she asked now.

'Napoli.'

'Naples? You mean you went to your parents?'

He looked embarrassed. 'I know what you think. But Mamma…'

'You went running to her because we'd had a row?'

He nodded. 'I wanted to explain why you aren't pregnant yet. I couldn't bear them to keep asking.'

'Oh great! Now they'll have me marked as that barren English girl.' Grace heard her voice getting louder. A man at one of the other tables was staring over at them. She looked back at Franco.

'Barren?' Franco shrugged. 'I don't know this word.'

'It doesn't matter. When did you get home?'

'I caught the first ferry over in the morning,' he said. 'But you'd already gone.'

'I probably passed you—' she wondered if he could hear her bitterness '—going the other way.'

For the next few days Grace and Franco skirted around each other. There was a late season surge in visitors so they were busy, which helped. Or Franco was. Grace couldn't shake off the lethargy, and now she was back in Italy she fretted about her family. She caught the bus into Ischia Porto and wandered down to the harbour.

She stopped for a slice of pizza at one of the taverns on the *rive droite*. From there, she admired a yacht, anchored a few feet away. It towered above her, two decks high. Its sleek blue paint gleamed where two uniformed sailors were washing its hull down with long-handled brushes. Its name was picked out in white copperplate script—Miss Mulberry, LONDON.

Her friend Lilian phoned and invited her to lunch at their favourite restaurant in Piazza Dante. Grace had met Lilian in a bookshop when she first began teaching in Naples. Lilian was Scottish, but had come to Italy with her husband, Nathan James, a diplomat at the British Embassy in Rome. When he died scarcely eight months into the posting, Lilian couldn't face the thought of life back home without him and settled in Naples. She was sixty, a tiny woman, barely five feet, with a shock of white frizzy hair. Theirs was an unlikely friendship, but when Lilian phoned, Grace realised that lunch in Naples was the tonic she needed.

The restaurant was a warren of rooms, each one opening off the other. Grace passed through them searching for Lilian. She found her near the back, engrossed in a book, a cup of rich dark coffee, one of her favourite cheroots nestling in the saucer, beside her.

She looked up as Grace arrived at her table, her face breaking into a wide smile. She snapped the book shut and stood up to embrace her. She barely reached Grace's shoulder and Grace always felt like a giant beside her. 'Let's order straight away. I'm famished. And you look as if you could do with a good square meal.' She pushed a menu towards Grace. 'I'm having pizza margherita. You can't get better than perfection.'

Grace scanned the menu. 'The same for me,' she told the waiter.

'I've ordered a litre of the house red.' Lilian gestured at the departing waiter. 'You should have seen his face. He made sure I had a bottle of water as well.' Lilian drank copious amounts, but remained stick-thin and sober. 'I could give up smoking and drinking and live till I'm ninety,' she liked to say, 'but I'd rather enjoy myself.'

'So, how are you dear child? I'm so sorry about your daddy.' Lilian fingered the cheroot longingly—she'd never got used to the smoking ban.

Grace had decided on the ferry coming over that she was going to confide in Lilian. Lilian had lived a bit and would probably have some advice. 'I feel so mixed up.'

The waiter arrived with a carafe of wine. Lilian poured them both a glass. 'Would it help to talk?' She waved at her ears which were permanently bright pink. 'These flappy old things do have some uses.'

Grace sipped her wine and felt its warmth tingle in her throat. 'It's complicated.'

Lilian narrowed her eyes as if against smoke drifting up from her cheroot. 'I don't have to be anywhere.'

'I wasn't there when he died.'

'I guess that makes it harder to believe.'

'Sort of. But I always thought one day I'd get a chance… a chance to ask him if he loved me.'

'Loved you? Daddies and their little girls. There's something special there, isn't there?'

Grace hesitated, while the waiter put their plates on the table. '*Bene grazie.*' She took a mouthful of pizza. 'Mm. Lovely.'

'Carry on.' Lilian tore off a chunk of pizza with her fingers.

'When I was a baby…' Grace rested her elbows on the table '… Mum came back to Italy because her mother was ill. She left my dad and my brother and sister in England and took me with her.'

'Difficult for everyone.'

'The thing is my nonna died, but Mum didn't go home. I only knew our life in Italy. I was four when we got back. I can still remember how much I hated it. I didn't know any

English. Rick and Isabel were big and scary. And every time my dad picked me up, I screamed.'

Lilian took a mouthful of wine. 'Surely he understood. You were a frightened little girl.'

'Not long after, my mother had another baby, George. And suddenly he was all that mattered.' Grace felt Lilian touch her arm. She stared at the brown splodges on the back of Lilian's hand. 'I can't remember Dad ever reading me a story, or playing with me, or even sitting on his lap.'

'You poor, wee thing.'

'That's why it was so awful not to get there in time. Now I'll never know.'

'I'm sure your daddy did love you, but it must have been hard for him as well. This little mite, spouting Italian, screaming blue murder every time he went near her.'

Grace couldn't help laughing. 'I suppose so, but I wish it had felt like it.'

'Things aren't always as they seem.'

'And I feel extra bad because I was horrible to my sister the whole time I was in England. I was… sort of jealous… of her closeness to Dad.'

'I've known people behave in all sorts of peculiar ways after a death.'

'But I usually get on so well with Isabel. She looked after me when I was little—when Mum and I first went back. I used to get in bed with her at night when I was scared… and she taught me English.'

'She'll forgive you.'

'But now she's left to deal with my mother, who is not the easiest of people. And Rick and George do nothing but argue.'

'Brothers, eh?'

'They've both decided they want Dad's piano. There was a terrible row.'

'Who did your daddy leave it to? I presume there's a will.'

'Apparently everything goes to Mum. And she wants to keep it.'

'No point them arguing.'

'That won't stop them.'

'I remember when my mother died. Her sisters argued about her watch—never spoke to each other again.' Lilian picked up the carafe. 'Have another of this fine stuff.' She finished off the remains of her pizza and drew a cigar from the slim gold tin. 'What about the divine Franco? Is he taking good care of you?'

Lilian was half in love with Franco, Grace sometimes thought. Perhaps she should know what he was really like.

'We're not getting on so well at the moment.'

'Tsck! Tell him I'll come over and personally chastise him.'

For once Grace couldn't smile at Lilian's humour. 'If only it was as simple as that.'

'Sorry, me and my big gob.' Lilian waved away the waiter who came to clear the table and sat back, the cigar held between her fingers. 'What's the problem?' she asked. 'Tell me to mind my own business, if you like.'

'No, it's fine. We've been arguing about children.'

'I suppose you want them and Franco doesn't?'

'The reverse, actually.'

'Now you have surprised me. I can see you with a brood of exquisite little ones, all long limbs and brown eyes, just like you.'

Grace smiled. 'Maybe one day… but for the moment I want to enjoy life a bit. Before I met Franco, I'd planned to travel.'

'There's nothing as precious as bringing up a child.'

Grace looked at her in surprise. 'Did you want children?'

'I would have loved a baby, but I had an ectopic pregnancy soon after we were married, and I couldn't after that.'

'Lilian, I'm sorry.'

'It's not something I usually talk about.' Lilian shrugged. 'I travelled the world with Nathan, but I still mourn that lost child.'

Eleven

Isabel waited in the entrance hall of Kenwood House. She could see at a glance that he hadn't arrived yet, but even so her eyes searched non-existent corners. Her stomach churned and her hand continually smoothed her hair: it always went fluffy in the rain. Why on earth had she agreed to this? She moved to the back of the hall and fixed her gaze on the entrance.

Kenwood was one of her favourite places. She and Brian used to come to the Saturday concerts in the summer. She would pack a picnic and Brian would produce a bottle of wine. He usually lay back on the picnic rug and dozed off once the concert started, but she preferred to listen to the music without his interruptions anyway, and the setting by the lake was idyllic. When they got home, they would make love, which made him more attentive for the next couple of days.

Isabel blinked back the tears that were never far away. It wouldn't do for her mascara to run. She looked at her watch. He was late. She'd give him another ten minutes and then she was going. It was her friend Sally who'd suggested the blind date.

'I'm not ready to meet anyone new,' Isabel had told her.

'It will do you good. Simon's into music as well. He used to play the violin for the BBC orchestra.'

'But not any more?' Isabel was curious despite herself.

'He had a skiing accident. Lost the top of two fingers,' Sally explained. 'It was his left hand, his fingering hand.'

'Can he still play?'

'He doesn't very often. He could probably teach, but he hasn't got the patience.'

Isabel recalled some of her students' half-hearted attempts on the piano. 'Especially not after playing in a world-class orchestra.'

'He retrained as a counsellor. Specialises in cognitive therapy, if that means anything to you. And his wife's left him, so you'll have lots to talk about.'

'Great! Cry on each other's shoulders, you mean.' But she'd found herself saying yes, when she meant no.

At least it had given her the chance to tell Brian she'd met someone else. Whatever happened today, it was worth it to remember the shock on his face. He was so complacent, so sure he could have his new woman and a bit on the side with her. She'd gone along with it because while they were sleeping together, he couldn't divorce her. And he'd have to come back eventually.

She checked her watch again: another five minutes. She pulled a sheet of paper from her bag: an email from Grace that had arrived as she was leaving the flat. She was missing everyone, Grace wrote. It was getting harder, not easier, to think about Dad being dead.

I'm sorry I was horrible while I was in England. I know I behaved badly. I was stressed, but I shouldn't have taken it out on my big sister! Sorry.

By the way, when you get a chance, can you ask Mum if she knows who Archie Stansfield is. Apparently he was a friend…

'You must be Isabel.' The voice made her jump. 'I'm Simon.'

She looked up to find a short, balding man standing in front of her. He was smiling. 'Sorry I'm late.' He held out his hand. 'Have you been waiting long?'

She stuffed the sheet of paper back in her bag. 'Only a few minutes.'

'I was afraid you'd have given up on me. The traffic was terrible. You'd better lead the way,' he went on. 'I haven't been here before.'

He sounded matter-of-fact and keen to get on with it, as if Sally had coerced him as well.

'Let's start in here.' Isabel turned into the library. 'The view's wonderful.'

'I suppose before those trees grew up, you'd have been able to see St Paul's.' Simon stepped back, turning his gaze upward to stare at the painting on the ceiling.

Isabel read from the guidebook. 'That was painted by Zucchi in 1769. It's Hercules between Glory and the Passions.'

'No contest there,' Simon said. 'Give me *the passions* every time!'

Isabel laughed. Perhaps the meeting wasn't going to be so bad after all.

They moved on to the dining room. It was a favourite of Isabel's with its deep red wall hangings and curtains. She cast covert glances at Simon. He seemed absorbed in the paintings so it was easy to study him. Sally had said he was about forty, but he looked older. Deep lines ran from his nose to his mouth. What was left of his hair was cropped short so that it was spiky on top. He wore a cream linen suit which rippled with creases. Dark splodges from the heavy rain that morning marked his shoulders.

He stopped in front of a painting. It was Vermeer's *The Guitar Player*. 'I like this,' he said. 'I didn't realise the original was here. My father had a book of reproductions of old masters, and I first saw this when I was about five.' He took a couple of paces back and studied the painting, his head on one side. 'You can almost see the strings vibrating under her fingers.'

Isabel didn't know whether to look at the painting or Simon. His expression, which had been one of wry amusement, softened. His mouth was fuller, his grey eyes warm.

He turned to her, his lips raised in a smile. 'It makes me long to feel the violin in my hands again.'

'Sally told me about your accident. I'm sorry…' Isabel saw the warmth fade from his eyes.

'Sally has been busy filling us both in.' He moved to stand in front of another painting. 'You play the piano, I gather.'

'Yes, but not to professional standards. I couldn't play in an orchestra like you did.'

'I wouldn't recommend it. All that travelling. Unsociable hours. Not conducive to domestic bliss.'

Isabel remembered Brian complaining if she gave piano lessons after he came home from work. And he'd hated Friday nights when she played for the amateur operatic society. Perhaps it was then he'd started seeing Anita. Perhaps it was all her fault, like he'd said.

She followed Simon through the dining room and into the music room with its pictures of Georgian ladies. He was knowledgeable about the paintings and the few moments of awkwardness about the accident were forgotten.

'Can I tempt you to something to eat or drink?' Simon asked as they returned to the entrance. 'They have refreshments here, I presume?'

They ordered coffee and cakes and chose a table in the corner. It was warm in the cafe and Simon took his jacket off. As he hung it from the back of the chair, Isabel caught sight of his injury. The middle and forefingers of his left hand were only stumps finishing just above the knuckle. The skin across the top was puckered and lumpy. She looked up and found him watching her. Her eyes slid away from his to the line of musical notes emblazoned in sparkling silver across the front of his black T-shirt.

'I can guess what you're thinking,' he said. 'When a man of my years wears a top like this, it's a cry for help!'

'No… no… of course I wasn't.' Oh God, he must be a mind reader.

'It's okay. You can say what you like.'

Isabel laughed. 'It *is* eye-catching.'

'All you need is love.'

'Sorry?'

'The music.' He pointed to the notes on his chest. 'It's the opening bar of the old Beatles' tune—All You Need is Love.' He met Isabel's eyes. She couldn't fathom his expression and again was forced to look away.

She searched for a new topic. 'You're a counsellor, aren't you?'

He smiled. 'Our Sal again, I suppose?'

'Yes, but I am interested. What sort of people come to you?'

'Teachers, dentists, plumbers… you name it, I've seen them. It certainly puts your own problems into perspective.' He reached across to his jacket pocket and took out a packet of cigarettes and laid it on the table. He drummed the packet with the fingers of his good hand. The two stumps on his left hand were stained brown with nicotine.

'I can see you don't approve,' he said.

Isabel felt the blush staining her cheeks. 'Is it so obvious?'

'Don't worry. I don't approve myself. Comes from all those years in the orchestra. These…' he tapped the packet '… and a taste for Glenfidditch. Too many late nights. Too many bars after the performance. Didn't do much for my marriage either.'

'What happened?'

'Helen, my wife, had enough of it in the end. I'd got a decorator in to paint the front of the house. She'd wanted it done for months.' He laughed, a harsh bark of sound. 'Silly bugger, I am!'

'What do you mean?'

'I came home one day to find a letter on the table. And she'd taken Edward, my lad.'

'You mean she'd left?'

'Yep. And I was too stupid to see it coming.'

'Where had she gone?

'Scotland. With the bloody decorator!'

She stared at the stumps on his fingers. They looked vulnerable, and she felt an urge to reach over and caress them. 'That was hard to take.'

With his good hand, he caught up the packet of cigarettes and crushed it against his palm. 'Listen, Isabel. I was a shit husband. I deserved shit.'

'I don't believe that,' Isabel said. 'Sometimes you get back more shit than you give.'

'It's funny, isn't it,' he said. 'You live with someone for years, think you know them as well as you know yourself and then…'

'I presume Sally told you my husband's left me?'

'She did, and I'm sorry. I know how much it hurts.'

Isabel shrugged. 'I'm still getting used to it.'

'Would you ever have him back?'

She shook her head. She and Simon weren't on a date exactly, but seemed tactless to tell him that she'd take Brian back tomorrow.

'It's the feeling of betrayal, isn't it?' Simon was saying. 'Once trust's gone…'

Her mother's secret reared up in Isabel's head. What had happened to the trust between her parents? She had never known her father tell a lie, not even the small white ones that everyone tells to get out of a fix. How many times as she was growing up had she heard him say 'honesty is the best policy'? But if it was true what her mother had said, then her parents had told the biggest lie ever.

'… so I dumped the bag of manure over his head.' Simon's voice intruded.

'Sorry. I was miles away.'

'I could see that.'

'What were you saying about manure?'

Simon laughed. 'I was testing you. Wanted to see if something shocking would get your attention.'

His grin was infectious and she couldn't help smiling back.

'I'm sorry,' she said. 'I'm rubbish company at the moment.'

'On the contrary.'

'I was thinking about my dad.'

'And I imagined my charm—'

'He died a few weeks ago.'

Simon frowned. 'Isabel, I had no idea.'

'It's okay.' She felt in her pocket for a tissue. 'I'm being stupid.'

'Stupid? It's tough to lose your dad, especially after your husband and…'

'It was sudden. He had a heart attack.' Isabel examined the surface of the table where some sugar had been spilt. As she pushed the grains to one side, she felt Simon's fingers brush hers.

'Talk if you want to.' His voice was gentle and she looked up. He shrugged in a self-deprecating sort of way. 'Try me.'

'After my dad died, my mother told me something.' Feeling tears coming, she dabbed at her cheeks.

'You don't have to…'

'I want to tell you.' Now she'd begun, she needed to get the story out. 'A few hours after he died, we were back at the house, and I was helping Mum get undressed. We'd been up all night and she was exhausted. She started talking about Dad and how much he'd loved her. They were always billing and cooing over each other. Then she came out with it.'

'Go on.'

'She told me that George, my little brother…'

'Are you sure you want to do this?'

Simon's question, something about the tenderness in his tone, caught at Isabel's throat. But she couldn't stop now. 'Mum said that George has got a different father. George is my half brother.'

There, she'd said it. 'You don't know what a relief that is. Actually to say the words aloud to another person—George is my half brother.'

'And you had no idea until that morning?'

She shook her head. 'They kept it secret all these years. George is thirty-five.'

'Do you think he knows? Perhaps they told him.'

'Mum said no one knows. She made me promise not to tell anyone.'

'Why? If she told you…'

'She said she was distraught or she wouldn't have said anything. She said it was Dad who made *her* promise never to tell anyone. He was ashamed that she was carrying another man's child.'

'Isabel, don't take this the wrong way, but is it such a big deal? I mean, lots of families these days have half brothers and sisters, or step brothers and sisters.'

'I know. And if they'd told us from the beginning… but, now… I mean, finding now, when Dad's dead… it sort of undermines all the certainties.'

'I know what you mean,' Simon said. 'It's some secret to spill the day he dies.'

'I even wondered if she'd made it up,' Isabel said. 'George is a brilliant pianist, and so was my father, and my grandfather. We assumed he'd inherited the talent.' She stopped. 'But it was Mum who told us that. She made us sit round the piano when George was playing. "George is a natural" she used to say. "Just like his daddy and Grandpa." And all the time she was lying her head off!'

'How do you explain the music then?'

'I don't know. Except I can remember George sitting on Dad's lap, even when he was a baby, and Dad playing to him and tapping out a tune with George's little fingers.'

Simon picked up the cigarette packet and turned it over and over. 'I see so many problems in my work because someone decided it was a good idea to keep something a secret.'

'Ever since I've known I can't seem to look the rest of the family in the eye. I keep thinking—if you knew what I know.'

'Tell your mother how hard this is for you.'

'I've tried, but she clams up. Acts as if it's my fault. Which is a bit rich, seeing as she's the one who screwed around.'

'What about a drink? You look as if you could use one.' Simon stood up. 'Is wine okay?'

'That would be lovely.'

'Excuse me… excuse me.'

Isabel became aware that someone was trying to attract her attention. She'd been so caught up in her thoughts and conversation with Simon that she hadn't noticed the two elderly women at the next table. She glanced round and saw one of them was leaning towards her.

'Forgive me for butting in,' the woman said. 'But I couldn't help overhearing what you were saying.'

Her companion looked embarrassed and kept her attention focused on her cream scone.

Oh, no, Isabel thought. What had the woman heard her say? Not about her mother screwing around. Please!

'Last year I found out I've got a half-brother.' The woman beamed.

Isabel looked towards the counter, willing Simon to come back.

'I was adopted, and I found out my birth mother had gone to Australia and she got married and had a son.' The woman started rummaging in her bag. 'Look—everyone says how alike we look.'

Isabel took the photo that was offered across the gap between their tables. A nondescript, white-haired man smiled out of the photo. 'Very nice,' she said, handing the picture back.

'The point is…' the woman leaned closer '…you don't need to worry about having a half-brother. It's wonderful. We email every week—I went to the college to learn how to specially—and talk on the phone once a month, and—'

Isabel spotted Simon carrying two glasses of white wine. Thank goodness! Not a moment too soon.

The woman followed her glance. 'Oh, my dear, here's your husband. He won't want to listen to me prattling on…'

'Sorry, it took a long time.' Simon put the wine down on the table.

'… and don't you worry about that half-brother. I'm sure you'll get on fine and dandy.'

'Thank you,' Isabel said. 'I'm sure we will.'

Simon sat down and raised his eyebrows. *Who's your friend?* his expression said.

'Don't ask,' Isabel mouthed back.

'Shall we drink to families?'

'To families!' Isabel sipped her wine. 'The horrible thing is… I always thought I liked my family, and now it's all gone wrong.'

'Strange how a death unsettles things. It's as if all those relationships are finely balanced, and then ping! They go off kilter.'

'What I don't understand is why they didn't tell us.'

'Perhaps they had a good reason. Or thought they had.'

'But what?'

'Only your mother can tell you that.'

'And if she won't?'

'You've got a tough decision to make.'

Isabel looked at her watch: the time had flown by.

'I suppose we'd better go. They'll think we've taken root here soon.' Simon pulled on his jacket. 'Thank you for today,' he said. 'I'm sorry you're having a tough time, but it's been great to meet you.' He leant forward and kissed her cheek.

She scrabbled under the table for her bag. Her skin seemed to burn where his lips had touched. 'It's been lovely,' she agreed. 'Sorry to burden you with my problems.'

He gave a little bow. 'All part of the service. Perhaps we can do it again sometime?'

She had set out this morning determined she would make some excuse if he suggested another meeting, but now she found she wanted to see him again. 'I'm going to visit my brother in Cornwall soon, but when I'm back…'

Simon reached inside his jacket and felt in a pocket. 'Here's my card. Give me a call.'

Twelve

Eva stopped in the bread aisle of the supermarket and reached out for a white crusty loaf.

Isabel caught hold of her hand. 'I thought you said you've been throwing bread away.'

Eva snatched her fingers from the loaf. 'Henry had toast every morning after his walk and a sandwich for lunch. I can't get used to not needing the bread.'

'Be strong, Mum. Dad wouldn't want you to go to pieces.'

'No. He used to tell me off if I was being "too Italian".'

As she unpacked the shopping from the car, Isabel remembered Grace's email. She waited until they settled down in the kitchen with a cup of tea. Her mother had spread some Florentines on a plate. Normally Isabel loved them, but when she bit into one, it tasted dry and stuck in her throat.

'Who's Archie Stansfield?' she asked.

'Why?' Her mother's mouth tightened into a thin line. 'Who told you about him?'

'Grace spoke to him at the funeral. She wondered who he is.'

Her mother swept crumbs from the table into her hand. 'He was a friend of Henry's.'

'I've never heard of him.'

'They hadn't seen each other for years.'

'Why not?'

'Your father never said.'

'I thought you told each other everything.'

'No wonder Brian walked out, if you pried into every part of his life!' Her mother reached towards the plate and took another Florentine. She bit into it, breaking it in two.

'That's cruel, Mum.' Isabel tried to keep her voice steady.

'You have to work to hang on to your man. Perhaps you spent too long on those piano students of yours.'

'You mean that justified Brian going off with some bimbo, do you?'

'Of course not, but a contented man doesn't stray too far from home. Look at Henry and me…'

Her mother's constant talk about how much Henry had loved her had a hollow ring now. 'Let's leave Dad out of this. Tell me more about Archie Stansfield.'

'Archie… Archie… What is all this about Archie Stansfield?'

'I'm intrigued. They hadn't seen each other for years and yet he turned up at the funeral.'

'You're giving me a headache with all these questions. I'll have to go and lie down.' Her mother leaned on the table as if to lever herself up. 'Help me, would you, *cara*?'

'In a minute, Mum.' Isabel felt stronger since the conversation with Simon. She wouldn't be fobbed off this time. 'Who told Archie Stansfield about the funeral?'

'How should I know?'

'It wasn't you?'

'Certainly not!'

'You must have some idea.'

'If I knew, Isabel, why would I say I didn't?'

'It wouldn't be the first secret you've kept, would it?'

The words were out before Isabel could stop herself. She hadn't planned to come out with it like that.

Her mother hands went to her hair as they always did when she was flustered. She took out some of the pins that held it in place. She gripped one between her lips while she repositioned the other. 'I don't know what you're talking about.'

'George, Mum. What you told me about George.'

Her mother stood up. The chair scraped across the floor tiles, setting Isabel's teeth on edge. Eva gathered the crockery together. She placed the saucers on top of each other and slotted one cup inside the other. She stacked them on the tray without a word.

Isabel had seen her behave like this before. It meant the subject was closed. 'You can't make me keep a secret like this,' she persisted.

Her mother picked up the tray and carried it to the draining board. She tipped the plate up, so that the remaining Florentines slipped into the biscuit tin. She turned on the tap and water splashed noisily into the bowl.

'I should never have told you.'

'No, you shouldn't. But now you have, you've got to tell the others as well. And if you don't, I will!'

Her mother swung round. Her face had gone white. Her hair was escaping from its pins and hung down over one shoulder. 'If your father could hear you.'

Isabel stared at the fine lines etched into her mother's top lip. She had never tried to defy her before.

Eva's rages were scary. Once, she'd stood at the top of the stairs and flung down a glass bowl Henry had given her as an anniversary present. It had landed on the tiled floor in the hall and smashed into pieces. Isabel had been the only one at home and she'd hidden in the garden until she heard her father's car pull up. She remembered now how she'd crept into the house and found him kneeling at the foot of the stairs, wrapping shards of glass in layers of newspaper. He'd put his finger to his lips and shook his head. 'Leave it, lass,' he'd whispered. 'Go and play.' It was the memory of the sadness in his eyes that day that spurred her on now.

'It's not fair to me that I know,' she insisted, 'and it's not fair to the others that they don't.'

'What is this *fair*?' Her mother's face creased as if the word had a nasty taste. 'Nothing in life is fair. How is it fair that your father's left me to cope on my own? How is it fair that my papa died and my brothers made me come to England? How is it fair that I hardly ever see my beloved Italia? How is it…'

Isabel caught hold of her mother's shoulders. 'All right, Mum. You've made your point.'

She felt her mother crumple against her. A stray strand of her hair tickled Isabel's cheek and her mother's brown eyes gazed into hers. 'I knew you wouldn't be cruel to your poor mamma. Not when her heart is breaking for darling Henry.'

Isabel recognised that wheedling tone in her mother's voice. She'd seen her get round her father so many times. She let her hands drop. 'You nearly had me there, Mum. But I'm not backing down on this one. I'll give you till after Christmas. If you haven't done something by George's birthday, I'm telling the others.'

Thirteen

Rick always relaxed once he turned off the A1 and left Newcastle behind him. Twenty minutes and he'd be home. He stretched his neck, easing it from side to side. He lowered his shoulders and massaged his forehead, his fingers moving in small circles, as Deanna had taught him.

Two days after he'd made Jim Foster, his marketing manager, redundant, Jim's father had died following a stroke. Rick had written to Jim to say how sorry he was, but there'd been no reply. He'd got Deanna to send flowers to the funeral, but when he asked members of staff who'd attended how it had gone, they mumbled an answer. He could see they blamed him in some way for Jim's father's death, but what was he supposed to do? He was hardly responsible for the downturn in the IT world. He was struggling to keep his company afloat when so many others had gone to the wall. And the new house had cost him far more than he'd bargained. The New York designer probably had been over the top, but Deanna had wanted it, and he found it hard to refuse her anything, especially since she'd been ill.

He turned left to Rothbury. This was his favourite bit of the journey. It was a clear night and his headlights picked out the occasional gleam of water where the River Coquet snaked its way along the left-hand side of the road. The woods of Cragside rose up on his right. He drove on into the village. There was hardly anyone about. He'd been worried Deanna would find it too quiet when they'd moved. After an unhappy start in Newcastle, she'd made lots of friends and worked in a boutique two days a week. But she loved Rothbury. Said she was a country girl at heart and felt more at home there than anywhere else they'd lived in England. Rick passed the war memorial and the market cross, drove along High Street and up the hill. He felt that familiar tightening in his chest. He would see Deanna in a few minutes. Even after all these years the thought excited him.

He dropped his briefcase on the floor in the hall. He bent down and unzipped the outside pocket. Slipping his hand inside, he felt for the envelope. Yes, it was nestling there safely. His first thought when he'd found his father's letter to George had been to destroy it. When the letter, with its hated words, had gone, the spears of anger might disappear too. But he decided to keep it—a symbol, an emblem of what he'd fought against all his life: his father had loved George more.

Deanna was lying on the sofa in the sitting room, her eyes closed. Some country and western music was playing. It wasn't his favourite sound, but it reminded Deanna of home. Homesickness afflicted her more since the cancer. As always these days, it took a few moments to adjust to her changed appearance. When he was away she became her healthy self in his mind. Her golden hair shimmered and her blue eyes shone. In reality, her face was pale and thin. Dark circles framed her eyes, and her wonderful hair had gone, leaving only a few unsightly tufts. Rick preferred it when she wore one of her turbans. Then he could pretend that nothing had changed. But tonight her head was bare. He leaned over and kissed her lips.

She opened her eyes and looked up at him with a wan smile. 'Hi honey.' Only her voice hadn't changed. It still held that deep sexy note that had captivated Rick the first time they met. 'How was your day?'

He sat down next to her and drew her feet on to his lap. He began to massage the soles in the way he knew she liked. They still hadn't made love, and he missed the physical contact.

'So so,' he said. He didn't like to worry her unless he had to. 'How about yours?'

'I slept off and on. Can't wait to finish the treatment.'

He rested his head against the back of the sofa. He loved this room. The drawing room was much grander, but they used this every day. It faced south with wonderful views across the river. The designer had chosen burnt ochre for the walls and curtains and two button-backed yellow sofas stood opposite on either side of the fireplace. He'd thought the pale yellow carpet hopelessly impractical when Deanna suggested it, but it looked good, especially against the wooden floor.

'When are you starting your piano lessons?'

Rick's head jerked forward like a hound scenting blood. 'Need a piano first.' He shifted Deanna's feet from his lap. 'I've seen one in Newcastle, but the bloke's asking too much.'

'You deserve a treat, honey.'

'I haven't got cash to burn.'

'I know, but you do so much for the girls and me and…'

'I'm not paying what he wants. But he'll come down.'

Deanna put her hand on his. 'I'm glad, anyway, that you've given up the idea of your dad's piano.'

'What makes you say that?'

'If you're buying one…'

He stood up, kicking one of Deanna's satin slippers as he did so. The vivid pink sat on the yellow carpet like a shadow on a pool of sunlight. Alicia had bought the slippers for her mother, and Rick thought they were hideous.

'Where are the girls?' he asked.

'Upstairs doing homework. Camilla's got coursework due in tomorrow, and you know Flavia never stops studying.'

Their daughters went to a girls' private school in Newcastle. Flavia was the most academic and was hoping to go to Cambridge to study art history. Rick was torn between pride and an obsessive fear that gnawed at his insides, when he thought about one of his princesses leaving home.

'Where's Alicia?'

'She rang a while ago. She's staying in Newcastle tonight.'

'Who with?'

'A friend, I guess. I didn't ask.'

'She'd better not be with that mechanic.'

Deanna patted the sofa. 'Come and sit down again.'

Rick perched on the edge. 'You're going to have to talk to her.'

'You could try.'

'She won't listen to me.'

'Darling, it's no good lecturing her.'

'I'm her father.'

'I know you adore her, Rick, but she's an adult. You've got to let her make her own decisions, and her own mistakes if it comes to that.'

'I'm not having her with that no-hoper,' he insisted.

'I've told you before: his name's Gary.'

'I don't give a damn what he's called.' Tension spiked the back of Rick's eyes. 'I've asked around at work and Samantha knows him. His brother's into drugs.'

'That doesn't mean Gary is. And Alicia would never do anything like that. She's promised us.'

'Like she promised us she'd get straight As.'

When Alicia failed her 'A' levels the previous summer, Rick had wanted her to go to a crammer to retake them. Instead, she'd got a job in the restaurant at the top of the Baltic Centre. She thought working there was glamorous with its views up and down the Tyne and the Millennium Bridge arching across the river below. And all sorts of famous people came to visit. She'd been full of some film star she'd served the other day. But Rick had been mortified when they'd gone there for lunch one Sunday and Alicia had waited at their table.

Deanna stroked her palm across Rick's forehead. 'Sit back. Relax.' Her hand was cool and smooth. 'Don't be such a cross patch.' Rick leant back and closed his eyes. The CD had finished. Only the tick of the clock, regular as a heart beat, and the muffled sound of music from upstairs disturbed the silence. He sighed. 'That feels just right, Deanna. You're so good for me. I don't know what I'd do without you.'

'Ssh.' Deanna touched his mouth with her lips. 'You won't have to do without me.'

She got up from the sofa. 'I'll fix us some supper,' she said. She crossed the room to the door. 'Hey, I almost forgot… your mom phoned today. She and Isabel are coming for Christmas. Isn't that just great?'

Fourteen

'You should have told me before we got married!' Franco leaned across the desk until his face was close to hers. The office was small and seemed airless. Grace felt frisked by fear as she looked up into his eyes.

'I didn't know myself then,' she said.

Franco turned on his heel, and the door swung to and fro behind him.

She tried to concentrate on the figures in front of her. In the summer she'd taken over running the books, but they'd got in a muddle while she was away. Franco's appearance in the office had unsettled her.

Last night they'd had another row. She thought about Franco's mother, a woman she couldn't take to, no matter how hard she tried. Mamma controlled her husband and six sons and expected her daughters-in-law to do what they were told too. Her approach to objection was to raise her voice an octave and talk at twice the speed. Grace could imagine what she'd been putting Franco through about the fact that they'd been married for two years and there was no sign of a bambino.

Suppose—just suppose—she agreed and had a baby. She imagined giving Franco the news. He'd dance that funny little jig he did when his football team won or the restaurant had a bumper week. The funny little jig she'd found so endearing at the beginning. He'd be happy, and his happiness was infectious. He'd cosset her; his mamma would fuss over her; she'd be included for the first time in the gossipy circle of his brothers' wives. But if she had a baby, she'd be stuck for the rest of her life: Franco, his family, Italy, would be her world.

This morning an email from Isabel had arrived. It was mostly about someone called Simon and how much she liked him, but at the end she'd added:

By the way I asked Mum about Archie Stansfield. She said he was a friend of Dad's but they hadn't met for years. She didn't know why, nor who told him about the funeral. She got stroppy. You know how she is when she doesn't want to talk about something. Anyway, why are you so interested in this Archie?

Grace got up from the desk and went into the restaurant. She moved among the tables, straightening cutlery, checking glasses. She crossed to the big window and gazed out. It was one of those rare grey days on Ischia, when the horizon had settled on the sea. The rain sheeted down so she could only just make out the castle rising up from its shroud of mist. Outside, flecks of white bobbed on the sea.

Her mind churned with the swelling ocean. *What happened then? Dottie fell pregnant.* She'd replayed the conversation with Archie Stansfield in her mind so many times that those three words were engraved: *Dottie fell pregnant.* She'd leapt up when he said them. Heard the little gasp escaping from her mouth. Felt her knee knock against the tray of tea and biscuits. Watched them land on the floor—brown liquid pooling on the carpet, bits of crockery, sugar, broken biscuits. Archie Stansfield had rushed to get help from reception, and in the mêlée, Grace had escaped.

She fixed her eyes on the castle, willing its walls to emerge from the mist. The contrast with her first view of Ischia could not have been greater. It had been a hot day in late May and her cotton dress was sticking to her. The heat of Naples was not yet as intense and debilitating as it would become in high summer, but it was still a relief when the ferry pushed out into the Bay of Naples and the wind flicked and lifted her hair from her face.

Grace hadn't been sure when Franco's parents first suggested buying them their own restaurant. But in the end she found it difficult to refuse Franco when his face crumpled in that way. He had plenty of experience from working with his parents and she—she had the elegance and beauty to charm their customers, Franco told her, gripping her hand as the boat bucked beneath them. He'd found the perfect place for them. Even the gods had adored Ischia, the 'green island'. Aphrodite, the goddess of beauty had bathed in its thermal waters, and the archangel Michael was said to have appeared there, giving his name to the island's southern tip, Sant'Angelo.

As the ferry drew closer to the island and first, Mount Epomeo and then, the Castello d'Aragonese came into focus like a developing negative, Grace had felt more positive. Her doubts about Franco were probably a result of the strangeness They'd got married quickly; there hadn't been time to adjust. She took in the green hills; pastel-coloured houses clustered around the harbour and the stretches of white beach, and decided she could be happy on this paradise.

But her father's death had catapulted her into a scary realm. She wasn't sleeping. Although she went to bed long before Franco finished in the restaurant, she feigned sleep when he finally slipped in beside her. Fears for her family, stricken with arguments, baited her brain. What was happening back in England? Her mother had been protected all her life. First by her father, then her brothers, and for nearly fifty years by the ever-adoring Henry. Grace sometimes wondered if her father had sacrificed something of himself when he married Eva. He'd always seemed happy enough, but…

Grace found Franco in the storeroom behind the kitchen. He was sorting through the chiller cabinet and the glassy eyes of a fish stared up at her. Franco glanced round as she touched his arm. He was wearing thick rubber gloves and his expression was as cold as the air that seeped from the cabinet.

'Franco…' The word came out in a breathless squeak and he didn't seem to hear her above the hum of the chiller. 'Franco, I need to talk to you.' This time she managed to control her voice. 'Can we talk?' she asked. With obvious reluctance, he closed the lid and slowly peeled off his gloves.

Grace poured them both a cup of coffee and they sat at a table. Alfonso looked round the door from the kitchen when he heard them, but she waved him away. Grace started to explain how she felt. How difficult it was to be far away from home and family with her father gone. She'd never been homesick before, had always loved travelling. Nothing had prepared her for this, she told Franco. She'd probably come back too soon after the funeral. She should have stayed longer and adjusted to his absence. As it was, she kept imagining her father was there as usual, kept seeing him sitting at the piano.

'I'd like to go home and stay with Mum.' The words spilled on the table between them and settled.

'I need you here!'

'Just for a week or two.' Grace cast a glance round the room. 'We're hardly rushed off our feet.'

'No, Grace, *I* need you.' Franco's mouth turned down at the corners in that sulky pout she was noticing more and more.

'A few days, then.'

'You're my wife. You should be here.' He kept his eyes fixed on the table, refusing to meet Grace's gaze. She took his hand in hers. It still felt cold. She held it between both her palms and rubbed until it was warmer. 'Isabel is going to stay with George, and I don't want Mum to be on her own.' She could see Franco was wavering. 'I'll be back this time next week.' She leaned across the table and kissed him. 'And then we'll talk about a baby, I promise.'

Fifteen

George lived in Penzance in a large Victorian house, five minutes from the sea front. He shared it with four friends, and on Isabel's first evening, they had supper round the big table in the kitchen. She watched George spooning out helpings of shepherd's pie and topping up people's beer. He seemed a different person: none of the brittleness and bravado he displayed to the family. Someone made a joke about his cooking and they all laughed.

Suzanne and Freddy were a married couple in their forties. He was six-foot five, with a mass of frizzy grey hair. She was tiny and as neat looking as Freddy was wild. Mark was sitting next to George. He was so good-looking, Isabel couldn't help staring. It was warm in the kitchen and he wore a tight white T-shirt that emphasised his thinness. Chloe was bubbly and pretty. With her dark hair scraped back in a knot and her paint-stained fingernails, she looked like a schoolgirl, but must have been in her twenties. She'd been working at the studio today, she explained to Isabel.

The evening was fun: no tedious piano lessons, no solitary supper by the television listening for Rose's key in the door, no waiting for a phone call from Brian. It was past midnight by the time George carried her bag up several flights of stairs to a room at the top of the house.

'Hope you sleep well.' He dropped the bag on the bed. 'The pipes are a bit noisy, I'm afraid.'

Isabel yawned. 'I'm so tired. I'd sleep through a tornado.'

'Chloe's next door if you need anything.'

Isabel peered out of the small sash window into the darkness beyond. 'Can you see the sea from here?'

'Just a hint between the rooftops and the sky.'

Isabel thought of the flat in London, hemmed in on three sides by buildings; a patch of garden and a glimpse of playing fields through the fence couldn't match the sky and rooftops.

'It was good to see you laughing this evening,' George said.

Isabel swung round.

'If it's any consolation, I never did like the bastard.'

'Brian?'

George grinned, the sort of grin you expected to come with missing front teeth and dirt-smudged cheeks. 'No need to look so shocked, Sis. I do have some taste, you know.' He put his arm round her shoulder and drew her to him.

Isabel didn't know what to do. Her arms got in the way of the hug, and the scent of his after-shave made her nostrils prickle. She moved her head and his lips grazed her forehead. She waited as long as she could and then eased away, hoping the movement was natural.

George sat down on the bed.

She sensed his eyes on her as she fiddled with the zip on her bag. She pulled out her nightie.

'I should have asked before,' he said. 'How's Eva? I've had some interminable phone calls with her since I got back.'

Isabel was conscious of the filmy material of the nightie. She'd bought a new one specially, but now the pale pink silk seemed stupidly glamorous, and she shoved it under the pillow. 'I'm glad to get away, to be honest.'

George took her hand in his. 'Poor you. Left to hold the fort.'

'She's obsessed at the moment with Dad's clock. She's latched on to it as some sort of symbol of the fact he's gone.'

'Can it be mended?'

Isabel felt her hand growing hot in George's grasp. 'I could take it somewhere, but I doubt it. It's in too many pieces.'

'Weird, wasn't it?'

'Was spooky that it fell down at five to four.'

George dropped Isabel's hand. He flicked the end of the zip on her bag backwards and forwards. 'I meant weird that it fell down at all.'

'The screws had worn loose, hadn't they?'

'Not Dad's ghost then?'

'Ghost?' Isabel clutched the headboard. 'Don't say things like that!'

George laughed. 'Isn't it supposed to be the unquiet dead who walk? The ones who can't settle.'

'Shut up! And don't start saying that to Mum.'

George got up and went to the door. 'I'm only joking, Sis.'

'Good.'

'Still weird though.'

Isabel climbed into bed. Despite her assertion to George, sleep didn't materialise. She wasn't used to a single bed and felt stifled by the sloping ceiling above her head, which she could sense even in the darkness. George was right. The pipes clunked endlessly as the central heating cooled.

It was strange to think her father had been here only a few months ago. What had he thought of this unconventional household? He hadn't said much when he arrived home. He'd carried the painting George had done of him in from the car and hung it above the mantelpiece in the dining room. 'I think the lad will make it work this time,' had been his only comment.

For the hundredth time since her father's death, Isabel turned over the thought that Henry was not George's father. She'd felt determined when she gave her mother the ultimatum, but she didn't know whether she'd go through with it. Usually she pushed it out of mind. But being there with George, she knew the secret was growing, tumour-like, inside.

The studios were bright and airy and after a second cup of coffee, Isabel began to wake up. Mark was in the room next door taking a life class. She helped George set out brushes and paper for his group of beginners. This was their third week and he told her how he was going to show them painting techniques, placing little pots of blue next to each of the eight easels. The class was mainly middle-aged women, and Isabel noticed George's popularity. He flirted, praised their work, listened to their anecdotes. She watched them gaze up at him adoringly.

George fitted the artist's image: dark good looks, torn jeans, a loose checked shirt, the hint of a beard. But he was a good teacher. Far more patient than she was with her students. He went from one easel to the next. 'Wonderful!'... 'Brill!'... 'If you try dragging that sponge over the paint...' She studied him as he moved round the room. He was attractive... sexy, she thought.

Next week the group was going to have a go at landscapes and she wished she could be there to see how they got on. She wondered if her father had enjoyed himself as much. She went into the kitchen to make coffee and set out the sandwiches and fruitcake Suzanne had prepared. Mark's class had finished and George was helping him clear up before the afternoon's session.

The sandwiches looked tempting—thick crusty bread and hunks of cheese with pickle. She was famished. She crossed the corridor and opened the door of the other studio. Easels stood in lines down the middle of the high-ceilinged room. Half-finished canvases were stacked against walls. At one end a low couch draped with a red throw stood on a raised platform.

Isabel's eyes were drawn to the huge window at the other end of the studio, which looked out on to the sea. The light was unexpectedly bright from the expanse of glass. George and Mark were silhouetted against the winter sunshine. They had their backs to Isabel as they gazed out deep in conversation. The sight of their arms clasped round each other jolted through her.

Over lunch, Isabel had to stop herself staring at Mark. She bit into a cheese sandwich. He and George were obviously close, but how close? George had never been short of girlfriends. He'd been with Eloise, a beautiful Argentinean, for several months when he was in his twenties. Henry and Eva had hoped he'd marry her. But she'd disappeared like so many others.

George stood up. 'That's better. Good old Suzanne. Knows how to keep a man happy.' He dusted crumbs from his jeans. 'Come on, you slacker.' He slapped Mark on the shoulder. 'Back to work.'

Mark caught his arm and twisted it behind his back.

'Get off, you brute!' George pulled free of his grasp. 'You've got a class to teach. Isabel, I'm going to St Ives to order paints and brushes. You're welcome to come, but Chloe will be here soon and I know she's hoping you'll model for her.'

For an awful moment, Isabel thought she was going to have to pose nude. The last thing she wanted was to appear the suburban housewife, but she cringed at the idea of revealing her lumpen body to the youthful Chloe. Since Brian left, she'd piled on pounds and could hardly bear to look at herself naked.

'Don't worry.' Chloe rearranged the throw on the couch 'I want to do a head and shoulders. I'm working on a project for my Master's, the seven ages of woman.'

Isabel perched on the edge of the chair Chloe had indicated. 'And I suppose I'm perfect for the middle aged frump!'

'Don't be so hard on yourself. You've got wonderful skin.' Chloe placed her hands on Isabel's shoulders. 'If you could relax… tilt your face so that the light catches it.' She took Isabel's chin in her hand and moved it up and to the side. 'Is that comfortable?'

Isabel was surprised she didn't feel more awkward at the younger woman's fingers on her neck. 'It's fine, but I'm not very good at staying still.'

'That's all right. I work quickly.'

Isabel didn't dare say a word. Only the sound of music from next door and the occasional scrape of Chloe's pencil on the paper broke the silence. Isabel felt a familiar blush spreading across her breasts and up her neck. Chloe would see the crow's feet, the lines either side of her mouth. She wished she'd put hair colour on before she left home. The roots were really grey.

She risked sneaking a glance at Chloe. She was standing back from the easel, her head on one side. 'How's it going?'

'Can you manage another fifteen minutes or so, while I get this first sketch down?'

'Yes, I'm fine.'

'You're allowed to talk.'

'I'm concentrating.'

Chloe laughed. 'That's my job, not yours.'

Isabel felt an itch developing on the side of her nose. 'How long have you known George?' Conversation might help take her mind off it.

'About five years. I met him when I was at Uni. He's a friend of one of my tutors.'

'We were surprised when he got involved in this art school. He's never really settled to anything before.' Isabel waited, but Chloe seemed absorbed in her sketch. 'He's got all of you to motivate him, I suppose.'

'Oh no,' Chloe said. 'He keeps us going. Mark's a brilliant painter and he's the one with the money, but he's got no drive, and I wouldn't have a clue how to teach if George hadn't given me some tips. No, it's George who holds this whole thing together.'

'How about Suzanne and Freddy?'

Chloe explained that Freddy had been a talented sculptor, but didn't do much these days. 'Drugs,' she said. 'It's such a shame. George has been so good to them. I don't know where they would have been, if it wasn't for him.'

This was a view of her brother Isabel hadn't expected. She'd come to Cornwall hoping to persuade George to give up his plans for Henry's piano, but her stay was turning into a different experience altogether.

As if she'd read her mind, Chloe said, 'George is determined to have your dad's piano, you know.'

Isabel watched Chloe's pigtails bobbing about as she sketched. She wondered if George had told them all about the row. It was horrible to think of them sitting round that kitchen table dissecting her family. Rick could be overbearing, but their father had always told them 'family squabbles don't go outside the front door'.

'I hope I don't seem cheeky,' Chloe said, 'but I think it's what your dad would have wanted.'

'What makes you say that?'

'When he was here in the spring…'

'What? You met my father?'

'Yeah. George and I were having a bit of a thing at the time, so I went out for a few meals with them—if you could keep your chin up for a couple more minutes—I thought your dad was great, and he and George were such mates.'

Isabel contemplated telling Chloe the secret. That would unsettle her smug assurance. How dare she talk about their father as if he was an old friend or interfere in their family's private affairs? As that last thought filled her mind, she imagined George's comment: *That's so bourgeois, Sis*. Even so she'd love to see the look on Chloe's face if she told her George was not Henry's son.

'Right!' Chloe announced. 'That's the first sketch done. If you'd sit again tomorrow, I should manage without you after that.'

Isabel was taken aback. She hadn't expected it all to be over so quickly. 'Can I see it?' she asked, but Chloe was already covering the easel with a sheet.

'Nope. I never let people see work in progress.'

That evening Suzanne cooked a delicious roast and Mark produced several bottles of champagne. 'In honour of our guest.' He bowed, as he held out a bottle. 'Comte Audoin de Dampierre 1990.'

'Mark, that's one of your best!' George exclaimed.

'Isn't your sister worth it?'

During the meal Isabel studied the others. If there was anything between George and Mark, or between George and Chloe for that matter, she'd definitely notice some sign as they relaxed with the alcohol. But the only meaningful glance she intercepted was between George and Suzanne when she asked where Freddy was.

'He's not feeling so good tonight,' Suzanne said.

As the evening wore on, Isabel was enjoying herself too much to worry about liaisons. She had several glasses of champagne and felt tipsy when she climbed the stairs to her attic room. She paused on the landing to call goodnight to Chloe in the room next door and flopped on the bed. She fell asleep instantly, but then the dream started…

She's walking with Josh. They are in the park and they're going to feed the ducks. Suddenly a forest appears in their path, dark and forbidding, like a forest in a fairy tale. Fir trees cluster densely, blocking out sunlight. Isabel doesn't want to continue, but Josh pulls at her hand. 'Come on, Mum.' His high childish voice echoes in the treetops. He runs on and reluctantly she follows. The path is narrow and thick with pine needles. Josh is shouting, filling his bag with cones. She glimpses a flash of his red anorak ahead. He is moving faster than she is. 'Wait for me, darling!' she calls.

And then she can't hear his voice. Only a soft moaning as the branches sway overhead. She starts to run, peering into the gloom, desperate to catch sight of that flash of red. She stumbles over a tangle of roots, which straddles the path. Her chest burns. 'Josh! Josh!' She screams his name, but no sound comes out. Then the murmuring starts. A low whispering around her. Faces appear high up in the trees. Their eyes shine, a fierce glare, and their mouths loll open. She's trapped. Her limbs feel weighted. She bends forward and clutches one thigh with both hands. She tries to lift her leg. It won't move. 'Josh!' She forces her lips open, but nothing comes out. 'Josh!' Gathering all her strength, she screams his name…

'Isabel. Isabel.'

From deep in her consciousness, an awareness of a voice surfaced: 'Isabel?' The door opened and in the light from the landing, she saw Chloe's face.

'You called out.' Chloe was standing beside the bed. 'Are you okay?'

'I had a dream.' Isabel covered her eyes, shutting out those horrible images. 'My little boy…'

'No need to explain. You need a hug.' Chloe lay down on the duvet and put her arm round Isabel. She stroked Isabel's hair back from her forehead. Her hand was cool on Isabel's burning skin. Isabel started to explain about Josh, about the dream, but Chloe put her finger to her lips. 'Ssh, don't try to talk. It will be all right.' Her weight felt heavy on the duvet, and it was oddly comforting. It reminded Isabel of Samson snuggling up to her on the bed at night.

Sixteen

On Grace's first evening back in London, she and Eva went out to dinner with Deanna and Flavia. They were combining Flavia's interview at Cambridge with a couple of days' shopping in London. Grace was glad to get out of the house. Her mother had followed her round from the minute she arrived, even waiting on the landing while she went to the loo.

They met at the hotel where they'd had dinner before. Grace was shocked at Deanna's appearance. In the weeks since Henry's funeral, she'd lost a huge amount of weight. When Flavia started telling Eva about the art history course, and how it would mean spending six months in Florence, Grace got the chance to ask Deanna how things were going.

'Not so well.'

Grace had never heard the normally upbeat Deanna so pessimistic.

'They think there's secondaries, probably in the lungs, as I've been kinda breathless lately.' Deanna glanced across the table to Eva and Flavia. 'The girls don't know.'

'How's Rick taking it?'

'I haven't told him.'

'But you can't carry this on your own.'

Deanna shrugged. The bones of her shoulders jutted out under the silky material of her red tunic top. 'He'll be devastated. He hasn't come to terms with the whole cancer thing yet.'

'You need his support, Deanna.' Grace pulled her chair closer to her sister-in-law. Deanna had the most beautiful blue eyes she had ever seen. Now they were ringed with dark circles.

'Things are not good for him at work right now. I call my mom every day. She sees me okay.'

'When will you tell him?'

'Not till after Christmas. Eva and Isabel are coming up and I want everything to be perfect. It might be the last Christmas we get together.'

'Oh, Deanna.' Grace felt helpless. 'I wish I wasn't so far away.'

Deanna smiled. It was easy to see why Rick was so in love with her.

When Eva and Flavia got up to go to the Ladies, Deanna turned immediately to Grace again.

'I didn't want to keep whispering while they were here. I'm sure Flavia suspects something as it is.' She sipped from her iced water. 'I think you should know Rick's not gonna back down over Henry's piano.'

'Not that wretched piano!' Grace stirred her coffee angrily and it splashed on to the tablecloth. 'I'd like to bang my brothers' heads together. They're both pig stubborn. Dad always said so.' The coffee seeped into the white fabric.

'Perhaps you could warn George off.'

'I don't know what makes either of them think they can have it,' Grace said. 'The piano belongs to Mum, and it means everything now Dad's gone.'

Deanna patted the stain with a tissue. 'I'm afraid Rick's got plans for your mom, as well.'

'What do you mean?'

Deanna shook her head, indicating Eva and Flavia who were coming back to the table. 'Not now.'

Eva and Deanna left the hotel restaurant first. They walked towards the waiting taxi. Eva had her arm in Deanna's and was leaning on her. It should be the other way round, Grace thought, as she fell into step beside Flavia.

'I'm glad of the chance for a quick word,' she began. 'I wanted to talk to you about that time I saw you and Alicia in the ladies.' They were almost at the taxi and Grace stopped.

Flavia fiddled with the strap of her handbag.

'I need you to promise that whatever was going on has stopped. Otherwise I'll tell your father.'

Flavia let out a big sigh, as if she'd been holding her breath since that night. 'I feel terrible about it, Auntie Grace. Thanks for not saying anything to Mum and Dad.'

'I don't want to upset Deanna, when she needs to concentrate on getting well.'

'It was a one-off, I promise.'

'And what about Alicia?' Grace tried to keep her tone casual.

'I'm sure it was that once for her as well.'

'But you don't know?'

'I don't see all that much of her. I've got so much homework and she's either working or out with Gary.'

Gary. Grace had overheard a row between Rick and Alicia about Gary the night of the funeral. 'What's he like?' she asked.

'Really cool. He's got tattoos of snakes up his arms, and he and Alicia are going to get each other's names done across their backs.'

Grace stood at the front door while Mrs Flanagan helped her mother into the car. She waved goodbye as they pulled away from the kerb. Bliss. A few hours' reprieve from her mother's saturating emotion. She had insisted on speaking only Italian, recounting memory after memory of her brothers and sisters and the life they'd shared back on the farm when they were young. Uncle Eduardo had phoned yesterday afternoon, and Grace heard the continual rise and fall of her mother's voice from upstairs for almost an hour. After that she cried all the more. When Mrs Flanagan from church had telephoned this morning and suggested taking her to an Advent lunch, Grace had urged Eva to go.

It wasn't only the peace she was looking forward to. There was an oak bureau in the sitting room where her father had kept photos and letters. With her mother safely out of the way, she was going to have a rummage to see if there was anything that related to Archie Stansfield.

But first Grace went into the dining room and sat down at the piano. She opened the lid and ran her fingers along the keys. It certainly had a beautiful tone. She loved the sound of the piano, especially this one, which had so many associations with her father. Grandpa used to relate the story of Elgar playing on it when he was a young man, but her father said that Grandpa was inclined to tell tall stories.

The third drawer of the bureau was deeper than the first two and it was this one she'd often seen her father open. It looked remarkably tidy and she wondered if her mother had already been through it and sorted out the contents. She felt like an intruder as she lifted up papers, trying to place them back exactly where they'd been. There was a heap of envelopes with her grandmother's forward-sloping writing, and underneath a smaller pile with her mother's elaborate script. She flicked through a few, noticing the Italian postmark and stamp on some. She hesitated but couldn't bring herself to read any. Her hand hovered over bundles of cards, each held together with a rubber band. They were birthday cards sent over the years from the four of them to their father. Grace checked for the ones with her signature in them, from the five-year-old's scrawl to the neat handwriting she had today. Funny to think she could hardly remember any of those birthdays now.

She started to replace the cards when her fingers touched something wedged in the back of the drawer. It was an old black and white photo. It had faded to a soft brown and a crease ran diagonally across the middle. The photo showed three people, a young woman with a man on either side of her. Each had an arm around her waist. They were smartly dressed and all stared into the camera with broad smiles. Grace recognised the man on the left of the picture as a very young version of her father. She'd seen other photos in which he looked similar and knew they were taken when he was still at school. She didn't know who the other two people were. She turned over the photo. Across the top were the names, Henry, Dottie, Archie, followed by the date—23rd August 1948. Underneath was the inscription—*For Henry, In memory of a wonderful day. All my love, Dottie.*

Seventeen

Rick couldn't believe he'd overslept. He stumbled about the bedroom looking for his running clothes. He hated Deanna being away and the night before he'd sat up drinking whisky. Alicia and Camilla were staying in Newcastle, and the house was lonely. Deanna usually put his freshly-washed track suit and running vest ready for him before she went to bed, but this morning, it was a good twenty minutes before he discovered his things in the laundry room. He was way behind schedule. It was getting light as he let himself out of the house and turned down the hill towards the village.

The morning was bitterly cold and he was glad of the woolly hat and gloves Camilla had bought him for his birthday. His legs felt wooden as he forced them into action. He had barely run half a mile before waves of pain sliced into his chest. He gasped for air, puffs of white issuing from his mouth like smoke signals. As the road sloped upward, his pace got slower and slower. His trainers felt as if they had weights in them. But as he left the village behind him, power surged through his legs. His breathing settled into a steady rhythm. Mentally he timed his strides —one a second, sixty in a minute. That was his goal.

There were few cars about at that hour on a December morning. He ran with the River Coquet on his right and he always felt better once the dark looming trees of Cragside fell away and a gentler landscape to his left opened up. He was making good time as he reached Pauperhaugh, turned right over the old bridge and headed back up to Rothbury along the disused railway track.

Barely a few strides into the return journey, an agonising pain stabbed at his left side. He bent double, hands on his knees. When he first started running, he had often abandoned a run because of just such a pain, but as he got fitter, it had happened less. Now, the pain defeated his attempts to breathe through it. He sank to his knees, curling over in a ball so that his forehead touched the wet grass.

He felt something nudging at him from behind. A heavy weight landed on his back, while the sound of breathing, even louder than his own gasps, echoed in his ears. He raised his head to find the face of a red setter inches from his own. Its foul smelling breath blasted his senses. He forced himself upright and struggled to his feet. He looked round to see if the dog was on its own.

About thirty yards away a man was coming towards him. He walked with a pronounced limp and wore an overcoat and a trilby hat pulled down low over his forehead. He whistled and the dog turned and bounded back towards him. Rick straightened up and made himself breathe as normally as possible. He didn't want anyone to see him looking so helpless. The dog circled the man a couple of times before trotting back to Rick, its tongue lolling from its mouth. It sniffed at his track-suit bottoms. Rick felt obliged to bend down and stroke its head.

As the owner approached, Rick prepared to greet him. He didn't recognise the man, but Deanna was always telling him he should be friendlier to the locals. The man raised his hat.

'Cold morning,' Rick said.

'It is an all.' The man didn't pause. He returned his hat to his head and limped past Rick without glancing in his direction. The dog galloped after him. But before he'd taken more than half a dozen paces, the man looked back. 'I should be careful with yon jogging,' he said. 'You don't want to drop down dead from a heart attack like your dad.'

The drawing room ran the length of the house. Deep bay windows at the front looked out on to a gravelled drive, while French doors at the back opened on to lawns, which sloped down to the river. It was the room that had first sold the house to him and he loved the pale green Deanna had picked for the walls. Three enormous sofas in rich cream brocade were grouped in the centre around the fireplace. Rick liked to sit in one of the armchairs at the garden end, especially on a Sunday morning when he allocated forty minutes to reading the papers. When it was sunny he timed himself by the patch of sunlight which edged across the carpet. It would start in the far corner and when it had reached his feet, Rick knew it was time to go and choose a bottle of wine to put in the fridge for lunch.

Their previous house in Newcastle had been spacious but modern and when they moved to Rothbury, he'd spent a considerable sum on antiques. The house dated from the 1860s and Deanna was always on the lookout for furniture to suit the period. A Victorian kneehole desk filled the space between the two bay windows. This was the spot Rick had earmarked for his father's piano. His original plan had been to wait until the piano arrived to begin lessons, but the row with George had made him realise it wouldn't go his way so smoothly. His mother was bound to support George. He'd win in the end, but in the meantime he'd bought another piano. It was being delivered this morning and his first lesson was in the afternoon. It was going to be a surprise for Deanna when she got home. But it meant he had to find another place for the mahogany desk.

When Mrs Crosby, the cleaning lady, arrived, the drawing room was in chaos. Rick had tried the desk in three different places, but none suited as well as its original home. Mrs Crosby stood in the doorway with her hands on her hips. 'It's a fine mess you've got here,' she pronounced.

'I'm changing the furniture round.' Rick was at a critical moment in a manoeuvre with a bureau.

'I can see that, but what will your good lady say? She's particular about what goes where.'

'If you could take this drawer from me for a moment Mrs Crosby, before I drop the lot…'

Rick would never have admitted it, but the room started to look better once he followed Mrs Crosby's suggestions. She had Deanna's knack of placing a chair or a vase of dried flowers so that you couldn't imagine the object ever being anywhere else. Soon order was restored and although the room didn't look as pleasing as it had, Mrs Crosby couldn't find too much to criticise. Rick cringed as he heard himself profusely thanking her.

She was always full of tittle-tattle about village goings-on and normally Rick couldn't stand to be in the same room, but whenever he complained, Deanna said she enjoyed gossiping. It reminded her of home and her mother's circle. This never failed to shut Rick up. He was paranoid that one day Deanna would say she'd had enough of him and of England and she was returning to the States. He would do anything to stop that happening. Now, he felt forced to offer Mrs Crosby a cup of tea. 'It was bad news about your dad,' she said as she dunked a ginger nut in her tea. She twisted her head to allow the sloppy mess to plop into her mouth. 'So sudden as well.'

He was usually at work at this time, so he hadn't seen Mrs Crosby since his father's death. 'It was a shock,' he admitted, hardly able to believe he was having this conversation with a cleaning lady.

'They do say it runs in families, heart trouble, that is,' she said.

Rick had a sudden thought. 'Mrs Crosby, do you know a man with a limp who takes his red setter for a walk in the mornings?'

'Know him?' She roared with laughter. 'I should do. Bert and me have been wed forty years come April. Why d'you ask?'

'I met him this morning while I was out running.'

'Aye, he said as he'd seen you. "That one will pop his clogs soon an all, if he's not careful" he said when he came home.'

His first piano lesson wasn't a success. For a start he'd had a job getting rid of Mrs Crosby. She'd followed him round filling him in with the life stories of all the residents of Rothbury. Then the new piano wasn't delivered until two o'clock, so Rick was hot and dishevelled when Mrs Dobson arrived half an hour later. He was proud of himself that he'd managed to find someone to teach him without Deanna's help. He'd called at the heritage centre one Saturday morning and the woman there had recommended her sister who lived at the other end of the village.

He sat down on the piano stool and rested his fingers on the smoothness of the ivory.

Mrs Dobson sat on his left. 'The first thing to remember is—don't lie over the keyboard.'

Rick snatched his hands away.

'Keep your wrists relaxed and hold your fingers just above the keys.'

He tried to let his wrists go floppy.

'Right, let's try the key of C major. Show me middle C.'

He pointed to the appropriate key, relieved that he could remember.

'Good. Starting on middle C, play me the five notes: C, D, E, F, G.' Mrs Dobson broke into a baritone that would have served her well in a male-voice choir.

Rick smiled. Dead easy. He let his fingers ripple up the keyboard.

Mrs Dobson drew in her breath. What was wrong with the old bat? He'd played that with the aplomb of a maestro.

'You'll have to get the tuner in. That middle C's way off.'

Rick started to protest, but she cut him short: 'Play that for me again and this time keep the volume and the rhythm the same for all five notes.'

'I did.'

'No, you banged on the C, and I could hardly hear the G.'

Memories of those childhood lessons jangled in his head like jailer's keys. The rest of the session was a torment as she barked out instructions and he struggled to fulfil them. By the end, he was sweating so much, his fingers skidded across the keyboard. At last she said 'Now if you could practise that scale for next time and don't forget to loosen up your wrists.'

He showed Mrs Dobson out of the front door, promising he'd be more prepared next week. He was following the progress of her pork pie hat as it bobbed down the road, when he saw Alicia strolling up from the village.

'Hi Dad,' she called. She looked round at Mrs Dobson. 'Does Mum know what you get up to when she's not here?'

Rick was furious at being caught out. The last thing he wanted was for Alicia to spill the beans about his piano lessons to Deanna before he got a chance. 'Don't be so stupid!'

She leant forward and kissed him on the cheek. 'Joke, Dad. Joke. Although I know you have little acquaintance with the funny side of life.'

'What are you doing here, anyway?' he asked, pleased that he managed not to make his usual comment about her appearance. She'd recently had her long beautiful hair cut and it was short and spiky.

'I live here, remember?' She pushed past him and dropped her bag on a chair in the hall.

'I meant how did you get here?' He picked up the bag and hung it from a hook on the hallstand. 'I thought I was collecting you from Newcastle later on.'

'I got the bus.'

'Bus? From Newcastle?'

'No, Dad, I got a bus from Newcastle to Morpeth. Then one from Morpeth to Rothbury. It's called public transport. It's how ordinary people get about.'

Rick spent the rest of the afternoon in his study going over figures for the next day's sales meeting. Last month had shown an upturn on the previous six and the signs were that the drop in shares had bottomed out. This was the world where he felt comfortable. You knew where you were with computers. They didn't get cancer; they didn't grow up and turn into strangers, and, most of all, they didn't die on you.

Rick knew his father would have winced at his feeble attempts on the piano. He had been so sure the morning of the funeral that his father would have wanted him to learn. His enthusiasm had seen him through the following weeks. In fact he'd been so preoccupied with arranging lessons and buying the piano that he'd hardly thought about his father at all.

'Dad!' Alicia called from the hall. 'I've made scrambled egg on toast. Do you want some?'

He settled himself at the kitchen table. 'What are you after?'

'Why should I be after anything? Can't I make a fuss of my dad if I want to?'

He paused with the fork half way to his mouth. 'You don't usually.'

She looked crestfallen and he regretted the words. 'How's work going?' he asked.

Alicia chatted away, regaling him with stories of the people she'd encountered in the restaurant. Apparently the wife of the prime minister had visited the day before, and a minor member of the royal family the previous week. 'The manager acts like he's really cool, but he was bowing and scraping like mad,' she said.

Rick wiped his mouth on a napkin and leaned back in his chair. Alicia told him that she was thinking of going to college. He smiled. She was a talented artist and he'd lost count of the times he'd said she shouldn't waste such a gift. He started to feel better. This was the first conversation he'd had with his daughter for months where they hadn't been shouting at each other.

'Dad,' she said.

'What is it, princess? If it's money you're worried about, you know I'll help you through college. You can give up this ridiculous waitress idea.'

'I enjoy being a waitress. And I get loads of tips.'

'But you're too good for it.'

'Dad, you don't know the first thing about me.'

'Of course I do. You're my princess and don't you forget it.'

'I'm not a little girl any more, but you can't accept that, can you?'

Rick stood up. He pulled open the dishwasher and banged his plate in. He turned back to look at Alicia. 'Try me.'

'You know what I want.'

'Do I?' He wasn't going to make this any easier for her.

'It's about Christmas…'

'What about it?'

'I did ask you before, Dad.'

'And I told you before—I'm not having that layabout in my house!'

Alicia folded her arms and glared up at him. 'He's not a layabout. He works harder than you've ever had to.'

'I've asked around, Alicia, and I know things about your precious boyfriend.'

She stood up then and he saw her lower lip droop. If she thought she could get round him by turning on the waterworks, she was mistaken.

'It's not worth being nice to you!' she shouted. 'I don't know how Mum puts up with you.'

Rick slammed his fist down on the table. The pepper mill jumped in the air, fell over and rolled across the surface of the table. It hovered on the edge for a moment before crashing on to the tiles, its glass shattering.

'Don't you dare bring your mother into this!' He was about to storm off, but Alicia reached the door before him. She stopped and turned back. Her long purple fingernails gripped the edge of the door.

'And you might as well know, Dad, If Gary's not welcome over Christmas, then I won't be spending the day here either!'

Eighteen

'Go on. Open it.'

The gold wrapping paper crinkled in Isabel's hands. The parcel felt soft and delicate. 'I ought to wait for Christmas Day,' she said.

'No, I want to see your face when you open it.' Brian's voice was as excited as a child's.

Isabel looked round the table. Brian was at the far end, Rose and Josh on either side. It was the first time since Brian left that they'd all sat down for a meal as a family.

'Hurry up, Mum. Let's see what you've got.' Josh's eyes shone in the candlelight that flickered round the room. Isabel hadn't seen his face so open and happy for months.

She pulled the sellotape from one side of the parcel. The paper tore. 'I haven't bought you a present, Brian.'

'Not to worry. It's good to be together. A family. Come on, Rose. Pull this cracker with me.'

Isabel looked at him. He showed no sign he was aware of the irony of what he'd said. His face was flushed from the wine and he was laughing at Rose as she read the joke from her cracker.

When he'd asked if he and Josh could come for dinner for an early Christmas celebration, she decided to push the boat out and have the traditional turkey with all the trimmings. She found her special tablecloth in a suitcase she had never got round to unpacking when she and Rose moved to the flat. It was white cotton with pink and green embroidered flowers decorating the middle of the cloth. She'd bought it from a market stall in Majorca and its vibrant colours brought happy memories.

She spent ages ironing it, but as soon as they sat down at the table, Brian knocked over his glass, spilling wine. The red stain inched across the white cloth. He dabbed at it. 'Sorry about that, Bel. It's your favourite as well.'

'Accidents happen.' Isabel forced her mouth into a smile. Why did he have to be so clumsy, forever knocking things over?

'Come on, Mum,' Rose said. 'Open that present.'

Isabel tore off the remainder of the gold wrapping. Inside was a layer of tissue paper. She pulled this off and found her hands full of something black and lacy.

'What is it?' Josh asked.

'Lingerie, stupid!' Rose said.

Josh screwed up his nose. 'Ugh. Girls' stuff.'

Rose leant over and picked up the pair of knickers that Isabel was holding. 'Hey, these are sexy, Mum. Not like your usual passion killers.'

Isabel heard the smirk in Rose's voice. A wave of heat surged across her cheeks as she held the matching bra between her thumb and her forefinger.

'You do like them?' Brian stood up and came over to her chair. 'I hope I've got the right size… I couldn't quite remember…'

'I'm sure they'll be fine.' Isabel snatched the knickers from Rose and bundled everything back into the wrapping paper. 'I'd better do something about that wine stain,' she said, escaping to the kitchen.

She crossed to the sink and opened the window. Icy air blasted in. She turned on the tap, holding her wrists under the jet of cold water. She took long deep breaths. From the sitting room came a shout of laughter. She heard Josh cheering. Isabel knew they weren't laughing at her—they'd been setting up the Monopoly board as she left—but the sound didn't make her feel better. Had Brian tried to humiliate her on purpose, or was he plain insensitive? It was hard to know which was preferable.

'Are you all right?'

She hadn't heard him coming into the kitchen and Brian's voice made her jump.

'Of course. Why?' At least the blush had died down from her face.

'You didn't seem very happy with your present.'

She turned to face him. 'The present's fine.'

'I can get a different colour.'

'I said, it's fine, Brian. Thank you.'

He took a step towards her. 'It's obviously not fine. You used to be pleased with lingerie.'

'That was then. Things are different now.'

'How?'

Samson appeared at the kitchen window. He stepped over the sill and on to the draining board. Drops of water clung to his paws and he lifted the front ones, flicking the drops away. She picked him up and put him on the floor. He nudged against her legs and she bent to pour milk into his bowl. She stood up again.

'For a start we were living together in a relationship.' She was able to meet his eyes at last. 'Then you left me for your tart.'

'Anita's not a tart.' His eyes clouded over as if he were genuinely shocked at the description.

'Never mind that now. You shouldn't give me underwear. We're not a couple any more. Remember?'

'But you want us to be.'

Isabel thought she'd been clever: keeping him interested by having sex with him, cool towards him at other times so he never knew where he stood. Had he really seen through her game?

'Dad!' Rose called from the sitting room. 'It's your turn.'

'You'd better go back.' She turned away to fill the kettle. 'I'll make coffee.'

She thought Brian had left the kitchen, but then he spoke: 'Who's the card from?' He was standing right behind her.

'What card?' Isabel asked although she could picture the postcard propped on the mantelpiece in the sitting room. It showed a picture of a sunset on a Cornish beach, pink light streaming across a milky sea.

'The one that says, "You're a star!" No signature.'

'Have you been reading my post?'

'I just turned it over.'

'It's private, Brian.'

'It better not be from some man, that's all!'

The car swept into the drive.

From the back seat, Isabel bent her head to get a better view of the house. 'It's huge, Rick,' she said, in spite of the warning she'd given herself not to show she was impressed. 'It must have cost a fortune.'

'A fair bit. It's got six bedrooms and three bathrooms.'

'Your brother's a successful man, Isabel,' Eva said as Rick helped her from the car. 'He can afford it.'

Isabel followed Rick round to the boot. 'You're a bit far away from Newcastle. What do the girls think?'

Rick lifted the suitcases and bags out on to the gravelled drive. 'There's more space, cleaner air, a healthy environment for them to grow up.'

Isabel laughed. 'Are you working for the tourist board in your spare time?'

Deanna was waiting for them at the front door. Eva embraced her daughter-in-law, showering her cheeks with kisses.

'You look tired, *carissima.* I hope you haven't been overdoing things.'

'Not at all. Rick's helped me, haven't you, darling?' She smiled across at him. 'Did you have a good journey?'

'Wonderful!' Eva said. 'So quick.'

Isabel and Eva had flown to Newcastle. Rick had insisted on paying for a taxi to the airport and first class seats. On the flight, Isabel sipped a glass of champagne. 'I could get used to this.'

'You must make sure you thank Rick,' Eva said. 'It's very generous of him.'

'Mum, you taught me to say please and thank you when I was two.'

'If only your father was with us.'

'But then you and Dad would have been going to Cornwall for Christmas.'

Eva's brown eyes flashed. 'Don't let Rick hear you say that!'

Isabel looked out of the window for the rest of the flight. For the first time in her life she'd stood up to Eva when she'd issued the ultimatum—'You've got till George's birthday'—but the end of January and her brother's birthday approached like an avalanche.

Near Newcastle, they hit some turbulence. As the seat belt signs came on and the plane bucked and heaved, Eva clutched her hand.

'You'll look after me, won't you, Isabel?' she said.

Rick carried the baggage upstairs, while Deanna showed Isabel and Eva into the drawing room.

'What a lovely room.' Eva waved her hands and the bracelets danced on her wrist. She crossed to the French windows that looked onto the garden. She beckoned Isabel over. *'Che meraviglia!'*

Set high above the Coquet Valley, the house commanded magnificent views. Outside was a stepped terrace, and then lawns curved down to the river. Rothbury itself, like a toy town from this distance, huddled in the valley. In the gathering twilight, a haze had settled over the village, as plumes of smoke drifted from numerous chimneys. On the other side of the river, there was a stretch of pasture land, before the hills rose steeply again. Isabel thought she would have bought the house for the view alone.

'The garden must be a lot of work, Deanna,' Eva was saying. 'I hope it's not too much for you.'

'Rick does some, and the gardener comes on Fridays. I haven't been able to do it since I started the chemo.'

Eva shuddered. 'Ugh! Chemotherapy.' She pronounced it in an exaggerated way, as if she'd been forced to use a swear word. 'My brother suffered so much.' She turned to Isabel. 'You remember Uncle Giacomo, don't you?'

Isabel glanced back to Deanna. She looked dejected. 'How's the treatment going?' Isabel asked, ignoring her mother.

'Real good. My consultant's pleased with me.' Deanna's mouth spread in a wide smile that should have suggested happiness and good health. 'Now you make yourselves comfortable. Mrs Crosby's left tea things ready for us.'

Isabel sat down on one of the cream sofas. She could imagine Samson's black hairs all over it. Her gaze took in the mahogany furniture and the low-lit alcoves lined with books. An immense Christmas tree dominated one end. Yellow-flamed candles cupped in gold holders adorned the branches. An arrangement of flowers stood on the glass-topped coffee table. Ivy leaves were entwined round fat cream candles, with golden pinecones interspersed. Christmas roses, their buds bulging, spilled from vases and bowls on every surface. A huge gilt-framed mirror hung above the fireplace. And they say there's no money in computers any more, she thought.

Deanna came in, carrying a tray of tea and biscuits. Rick followed. He piled logs on the fire.

'Winters are colder up here,' he said.

'Say if you're not warm enough.' Deanna placed the tray on the table and poured the tea. Fine bone china, Isabel decided, as she took a cup.

'I know you normally go to Midnight Mass,' Rick said, 'but I want to take you to the service on Christmas morning at All Saints. I've been every Sunday since Dad died and I've been asked to read the lesson tomorrow.'

'That sounds lovely, *caro*, but I'd rather go to Mass.'

Rick perched on an arm of the sofa next to his mother. 'You'll like All Saints,' he said. 'The panelling is magnificent.'

'I've never missed Midnight Mass.'

'They're so ecumenical nowadays, you'll scarcely know the difference.' Rick moved to an armchair and leant back with his hands behind his head. 'So, you like the house?'

'It's *bella, magnifica*.' As so often when Eva was excited, her English failed her.

'It's all down to Deanna.' He turned to Isabel. 'What do you think?'

'It's lovely.'

'I bet old Brian would be jealous as hell,' Rick said.

Deanna switched on the table lamps. 'Would you pull the drapes, honey?'

Rick crossed to the windows that looked onto the drive at the front of the house. As Isabel watched him reaching up and pulling the cord at each side of the curtains, she noticed the piano, standing between the two huge bay windows. Eva's gaze must have followed hers, because at the same moment, her mother cried, 'A piano! How wonderful. Is it for the girls?'

'It's Rick's,' Deanna told her. 'He's having lessons.'

Eva clapped her hands. 'Wait till I tell your brother. He could give you some tips. You know what a brilliant musician he is.'

'Deanna told you—I'm already having lessons.'

'And Isabel could help while she's here,' Eva went on. 'She teaches little ones, but I'm sure she'd cope with you.'

Isabel didn't dare glance at Rick. She wondered about the acquisition of the piano. Somehow, she didn't think it meant Rick had given up the idea of having their father's.

'Where are the girls?' she asked Deanna quickly.

'Flavia and Camilla are doing last minute Christmas shopping in Morpeth. They'll be back soon.'

'Will Alicia be home?'

'She's staying in Newcastle tonight, but she's promised to be here in time to open presents tomorrow. It'll be the first Christmas morning we haven't all been together.'

'She'd better be here when we get back from church,' Rick said.

'She will, honey.'

Just before supper, Flavia and Camilla arrived home.

'You'll love your present, Mum.' Camilla put her arm round Deanna's shoulder. 'I've been searching for one like it for ages.'

'She more than spent her pocket money,' Flavia said. 'I had to loan her some.'

'That's lovely.' Deanna was standing at the Aga stirring something. 'You'd better get changed. Supper's nearly ready, and Dad will be cross if you're late.'

'Dad needs to lighten up.'

'Camilla! That's not very nice. Especially in front of your grandmother.'

Camilla kissed Eva's cheek. 'Sorry Nonna, but it's true.'

Although smaller, the dining room was as splendid as the drawing room. Its wallpaper was dark red with a gold stripe and the gold was picked up in the curtains, draped in elaborate swirls around a metal rail. Alabaster carvings of lions stood waist-high at either side of the windows. An oak sideboard lined one wall, while most of the room was filled by the long dining table laden with dishes of cold meats, cheeses, salads, quiches and a tureen of steaming soup.

'We thought we'd keep it simple tonight,' Deanna said. 'Mrs Crosby prepared some of it before she went home.'

*

When Deanna wanted an early night to be fresh for Christmas Day, Isabel was glad. Her room was at the back of the house across the landing from her mother's. It was small by the standards of the rest of the house—a king-size bed with a black wrought iron frame took up most of the floor space—but it was still twice the size of her bedroom at home. She checked her presents for the next day, hung up the red dress she'd bought especially and climbed into the high bed. The white cotton sheets felt beautifully cool as she pushed her legs down to the bottom of the bed.

She hadn't had much sleep the night before. Brian's gift had upset her. She'd been so sure he would come back one day, but his certainty she still wanted him had made her feel stupid, and his sneering comment about Chloe's postcard had been the final straw. The empty bed in Rose's room had also unsettled her. Once the game of Monopoly finished, Rose said she might as well go with her father and Josh that evening, rather than Brian having to return for her on Christmas Eve as planned. Isabel didn't want to make a fuss —what difference would a few hours make? She stood at the gate to wave goodbye to the three of them, trying to make herself smile. Her jaw ached and her lips stuck to her teeth. She went straight to bed and pulled the cover over her head. Another woman would spend Christmas with her babies. She would be the one to listen to their excited whisperings early on Christmas morning, hear them laugh, watch their faces as they opened their presents, smell their sweet scent as they came close to say thank you.

It was late, but she'd thought about phoning Chloe. She remembered her words on that last night in Cornwall: 'Call me, day or night. I'm here for you.' She even got up at one stage to find her phone number. But as she searched through her address book, something fell from between the pages. It was the card Simon had handed her at Kenwood House.

and although he was poised to continue counting, it didn't appear again.

'Dad taught me how to do that.' He picked up several more stones, examining each one. '"It's all in the selection process" he used to say.'

'It's funny, isn't it?' Isabel said. 'It's the little things that get you.'

'I remember him taking me to see Arsenal play. It was the only time. I think Mum was still away in Italy and Grandma looked after you. I'd been picked for the under-10s team and I was sure I was going to be a professional footballer.'

'Did Arsenal win?'

'You bet!' Rick smiled, and for a moment Isabel saw the little tow-headed boy he must have been. 'We went to a café in Highbury afterwards to celebrate. We had fried egg and chips. "Don't tell your gran," he said. "This is our secret."' Rick looked sheepish.

He had three separate piles of stones by then. Judging by the different shapes, they were definite skimmers, possibilities and rejects.

'What do you think about me learning to play the piano?' he asked.

'If there's something you want to do, go for it,' Isabel said. 'Dad dying has made me realise how short life is.' As she heard the cliché emerge, Isabel wondered what her dream was. All she'd thought about for months was getting Brian back. There must be something she'd like to do with her life.

'George thinks it's a joke. I expect you do as well, only you're too polite to say so.'

'I don't think it's a joke, Rick.' Isabel hoped she sounded convincing.

'In a year's time I'll be able to play like Dad.'

'He had been playing all his life.'

'See!' Rick kicked his pile of discarded stones into the water. 'You don't think I can do it.'

'It's not that.' Isabel was getting cold. There was a lovely fire in the drawing room and she wanted to go in. 'But it's much harder when you're older. Like any new skill.'

'I'm going to do it, Isabel,' Rick repeated. 'And because I've bought this piano, it doesn't mean that I'm not going to have Dad's.'

'Mum wants to keep it. You know it reminds her of Dad.'

'I'm prepared to leave it for a while. That's why I've got this one in the meantime. But when she moves house, there won't be room for a piano.'

Isabel stared at him. 'You're not serious about her moving?'

'I'll wait until she's stronger. But I want her to sell up and move here. She'd be better off out of London, and Deanna and I will take care of her.'

'But I'm only ten minutes away. I'm always popping in and out.' Angry words leapt to Isabel's lips, but she clenched her teeth. It was Christmas Day, she was a guest in his home and for her mother and Deanna's sakes, she wouldn't cause a scene.

'I've already put in an offer on a house in Hexham for her,' Rick said. 'It's only thirty minutes from here.'

From the terrace came the sound of Deanna's voice calling them.

'Thank goodness. That means Alicia's home.' Rick turned towards the house. 'I knew she'd see sense when the time came.' He started to clamber up the bank from the river. He turned back and reached out to Isabel. 'Give me your hand.'

She was about to refuse, but the bank was muddy and she didn't want to give him the satisfaction of watching her undignified scramble.

Rick strode up the lawn while Isabel trailed behind him. By the time she reached the house, he was already several yards ahead, but she still heard his explosion of anger. She arrived at the door of the drawing room to find the others looking as if they'd been interrupted in a game of musical statues. Her mother sat huddled in a corner of the sofa. Deanna was standing at the drinks tray. She was deathly pale. Flavia and Camilla were at the other end of the room by the Christmas tree. They were on their knees, a present in each hand.

Rick held his eldest daughter by the arm. A young man stood behind Alicia. He was very tall and gangly. He wore a short-sleeved T-shirt with the words *Piss Head* printed across the front and jeans, which were torn at the knee. Tattoos covered his spindly forearms. His hair was stringy and greasy looking.

'If you'd let me speak...' Alicia was saying. 'This is Gary.' She turned to her right, but Rick's eyes didn't even flick in the boy's direction. His gaze bored into Alicia.

'I told you never to bring that lout here!'

'And I told you I wouldn't come today if he wasn't welcome.'

'Then why are you here?' Rick's bellow was terrifying. Isabel looked towards her mother. She'd shrunk into the cushions that enveloped her and her eyes were squeezed shut.

'You needn't think it was to see you.' Alicia spoke quietly. Every word was carefully enunciated. 'I came to see Mum and my sisters.'

Rick lifted his right arm in the air. Oh God, he was going to hit her.

Alicia laughed. 'Go on. Do it. Isn't that what bullies do when they can't get their own way? You bully the people at work and you think you can do the same to your family.'

'How dare you!' Rick clenched his fist above his head. Isabel could see his arm was shaking.

'Dad!' From the far end of the room, Flavia came to life. She pushed Camilla out of the way, knocking a present from her hand. The sound of glass splintering on the polished wooden floor filled the few seconds' silence. Deanna, too, seemed to wake from a dream. She and Flavia reached Rick at the same moment. Deanna put her arms round him. 'Honey, calm down. Alicia's your princess. Remember?'

Rick was still glaring at Gary, but he lowered his fist.

'I wanted Alicia here. I told her to bring Gary rather than stay away.' Deanna's voice was silky as she stroked his hair back from his forehead. 'I needed us to be together, Rick. This year, especially.' Deanna reached up and wound her arms round Rick's neck. She began to kiss his mouth. It felt wrong to watch, but Isabel couldn't tear her eyes away.

She wasn't sure what happened next. Whether Deanna tipped her head back too far, or Rick accidentally knocked her turban as he cupped her face in his palms, she didn't know. But Deanna's yellow turban slipped. It hung from the back of her head and then as she clutched at it, it fell to the floor. Unsightly tufts of grey hair sprouted from the largely bald dome of her head. Isabel saw the horror on Rick's face.

It lasted only a matter of seconds. Deanna bent down, swept up the turban and repositioned it on her head. 'Darling, don't look so scared.' She stroked his cheek. Rick pulled away from her embrace, and Camilla had to catch her arm to steady her. He didn't seem to notice. He went over to the sideboard and poured himself a large measure of whisky. He turned back to where the others remained mesmerised. 'I'll be in my study when dinner's ready,' he said. 'And he…' he jerked his head to where Gary stood '… had better be gone.'

Twenty

Grace poured herself a glass of water from the bottle in the fridge and stepped on to the balcony. Franco was still asleep, and she relished these moments alone. Below her, the sea was calm. It was a cold morning, but the sky was a bright blue with only the occasional cloud rolling across. Grace pulled her wrap closer round her shoulders. She was so tired; her whole body ached. Christmas was spent with Franco's family, while the restaurant had been fully booked since New Year's Eve. It would be the same now until the Epiphany.

Her eyes were drawn, as always, to the *castello* and she was just in time to see a halo of sunlight illuminate the fortress. She wondered if it had been a morning like this on 27th December 1509 when Vittoria Colonna married Count Ferrante d'Avalos in the castle cathedral. The *Castello d'Aragonese* had been a great Renaissance court, a magnet for artists and poets with Vittoria at the centre. Despite Grace's fascination with Vittoria, a sense of what it would have been like to be her remained elusive. A great beauty—Michelangelo was said to be in love with her—she was a romantic figure from a remote world. Yet she stared out from her portraits like a woman from the twenty-first century.

The light made Grace's eyes water and she raised her hand to shield them. Thoughts of Vittoria's life sent her back to when she was nineteen. She'd had a terrible row with her father. It was the summer holiday and her first year at university was over. She wasn't enjoying her degree—studying Italian was a step back instead of a new adventure. There was a boy on her course who was going to drop out and travel America. Grace had slept with him a few times and he asked her to go with him. Her father wouldn't hear of it, and when October came, Grace went back and continued her studies.

She stared across the narrow stretch of sea to the castle. Suppose she had abandoned her course and travelled to America? She would never have been in Naples teaching English. She would never have met Franco and fallen for his brown eyes and long lean body. She would never have been on a small island which—for all its beauty—imprisoned her. She would never have married Franco and felt as caged by his demands and expectations as the thick walls of the *castello* might have held her captive in earlier times.

A few nights before, the castle had been the backdrop to a spectacular show of fireworks to welcome *il nuovo anno*. Franco had gone up on the roof about eleven o'clock when the evening in the restaurant was in full swing and let off their own display. Everyone had swarmed outside on to the pavement to watch. Grace remained in the kitchen. The fireworks reminded her too much of the previous summer. Her parents had come to Ischia for the first time and together they'd watched the island's annual celebration for the feast of St Ann. The balcony provided a perfect view.

Lights had shone out from hundreds of lanterns placed around the castle and on the rocks that stood in the sea below. They cast a glow that trembled across the stretch of black water between the castle and the reefs. The sea was filled with boats of all shapes and sizes, rocking in the waves. People crammed on to the bridge that linked the castle to the island to watch the parade of decorated carnival rafts. Just after midnight, the firework display began from a boat moored out in the bay. Arcs and swirls and spirals of greens and golds and colour after shimmering colour filled the sky. Then the castle began to glow. One patch of red appeared in the darkness and then another sprang up, and another, until the whole *castello* was fired with crimson and flames leapt into the black sky. Grace remembered her mother's gasp.

'It's all right,' she'd whispered. 'It's not real. They pretend to set fire to the castle to recall the pirate invasions.'

They'd been standing close, her father in the middle with his arms round Grace and Eva.

'They don't do fireworks as well as us,' he said, 'but they're pretty nonetheless.'

'Pretty!' Eva exclaimed. 'How can you be down-key about something so magnificent?'

'You mean low-key.'

'What?'

'You said down-key. It's low-key.' Henry was the only one who dared correct Eva's mistakes. She often got annoyed, but that night she laughed.

'Down... low... who cares?' she'd said. 'I adore fireworks,' and she'd kissed Henry on the cheek.

Grace turned back to the darkened bedroom. She pulled on some trousers and a jumper. Franco was snoring. Usually he was up ages before her. He worked hard, determined to make a success of the restaurant. He wanted to extend it. In the early hours of the morning, he'd made Grace sit down with a glass of prosecco while he outlined his plans. The building next door was up for sale and Franco intended to put in a bid. He paced between the tables, as he explained how they could create three or four en-suite rooms and offer accommodation. The extra space would also be useful for the bambini.

Grace smiled awkwardly. When she came back from England the second time, she'd expected a cold reception. They'd parted on such bad terms she'd almost reconciled herself to the fact that her marriage was over. Instead Franco had been warm and loving. Asking her lots of questions about her mother, holding her tight when she woke in the night crying. In the morning, when she opened her eyes, he would be leaning on one elbow watching her, a smile on his lips. '*Mia cara*,' he would murmur, '*bella, bella*.'

One morning she had whispered the word 'Yes.'

'Yes?'

'Yes, I will.'

His dark eyes looked puzzled. 'You will what?'

'I'll have your baby.'

Perhaps it would work out. Her father had gone and nothing could replace him, but a new life growing inside her might make the pain less raw. At Christmas, when Franco had revealed the news to his family, Grace had been showered with attention. His mother could not have made more fuss of her if she'd been Our Lady herself. And for a few days she too had been consumed with joy. It was as if she was already pregnant. But in spite of that, every morning she'd continued to remove the packet of pills from the back of her underwear drawer where she'd hidden them, press one from its foil wrapping into her palm and swallow it. One day soon she would stop taking them, she told herself. One day soon.

Franco had told the staff to come in later this morning after all their hard work, and the office and restaurant were deserted. Grace opened the shutters in the office. Light streamed into the room, bouncing off piles of papers on the desk. It would be good to have more space if they expanded into next door. She turned on the computer to check her emails, hoping for something from home. She hardly ever heard from Rick, but George was an avid email and texter—sometimes sending several a day—and Isabel had been in touch a lot since their father died.

But not since Christmas. Grace watched the little icons ripple on to the screen. Since her mother and Isabel had come back from Newcastle, she'd hardly heard from her sister. She had never got used to the Italian custom of the big event being on Christmas Eve. It left her feeling flat and longing for home on Christmas Day. She used to picture the scene in her parents' dining room while she waited for them to answer the phone: him at one end of the table nearest the piano, her at the other with the light from the window gleaming through her hair. When the phone was picked up, it was always her father's voice: 'Happy Christmas, love.' 'I miss you,' she used to say. 'Aye lass,' he would answer. 'I expect you do.'

Grace hadn't been to Rick's new house, so this year she hadn't been able to visualise them all. Her mother sounded subdued when she rang and even Deanna wasn't her usual bright self. There was a lot of noise in the background—Deanna said she'd have to go as Alicia had arrived with her boyfriend—and Grace had hung on waiting for someone else to pick up the receiver. But no one had and eventually she'd been forced to hang up, disappointed that she hadn't been able to speak to Isabel.

'*Buongiorno, Signora*!'

Grace's head whipped round at the unexpected voice. Benito, the postman, was standing in the doorway. He was grinning. '*Un bel mucchio di posta oggi*!' He dropped a huge pile of mail on the desk with a wave and then Grace heard the whine of his scooter as he accelerated up the road.

She flicked through the envelopes, mostly routine stuff. But half way through the pile, she stopped. It was a blue envelope with an English stamp. The writing was small and neat and sloped backwards. She raised the envelope to her face. There was a faint smell of cigarettes. Could it be the reply she was waiting for?

On that last visit to England, Grace hadn't known what to think when she found the photo in the bureau. Seeing Henry with two people called Archie and Dottie seemed to confirm Archie Stansfield's assertion that he and her father had once been friends. *For Henry… All my love, Dottie.* What did that mean? Her father and Dottie were lovers? Dottie fell pregnant. Whose baby? She must have been having an affair with someone else—that's why the relationship had ended. But Archie had hit him. It didn't make sense.

She'd studied her mother's face when she arrived home from the Advent lunch, trying to view her with a stranger's eyes. Eva had admitted to Isabel that Henry and Archie had a row many years ago, just as Archie himself had said, and Grace was sure she knew more.

The day before she returned to Ischia, when her mother went upstairs for a rest, Grace searched the bureau again. There might be something she'd missed. She'd been about to give up, afraid her mother would come downstairs and catch her, when she'd found it. Right at the back of the bottom drawer, hidden under a pile of Granny's knitting patterns, was a scrap of paper. It looked as if it had been torn from a child's exercise book, and on it was Archie Stansfield's name and address.

She'd written to him as soon as she arrived home. His reply arrived almost by return of post. It contained only a few lines in which he politely, but firmly, refused her request for more information. It was best that things remained as they were, he'd written. He should never have come to the funeral. Shouldn't have spoken out as he did. *I trust you'll understand and respect that the past doesn't belong to us and we shouldn't meddle with it.*

It had been too tantalising. Something had happened all those years ago that her father had concealed. Grace had to know. Before Christmas she'd written a second letter to Archie Stansfield, offering to come to England to meet him again. *I need to clear up these doubts,* she had written, *so that I can grieve for my father in peace. I shouldn't have run away when we met before.*

It was Archie's reply to this letter that had just arrived. For a moment she was tempted to burn it, but she'd gone too far. Whatever Archie Stansfield had to reveal, she needed to know.

She drew the two sheets of closely written script from the envelope.

My dear Grace,

I have thought long and hard since your second letter arrived. I might not be doing the right thing, but I don't like secrets and I think you should know what happened.

Henry was my friend from the day we started school. I left when I was 14. My family didn't have any money and I went to work in the mill. But your dad was clever and his mam was determined he would stay on until matriculation. I thought he would forget about me, but he didn't. He used to call for me every Saturday afternoon and we'd go fishing down at the river. To tell you the truth, he didn't really enjoy fishing. He'd spend all his time gathering a pile of stones that he'd skim across the water. I remember the day he managed to make his pebble leap seven times. He made so much noise, whooping and cheering; I shouldn't think I got another bite for the rest of the day. We were forever quarrelling about that—I'd want it dead calm so as not to disturb the fish, and his stones would be plopping into the water all over the place. I smile now when I think of it. We were an unlikely pair to be friends. My mam said his family was posh, and some people in the town thought your grandfather was racy, what with him playing the piano at the pictures, but I didn't care. Henry was the best friend ever.

The page dropped on to Grace's lap. The computer screen told her that she had four new emails, but she didn't click on them. She was lost in thoughts of her father as a boy. The best friend Archie Stansfield ever had. She could picture the look on his face the day his skimming stone had leapt seven times. His mouth would have been drawn tight in concentration, but his eyes would have sparkled. She'd seen that look when he'd mastered a difficult piece of music.

Part of her wanted to hang on to that image of her father, as she'd always known him. It wasn't too late to destroy the letter. But deep down, she knew it was. Her eyes returned to the blue pages.

Twenty-one

After Isabel returned from Rick's, thoughts of Simon preoccupied her. Last thing at night, she'd take his card from the top drawer of her bedside table and stare at his name. She would phone him the next day, she told herself, but come the morning her resolve always weakened. It was weeks since they'd met at Kenwood and he'd probably forgotten her by now. She could imagine the call: 'Hello, it's Isabel here.' Isabel? Who on earth is Isabel? he'd be thinking. She tucked the card back inside the drawer underneath her underwear.

It was well into January when she gained the courage to ring.

'Hi, it's Isabel.'

'Hi! Great to hear from you.'

'Sorry it's been so long.'

He laughed. 'I thought the famous Franklin charm had failed to work its magic!'

'I was wondering…' This was the difficult bit. She'd never asked a man out. Well, she wasn't inviting him out exactly, but… seconds passed as all the phrases she'd rehearsed evaporated.

Simon's voice sounded again in her ear. 'If you were going to ask me if I'd like to meet…'

'Yes, yes, I was,' she said, and before her nerve went again: 'Do you? I mean would you like to?'

'Isabel, I'd love to.'

They met for lunch in a pub in Highgate. She arrived first and ordered a diet coke, trying to look as if she always propped up bars on her own. Simon rushed in with apologies. When he kissed her cheek, her heart beat faster. She was acutely aware of the warmth of his hand on her back and forgot he was late.

'How about a nice chablis?' he said.

'Wine goes to my head at lunchtime.'

'Just one glass for you then. Shall we sit at that table by the fire?' Isabel bagged the table, while Simon went to the bar.

He poured out the wine and raised his glass: 'Here's to a blue-sky, yellow-sun, green-grass day.'

'What's one of those?' The wine tasted cool on her tongue.

'You know… hunky dory, tikkety boo…'

'Oh, I've got it—a white-snow, brown-chocolate, red-bus sort of day.'

Simon laughed—a barrelling sound that made her want to join in. 'I love it, Isabel. You're on my wave length!'

This was new territory. She'd never been on anybody's wavelength before. She took a few more sips and looked at him properly. He was wearing a thick blue cotton shirt and jeans. His hair was even shorter than she remembered and it seemed to make his ears stick out. He rubbed a hand across his head when he saw her glance. 'It is drastic, isn't it?' He grinned. 'I wouldn't have had it cut if I'd known the call was going to come.'

'Sorry I didn't phone before. But I went to Cornwall to see my brother, and then there was Christmas…'

'It's fine, but I'm glad you rang in the end.' He smiled. 'Shall we eat? I'm starving.' He handed her a menu, and the tips of his fingers touched hers.

Isabel stared at the drops of condensation slipping down the neck of the wine bottle. She was sure he'd touched her on purpose. But they were meeting as friends, right? Two lost souls, rejected by their partners and sharing the hurt. She lowered her eyes to the menu. 'I'd like pasta with mushrooms.'

'I'll have the cod and chips.' Simon patted his waist. 'One day I'll take myself in hand.' He reached into the pocket of his leather jacket, which he'd hung over a chair, and pulled out a packet of cigarettes. 'I know. I know,' he said, catching her eye. 'I've given up, but I like to have them near me.'

'How was Christmas?' Simon asked as he chased the last few peas around the plate. 'Hope yours was better than mine.'

'Were you on your own?'

'Yep. I had a steak, half a bottle of whisky and watched the box all evening.'

'What about your son?'

'Helen won't let me see Edward at the moment. Says it will unsettle him.'

'It's hard, isn't it? Rose and Josh went to Brian's and I hated it.'

'And your first without your dad.'

'Thanks for remembering. People don't generally.'

'I try not to forget what people tell me—especially nice people.' Simon looked down at his food and Isabel thought she saw his cheeks flush.

'Mum and I went to Northumberland to stay with Rick and Deanna,' she said.

'Is he the brother with a big house?'

'I'll say! It's a mansion.'

'Sounds nice.'

An image of Deanna standing at the front door waving goodbye to Alicia invaded Isabel's mind. Alicia had refused to stay without Gary even though Deanna pleaded with her. Deanna had looked so lonely and frail in her yellow turban.

'It wasn't nice,' Isabel said. 'Pretty awful actually.' She drank some more wine and looked over her glass to find Simon's eyes on her.

'You know I'm a good listener,' he said.

'It's boring. I went on about family stuff too much last time.'

Simon refilled their glasses. 'I'm into living Christmas vicariously at the moment.'

'You wouldn't want to live this one. Rick had a fight with his daughter because she brought home some boyfriend he didn't like; she walked out, leaving Deanna distraught; a present my niece had bought for her mum—a little horse made from Venetian glass—got broken in the scrum; I told Deanna that Rick is a complete boor…'

'Wow! Sounds some party.'

'That's why I don't want to talk about it.'

'Okay—let's talk about how long you're going to leave it till you ask me out again.'

Isabel realised she'd nearly finished her second glass of wine. She hoped her cheeks weren't too pink. 'I did have an idea…' God, had she really said that? A vague thought that she had rejected in the night had sprouted from her lips.

'Ah! I like ideas.'

'It would just be as friends.'

'Friends—definitely.'

The doorbell rang. Isabel glanced in the mirror in the small hallway. She reached up to smooth her hair. She regretted choosing the new green trousers. George and Chloe were sure to be casually dressed. Jeans would have been better. The bell rang again. She jumped as the letterbox snapped open.

'Come on, Sis!' George called through the gap. 'It's freezing out here!'

With a final nervous glance in the mirror, she opened the door. The hall filled with cold air and jostling bodies.

'At last.' George kissed her once on each cheek and then a third time, as their mother always did. 'We were about to go to the pub up the road.'

'Hello Isabel.' Chloe smiled as she and Isabel aimed for the same cheek to kiss and there was an uncomfortable moment as their noses collided and their lips puckered fruitlessly.

Chloe laughed. 'Shall we try that again?'

Isabel was relieved. George and Chloe were her first real visitors and she'd been fussing for hours before they arrived. She'd almost cried off, but she wasn't sure where they were staying, and George wasn't answering his mobile. But the mistimed kiss broke the ice.

Isabel took the bottle of wine George was holding out.

'Come in and get warm.' She led them into the small sitting room. She'd pushed the nursing chair into an alcove and moved the *chaise longue* into the bay window to make the room look less cramped. She borrowed a small coffee table from Sally and set out crisps and nuts in little glass bowls, like she used to when she and Brian entertained. Then she had second thoughts. She could hear George's mocking voice, 'Ooh! Nibbles! How twee!' She cleared the lot away, only to have to rush round refilling the bowls before they arrived.

She opened one of the bottles of wine she'd already put on a tray. She managed to break the cork and one bit got stuck in the neck of the bottle. Damn! Just when she wanted to look in control. She pushed that bottle to one side and inserted the corkscrew in another. Great. Success this time.

From the corner of her eye, she saw Chloe helping herself to peanuts. George was sitting at the piano. He ran his fingers over the keys. 'Mm. Nice tone.'

'It needs tuning.'

George played a few more notes. 'C's a bit out, but it's not too bad. That piano of Dad's is forever going off.'

'Do you want to choose some music, George?' Isabel indicated a pile of CDs on the floor in the corner.

'Can I?' Chloe asked. 'George hasn't got any taste, if it's not classical!'

Isabel watched her brother and Chloe on their knees, squabbling about which CD to play. For the moment at least, discussion of Henry's piano was shelved.

The doorbell rang again. This had to be Simon. He was late —she'd hoped he'd be here before George and Chloe. When George had emailed that he and Chloe were coming up to London for his birthday, and it would be nice to see her, Isabel had panicked. She couldn't do it on her own, and they'd feel sorry for her in her poky flat. She'd asked Rose, but she was going to a school disco. She even considered getting Brian round, but that wasn't a good idea considering George's scathing comments, and she'd feel pathetic. Then she had a brainwave: invite Simon.

When she opened the door and saw his crinkly face and sparkly eyes, she felt a soppy smile spread across her face. She didn't feel shy introducing him to George and Chloe. 'This is Simon. He's a friend of mine.' It was okay: she'd done it, and nothing terrible had happened. Nobody laughed. Nobody seemed surprised that she should have Simon as a friend.

Somehow his easy manner, his casual request that George play the piano, the interest he showed in Chloe's work, made her relax. It was easier than when she was with Brian. 'I'm a man's man,' he used to say. 'A few pints with the lads on a Saturday and discuss the match. Can't be doing with all this namby pamby music and painting and bollocks to your computer whizz kids. With me, what you see is what you get.' She'd always been on edge at family get-togethers in case Brian said the wrong thing.

'Isabel tells me you've set up an art school, George,' Simon said as she was opening another bottle of wine. 'How's that working out? I imagine there's a lot of competition in Cornwall.'

'We've broken even this first year.'

Isabel was astonished. She wouldn't have imagined George understood the concept of breaking even, let alone was able to achieve it.

'And what about your own work?' Simon went on. 'It's supposed to suffer if you teach others.' He held up his damaged hand. 'That's why I didn't bother after this put paid to my musical career.'

'You're a musician?' George asked.

'I played violin with the BBC Phil.'

'What happened?'

Isabel tensed, but Simon didn't show the edginess about his injury that he had when she first met him.

'I was skiing—stupid thing for a violinist—when I hit a tree stump. I fell and the bloke behind me—silly bugger was too close—crashed into me. His ski sliced straight through my fingers, cut through the glove and everything.'

'That's tough,' George said. 'I don't know what I'd do if I couldn't play the piano any more, or paint for that matter.'

Simon shrugged. 'You adjust.' He turned to Isabel who was leaning over him refilling his glass. 'And compensations come along.'

Twenty-two

'I don't like these any more, Mum.'

Isabel looked at the plate in front of Josh. Spaghetti hoops had been all he would eat on his weekly visits. The kitchen cupboard was crammed with tins of them. 'Don't you? What do you like?'

'Jackets with grated cheese. They're ace.'

Isabel turned back to the sink. 'Okay. Eat the spaghetti for today. I'll do a jacket next time.'

Not so long ago she would have gone on at Josh. Why didn't he like spaghetti hoops any more? When had he gone off them? She would have blamed Anita. Now it wasn't important. She finished washing-up the saucepan and sat down at the table. Despite what he'd said, he was shovelling spaghetti into his mouth. A streak of orange sauce ran down his chin. His hair had grown longer and looked as if it needed a brush, but she knew it took a good ten minutes to achieve that effect. He scraped the plate with his spoon, chasing the last spaghetti hoop. The spoon clattered on to the plate. He looked up at her and smiled.

Isabel couldn't believe it. The scowl that had been etched on his face for months had disappeared. His eyes shone and she noticed the long fringe of eyelashes that had always been a source of admiration. 'He'll break a few hearts with those lashes,' she remembered people saying when he was younger. He'd had a gap between his milk teeth at the front, which she'd loved, but now she saw his second teeth looked white and strong.

'Guess what?' he said.

'What?'

'I've been picked for the football team.'

'That's fantastic. I'm so proud of you.'

'Will you come and watch me, Mum?'

At last. A sign that she still meant something to Josh.

'I'd love to. When is it?'

'Saturday afternoon. Oh, I forgot.' His eyes had that hooded look again. 'Anita will probably be there.' It was the first time Josh had voluntarily referred to her.

'That's okay, love,' Isabel heard herself saying. 'I won't bite her head off.'

'Kick off's 2.30. Shall I let Samson in? He's soaking.'

Isabel followed Josh's glance. Samson was sitting on the windowsill, his mouth wide in a silent miaow. His fur was thick with raindrops and his pleading eyes met hers.

'Just wipe his paws on that old cloth. He's bound to make a beeline for my bed.'

Isabel was watching television in the lounge when the bell rang. Rose had gone to a friend's after school, as she seemed to so often now, and Isabel presumed she'd forgotten her key. But as she went to the front door, she could see through the glass that the silhouette was much bigger than Rose's. It was Brian.

She pulled open the door. 'What is it? Is Josh okay?' Brian had only picked him up a couple of hours ago; surely nothing could have happened.

'He's fine. Tucked up in bed.' Brian held up his hands. 'And before you say anything, Anita helped him with his homework.'

'He told me he didn't have any.'

Isabel saw the smirk on Brian's face. Damn! She'd fallen into the trap again. 'What are you doing here then? Rose is out.'

'It's you I've come to see, Bel.' Brian leant against the doorframe. The outside light shone down on his face, highlighting his unshaven cheeks. 'It feels as if you've been avoiding me.'

'I'm busy.'

'Don't mess about. It's brass-monkey weather out here.'

Isabel opened the door wider, and Brian pushed past into the lounge. He pulled off his anorak and sat down.

Isabel hesitated in the doorway. 'Don't get too comfortable.'

Brian patted the space on the sofa next to him. 'Come and sit beside me.'

'What for?' After the humiliation of the lingerie present, Isabel had been much cooler towards Brian. It was obvious she wasn't going to get him back if she gave in to his sexual demands too easily. In any case, she didn't only want him back, she'd decided, she wanted him less cocky, more loving, more appreciative.

'Come on, Bel.' Brian stretched out his hand. 'Give a man a break.'

Isabel sat down on the edge of the sofa.

'I'm glad to have a few minutes on our own.' Brian leant forward, his elbows resting on his knees. His hands were clasped, his fingers interlaced. They were thick and powerful looking. Grease from the cars he worked on was ingrained in his fingers and the skin was split across the tips. Isabel used to rub cream into them. Once she'd bought him a hand massage as a birthday present, but he'd laughed at her and refused to go.

She fixed her eyes on the television set. 'I'm not going to bed with you, if that's what you're angling for.'

'Okay.'

She glanced across at him and caught a look of irritation on his face, but it was gone in a second.

'We need to talk about things,' he said.

'I thought talking was for wimps.' Images of Brian sprawled on the sofa, television control in his hand, sprung into her mind. How many evenings had they spent like that? She'd be perched in an armchair to Brian's right, waiting for his next request—a can of lager, cheese on toast smothered in tomato ketchup. 'Talk to me, Brian,' she'd say when she couldn't bear the gulf between them any longer.

And he'd look round, his eyes bleary with alcohol. 'Bloody hell, give a man a break, will you?'

'I've changed.' He was leaning so close to her she could feel his breath on her arm. 'Aren't you pleased I want to talk?'

'What's there to talk about?' It was some sort of quiz show on the television, but the figures jumped about in a blur before Isabel's eyes.

'We've got loads of things to sort out.'

'It all seems clear to me. You've got a nice house, Anita, the baby, Josh. And I've got this flat, and Rose who doesn't really want to be here.' Isabel's eyes travelled around the small room crowded with furniture. 'And who can blame her?'

The front door of the neighbouring flat slammed. The monotonous beat of rock music thudded against the party wall. The room vibrated with the sound. Brian was across the floor in two strides. He hammered his fist against the wall. 'Shut that bloody row up!' He raised his fist again, but as suddenly as it had started, the music stopped. He looked back at Isabel. 'How do you stand that racket?'

She laughed. 'You ask me that?'

He sat down again. 'I'm sorry, Bel. This is why we've got to talk. Will you meet me on Sunday? I can get away for a couple of hours around lunchtime.'

Isabel felt herself soften. He looked just like Josh struggling with his homework, all creased forehead and earnest expression. He wanted her, she could see that. It would be so easy now to let him kiss her. To feel needed again. She moved towards him on the sofa.

'You've got lovely eyes,' Brian said.

Isabel gazed at him. She wanted to believe him. Every bit of her wanted to trust him. She could have her life back. Give Rose and Josh their family again. She stared at the broken veins on his cheeks. 'You've never said that to me before.'

He took her hand. 'There's a lot of things I didn't say. I'm not proud of myself. You were a good wife.' He reached out and stroked her cheek.

This was it. This was the tenderness she'd craved.

He brushed his hand over her hair, easing it back from her face.

She ran her fingers along his thigh, and he smiled. 'That's nice.' He pushed her blouse back from her shoulder and she felt his mouth on her skin, in that little hollow above the collarbone. She shivered. He freed her arm from the blouse and lowered her bra strap. Her nipple was in his mouth, and he was sucking on it. She gasped.

He lifted his head.

'Don't stop.'

His fingers were stroking her breast. His face was close. She could see her reflection in his eyes.

'It's you and me, isn't it, Bel?'

She nodded.

'Always has been. Always will be.'

'Yes.'

'You don't want anybody else?'

'No.

His fingers moved to her other breast. 'That's the end of this man you've met then?'

'What man?'

'This bastard Simon.'

It was as if he'd spat at her. She lifted her hand to cheek, almost expecting to find a globule of spittle.

'What do you know about Simon?'

'Aha! I was right.' His fingers circled her nipple. 'Simon? What sort of poncy name is that?'

She pulled away from him. It was horrible. Her breast was exposed. She felt as if a spider was trailing over her skin.

'What? What have I said?' Brian's voice had that hurt tone that reminded her of a child's whining.

She got up from the sofa, dragging at her blouse. The bra strap was in the way and she couldn't cover herself. She could still feel the sensation of hairy feet on her breast. 'Get out, Brian.'

He stood up, fiddling with his groin. 'Christ, what am I supposed to do with an erection like this?'

'You should have thought of that before.'

He tucked his shirt into his trousers. 'I don't get it.'

'No, you don't, do you?'

'All I said was that I didn't want you to see this other man. You can't blame me for wanting you to myself.'

She pulled the edges of the blouse tighter. 'I'd like you to go now.'

He put his hands on her shoulders. 'I can see you're upset. Why don't we have another chat when you've calmed down.'

'I don't want another chat.'

He squeezed her shoulders tighter. 'Meet me on Sunday. We could go to Hampstead Heath. You always liked it there.'

Isabel backed away from him. 'I'm going to Italy on Sunday to see Grace.'

'You didn't say.'

'I don't have to inform you of my movements.'

'What about Rose?'

'It's all taken care of. And I've explained to Josh what's happening.' She crossed to the television and turned it off. The scent of some cheap after-shave he was wearing was making her feel sick.

'What about Saturday?' he said. 'Are you coming to Josh's match?'

Her head jerked up. 'How do you know he's asked me?'

Brian smiled. 'Because I persuaded him to.'

Isabel swung her arm wide and clapped her palm against Brian's cheek. Her ears rang with the crack. She clutched her arms against her chest. Her palm tingled.

Brian cradled his cheek in his hand. The blue of his eyes was intense. She thought she could see tears.

'You bitch,' he snapped. 'You complete bitch.'

'You deserved it. You can't treat me like that.'

He straightened his shoulders and moved to the door. He was going. Thank God, he was going. Her legs were trembling. She couldn't collapse yet.

He looked back at her. 'Pleased with yourself, are you?'

'I told you—you deserved it.' *Please go now. Just go.*

'This… Simon.'

What now? How on earth had he found out about Simon?

'Tolerant sort of bloke, is he?'

'Leave it, will you? I've got nothing to say.'

'I hope he's tolerant.' The shock had gone from Brian's face, but a red weal marked his cheek. There was a cut on the cheekbone where her ring must have caught it. 'He'll need to be when he hears about your dirty little secret.'

'I haven't got any secrets.'

'No?' Brian laughed; a sound that grated. 'So he knows you've been fucking me behind his back, does he?'

Twenty-three

Isabel's eyes flicked to the departures board: Amsterdam. Berlin. Ottawa. Still no sign of her flight. They'd arrived far too early.

Simon must have sensed her impatience. 'Shouldn't be long now.'

'I hate waiting around like this.' She bunched her fists together in her lap.

He put his hand over hers. His skin felt cool, and her anxiety ebbed with his touch.

'I wanted to make sure I got you here in plenty of time,' he said. 'You know what I'm like.'

It was true he'd been late every time they'd met, and last time she'd teased him: 'Is your alarm permanently set on snooze?'

He laughed. 'It is a bad habit of mine. I promise I'll do better.'

So today he'd arrived at the flat to drive her to the airport an hour early, and they'd been waiting for an eternity for the flight to appear on the board.

'I think I'll go through passport control now.'

She felt his hand tighten round hers. 'Stay a bit longer. Till your flight's up at least.'

'I get jittery hanging about,' she said. 'At least if I go through—'

'I wish you weren't going.'

'Do you?'

'I'm going to miss you.'

She knew from the tension in his hand that he was waiting. There was an implicit script for this conversation. The gap for her reply strained between them. 'Simon, we're just—'

'I know. I know. We're just friends.'

Isabel couldn't think of anything to say. She opened her handbag and checked her passport and ticket again. *Dirty little secret… dirty little secret…* the words circled in her head. Her fingers gripped the passport.

'I know it's a difficult time for you, Isabel. But when you come back… I wondered… oh, hell… I'm not very good at this.' Simon put his head in his hands.

She gazed at his damaged fingers, at the puckered skin over the stumps. She longed to put her lips to them.

'You know what I'm trying to say, don't you?' With his head buried against his chest, Simon's voice was almost inaudible. She inclined her head towards his. He looked up and she found herself staring into his eyes. She felt the current race between them.

Dirty little secret … dirty little secret.

There it was: Naples. Her destination on the board at last. She jumped up. 'I've got to go—the flight's showing.'

The plane approached Naples just before two. They circled over the city and Isabel had her first glimpse of Vesuvius. It rose from the plains like a monster from the depths. A haze hung over Naples, obscuring much of it from view. But beyond, she could see the sea glittering in the spring sunshine. Despite her heritage, it was only her second trip to Italy. There had been a disastrous honeymoon in Venice: mosquitoes had mercilessly bitten Brian, and he'd driven her mad with his complaints about the crowds and the smell of decay he insisted hovered over the canals.

Isabel glanced from side to side as she walked through the arrivals gate: crowds were crammed against the barrier. Some were holding up name cards; others waved at passengers behind her. Everyone seemed to be in intense discussion—the volume was deafening. There was no sign of her sister.

Then, from behind, her case was yanked from her hand and an arm thrust through hers. 'Bel! So sorry I'm late!' It was Grace.

Isabel turned and hugged her. 'Am I pleased to see you!'

'Crisis at the restaurant. I had to catch a later ferry.'

'I've had any numbers of offers while I've been waiting.' Isabel jerked her head to indicate the men clustered round them.

'Bel!'

'Joke, Grace.'

'Sorry.' Grace screwed up her nose. 'Sense of humour by-pass.'

She headed for the exit and Isabel had to run to keep up. Her sister's normally shiny hair was lank and her black jumper had a yellowish stain across the front. She studied Grace, as she hailed a taxi and dumped the case in the boot. Under her olive-skinned complexion, she was pale and tired looking and her brown eyes were ringed with even darker circles.

'I thought we'd have lunch in Naples.' Grace leant forward to give instructions to the taxi driver. 'They say you've never tasted pizza until you've had one in Napoli.' She pointed out places of interest as they sped down the dual carriageway.

'What's up?' Isabel interrupted Grace's description of the statue they were passing.

'What do you mean? What makes you think something's up?'

Isabel pointed to Grace's right thumb. Around the base of the nail, the skin was red and inflamed. One part had a brown scab where it was starting to heal, but congealed blood had settled on the remainder like a fly. 'You haven't done that to yourself for years.'

'Don't.' Grace clutched her thumb with her left hand. Her father used to tell her off constantly for chewing her fingers. But once she left home to go to university, it stopped. For years the skin had been smooth, her nails beautifully manicured.

'There's got to be a reason for that,' Isabel said.

'I'll tell you when we get to the restaurant. It's not far now.'

They settled at a table in a small pizzeria. The waiter, a short man enveloped in an oversized apron, arrived with the menus and a crisp white cloth, which he spread on the table with flourish. Grace waved the menus away. She ordered two pizza neapolitana and a jug of vino locale. The waiter reappeared with the wine almost immediately. He poured two glasses and backed away, bowing at each of them.

'Salute, Bel.' Grace held up her glass. 'It's good to have you here.'

Isabel sipped the wine. 'It's not bad news, is it?'

'What are you on about?'

'I can see there's something,' Isabel said. 'I'm imagining all sorts of things.'

Grace reached into her bag and drew out an envelope. 'Read this.' She pushed it into Isabel's hand.

The letter had an English stamp. That made sense. Grace had come to England just before Christmas. She was ill and she'd had tests done. If Isabel opened the letter, was she going to be reading her sister's death sentence? She studied the front of the envelope. It was creased as if it had been handled many times. She didn't recognise the handwriting, but surely it would have been typed if it was from a hospital.

'Go on,' Grace urged. 'Read it.'

Isabel drew the blue pages from the envelope and sought out a signature. She raised her eyebrows. 'Archie Stansfield?'

'Read it.'

Isabel's eyes raced across the lines of elaborate heavily looped writing. Archie Stansfield's letter made her father seem so vivid. When she got to, *Henry was the best friend I ever had*, she thrust the pages back at Grace: 'I don't want to read any more.'

'Go on. You've got to read the rest.'

As you know, that friendship ended. Well, in a way it ended. I hated him for what he'd done, but in a way I still loved him. Hope that doesn't sound too soppy. I don't mean nothing by it. I loved my wife dearly. It's lonely since she passed on last year. But any road, it's your dad as you want to hear about.

Even though we didn't speak, I always knew what was happening. How he was getting on. There was the odd letter from him, and his mam and dad still lived nearby. Not that I spoke to them. I blamed them for what happened, especially her—she was a hard woman, his mam—but it's a small town and people talk.

Course he won his music scholarship—our Dottie always said he would—and he went off to London. He wrote to me, inviting me down to his graduation concert. But I didn't go. Then I heard he'd got married. Richard was born and then Isabel. It's all right for him, I used to think. Then you came along—'his little Grace' he called you in his letter. And I saw you that once when he came to the house. Pretty little mite, you were.

Next I knew Eva had left him. I know as you said she went to Italy to nurse her mother, but his mam told my auntie Joan that she'd left. She took you with her, and his mam went down to London to look after Richard and young Isabel. I had a letter from Henry while Eva was gone: 'She's not coming back, Archie. I've lost her,' he said. In spite of everything, I felt sorry for him. I wanted to write and tell him 'You've got to fight for her, like you should have done for our Dottie. Go over there and bring her back.' I didn't write, but he must have gone, cause next thing I got a letter and he said 'she's back, but she's pregnant and it's not mine.' Happen he's got his comeuppance, I remember thinking. I didn't hear from him again, but his mam came home, so I presumed Eva had stayed.

I only saw him once more at his mam's funeral. I sat at the back, but I'm positive he knew I was there. I was surprised how different he seemed. He looked like his dad.

It was a shock when your mam phoned to say he'd gone. I'd never met her, but she said Henry had told her about me and she thought I should know. I don't know how she got my number—it was hard to understand everything she said. I wish now I'd made my peace with him before he went.

Yours truly,
Archie Stansfield

Isabel dropped the letter on the table and looked up.

Grace was staring at her. 'Well? What do you think?'

Isabel couldn't believe it: 'pregnant, and the baby is not mine.' She was off the hook. She wasn't going to have to betray her mother's confidence. Someone else had done it for her. 'I don't know what to say.'

'Aren't you shocked? Do you think…' Grace began to prompt her.

'I'm shocked at the letter. Not what it says.'

Grace didn't seem to take in what Isabel was saying. 'But Bel…' Two spots of colour had appeared on her cheeks as if she'd applied dollops of rouge. 'Don't you realise what this means: Mum had an affair; Dad colluded in covering it up and…'

'George is our half brother.'

'It can't be true!'

'Grace…'

'Not Mum and Dad. They were madly in love till the day he died. We all knew that.'

'Grace…'

'I reckon Archie Stansfield's got this grudge against Dad and he wants to make it look bad for him.'

Isabel put her hand on Grace's arm. 'It's true,' she said. 'I think the letter is true.'

Grace started to cough. Some of her wine must have gone down the wrong way. She waved her hands about, as she tried to get her breath. Eventually the spasm subsided. She took a sip of water. 'What makes you say that?'

'Mum told me.'

'Mum? When?'

'The day Dad died.'

'What, months ago?'

'That morning after we got back from the hospital. I was helping her get into bed, and she told me then.'

'What exactly did she say?'

Isabel took a deep breath. She should have anticipated all these questions. 'I can't remember. She just said it.'

'What? By the way, Isabel, I know you think I loved your father but actually I had a baby by some other creep.'

'Grace, it's not my fault!'

'I'm sorry, Bel.' Grace's eyes were huge. 'But I can't believe you've known all this time and you didn't say anything.'

'Mum made me promise not to. I went along with it, but it's been torment.'

'That's awful.'

'I had a row with Mum in the end. I told her she had until George's birthday to come clean—'

'But that was in January.'

'I couldn't bring myself to say anything in the end. I was scared what would happen. But I decided before I came over that I was going to tell you.'

'I don't know whether I'd have believed you without Archie Stansfield's letter. It's really weird to think George has got a different father.' Grace filled her glass again. 'Everyone always says he and I are like twins.'

'I know what you mean. When I was in Cornwall, I kept looking at him as if somehow I expected him to be different.'

'It's finding out now, isn't it? If we'd known from the beginning…'

Isabel dipped a bread stick into the bowl of olive oil the waiter had put on the table and chewed on it. 'Mum said Dad had made her promise to keep it a secret.'

'I don't believe it. "Own up and shame the devil" he always said.'

'She said Dad couldn't cope with people knowing she'd been unfaithful.'

'So why did he tell Archie Stansfield?'

The waiter arrived with their pizzas and they were silent while they ate. Afterwards they went over the story again.

'I suppose technically they didn't lie,' Isabel said.

'They didn't tell the truth though, did they?'

'Perhaps they thought it was for the best… you know… difficult for George to come to terms with.'

Isabel watched Grace's changing expressions as she considered the idea. She hadn't changed all that much from the little girl struggling to learn English, her face screwed up in concentration.

'I suppose we all tell lies sometimes,' Grace said. 'But it's not really their secret to keep, is it? Surely George has a right to know who his father is.' She put her hand to her mouth. 'I've just thought… did she tell you who?'

Isabel shook her head. 'She wouldn't budge on that.'

Grace beckoned to the waiter. 'Let's have coffee and we'd better head home. Franco will be wondering where we are.'

When the coffee arrived, Isabel stirred it slowly. If it was anything like the coffee Mum made, it would be too strong for her. 'I've been thinking,' she said. 'We got so caught up in the George mystery, but there's loads of other stuff I don't understand in that letter.'

'I know. He told me he and Dad had a terrible row and I thought his letter was going to explain why. Instead of that, he seems to skirt round the subject.'

'Yeah. What does he mean Dad got his comeuppance, and "fight for her, like you should have done for Dottie"?'

Grace shrugged. 'Search me. He told me Dad and his sister, Dottie, were sweethearts when they were young, and Dottie got pregnant.'

The weather was cold and grey for the first couple of days of Isabel's stay in Ischia. Grace and Franco were busy—meetings with the architect about the building next door and a big family party who took over the restaurant each evening. Isabel didn't mind being left to her own devices. She was staying at a pensione not far from the *ristorante*. It was quiet and each morning she slept late. She hadn't realised how tired she was.

After breakfast, she walked into Ischia Ponte. She crossed the small causeway leading to the castle and stopped at a bar tucked away next to a pebbled beach. She ordered a cappuccino and gazed at the waves, tiny ripples like crimped hair. She wondered what Simon was doing. Was he thinking about her? He'd looked bewildered when she rushed away from him at the airport. He'd probably been steeling himself to make that speech. Strange to think she hadn't found him attractive when they first met. Now his steady grey eyes and full lips spread tingling warmth through her. He would watch her when she was talking and his interest made her feel special.

She sipped her cappuccino and took her mobile from her bag. She sent texts to Rose and Josh. She'd recently bought Josh a mobile, so that it was easier to keep in touch. *R u in the team this week?* she wrote. She'd loved watching him play last Saturday, and when he scored a goal, she screamed his name as loud as she could. There was no sign of Brian, or the baby, but she met Anita, a thin woman with mousy hair, who darted timid glances at Isabel as they stood on the touchline. After the game Josh had rushed up to Isabel and ignored Anita.

*

Three days into Isabel's stay the clouds lifted and the sun appeared. Grace was free and she took Isabel on a tour of the island. From the square at the foot of the castle, they caught the bus into Ischia Porto. 'I won't drive you,' Grace said. 'The roads terrify me.' So they boarded the *circulare*, a bus that would take them all round the perimeter of the island. 'We can go in either direction,' Grace explained, 'but anti-clockwise gives better views.' They passed through places with exotic names, Casamicciola and Lacco Ameno, towns sandwiched between the sea and the mountain that towered over them. Sandy beaches, deserted in the thin February sun, stretched away to the right, while to the left the road was fringed with trees behind which stood hotels and small pensione. The bus lumbered on into Forio. The haunt of poets and artists in the fifties, Grace explained. 'Let's stop for lunch. There's a good *trattoria* near the church.'

It was warm enough to sit outside now and Isabel lifted her face to the sun. 'Mm, this feels good.'

Grace ordered them each a glass of wine and a plate of spaghetti pomodoro. 'Sorry, Franco and I have been so busy.'

'The relaxation is exactly what I need.' Even with her eyes closed, Isabel could feel Grace appraising her. She opened them. 'Well, what's the verdict?'

'Was I staring?' Grace fiddled with cutlery the waiter had put on their table. 'You've lost some weight, haven't you, Bel? And that strained look's gone from your face.'

'I've had a minor breakthrough with Josh. That's helped.'

'I thought he'd come round. And what about Simon?'

Isabel looked up towards the sky rather than meet Grace's stare. Answer in a normal way, she told herself. You're not a teenager—you don't need to blush and stumble around for words. 'He's nice,' she said. That should do it. Nice: a safe bland word. Pleased with her note of offhandedness, she added 'How do you know about Simon?'

Grace laughed. '*He's nice*—I knew you wouldn't be able to leave it at that.'

'I wondered how you knew, that's all.'

'You mentioned him in an email, and George told me you'd found yourself a new man.'

'George should keep his big mouth shut! Simon is a friend.'

Grace raised her glass to Isabel. 'Here's to friends, I say.'

Their lunch was simple, but delicious. The tomato sauce was rich and creamy and the pasta had the right amount of bite. The wine made Isabel sleepy. She pushed her plate to one side and leaned back. She felt as if she might have dozed off when she heard Grace's voice: 'I said—what are we going to do about George?'

Isabel was instantly awake. 'Can't we put that on the back burner?'

'I've been thinking about it. George and Rick should be told.'

'Let's wait and see what happens.'

'They've got a right to know,' Grace insisted. 'How would you feel if you found out we were all keeping some secret from you?'

'I'd hate it but—'

'There's no but. We've got to tell them. Apart from anything else there's the piano.'

'What's that got to do with it?'

'They both want Dad's piano, right?'

'Right.'

'If Rick finds out George is not Dad's son—'

'Only biologically, Grace. In every other way, Dad was his father.'

'That's not how Rick will see it. Better he finds out now than later.'

'He'd make George's life a misery. You know what he's like.'

'He's got too much on his plate to bother with George,' Grace said. 'The news is not good about Deanna.'

Isabel felt her scalp prickle at the thought of her brothers. 'I can't do it, Grace. I can't bear the thought of George's face when he hears about this.'

On the southern side of the island, most of the other passengers got off at Ponte Grado. The buses waited there for a few minutes before completing the trip back to Ischia Porto. Isabel and Grace stayed on while the driver leant out of his window to chat to one of his colleagues. Grace gestured down the hill. 'Sant'Angelo.' Isabel glimpsed the sea and a huddle of houses, washed in delicate pinks and blues and yellows.

'We'll go there one day. It's beautiful, especially in spring and autumn when it's cooler and not besieged by tourists,' Grace said. 'God's own hideaway on earth.'

Isabel heard a strange note in her sister's voice and turned to look at her. A smile lifted her mouth, emphasising the tiny lines at the corners. She was distracted.

'You love it here, don't you?' Isabel said.

'Very much.'

'Would you and Franco ever leave?'

Grace shrugged. 'Who knows what the future holds?'

Isabel pulled her jacket round her. She suddenly felt cold. The driver restarted the engine and the bus pulled away up the hill to Panza.

It was late morning and Isabel and Grace sat at one of the tables in the restaurant with Franco, enjoying coffee and *pastiere*.

‘I think we’ll go over to the *castello* today,’ Grace said. ‘I want to show you the cathedral where Vittoria Colonna got married.’

Franco picked up one of Grace’s hands and kissed the back. ‘My wife…’ he said turning to Isabel. ‘I think she’s a little… *innamorata di Vittoria*.’ Grace pulled her hand free of his. ‘Don’t be silly, Franco.’

Isabel stood in the ruined cathedral, examining the columns and archways where the remains of statues and intricate carvings were visible in the blighted stonework. The high vaulted roof was largely open to the sky, clumps of moss and other vegetation its main decoration. Grace was standing close to where the altar would have been. She gazed up as if praying. Isabel wondered if Franco had a point. Grace was obsessed with this Vittoria.

A cold wind was blowing across the cavernous space. The *scirocco*, Franco had told her that morning. She watched her sister’s slim back. Even from a distance, she could see her shoulders were hunched under her coat

Twenty-four

Rick picked up the phone to ring Deanna. She hadn't been so well over the last month, and he'd been trying to get home earlier. She answered on the first ring.

'I'm afraid I'll be late,' he told her. 'I've got these wretched figures.'

'Don't worry,' she said. 'I'm watching TV, and Camilla's here.'

'Where's Flavia?'

'She's working on a project with a friend. You remember Sophie. She'll probably stay the night.'

'Are you sure you're okay?'

'I'm fine, honey. Don't fuss.'

Rick let the receiver drop into its cradle. He stared at the spreadsheet on the computer screen. He had the chance to take over a technology company in the Midlands, but when he looked at the increased staffing costs alone, he realised his gross turnover would have to double. His accountant said there was no way he could make it work. But if he made the Midlands, it wasn't such a leap to the south.

There was also the bungalow in Hexham he'd bought for his mother. They hadn't accepted his first offer and he'd had to go higher than he could afford. Still, once she sold the house in Highgate, he could recoup most of that and she'd still have a tidy amount left over to boost her pension.

Deanna wasn't sure. 'Honey, don't you think you ought to talk to your mom before you spend money on a house she might not even want?' she'd asked the day he went to sign the contract.

'Dad always looked after her and I'm going to take over now he's gone.'

'You can't fill your dad's shoes, my precious.'

'You don't always know what's best for me!' he'd shouted.

He cursed himself now remembering the tears in her eyes. Why was he on such a short fuse all the time? And he had to admit, she was often right. Perhaps she was this time. Perhaps Eva would take convincing that the move was a sensible step. He'd written to her to explain what was happening, but perhaps he'd need to see her too. That might not be a bad idea. It would give him a chance to talk to her about the piano. He'd held off long enough and she'd need time to get used to the idea of him having it.

He turned back to the computer. There had to be some way he could make this new company work. If he moved some of the Newcastle staff to Birmingham… no, they were down to the bone as it was. He picked up the photo of Deanna and the girls he kept on his desk. He ran his fingers lightly over Deanna's face. He wouldn't let anything happen to her. He loved her so much.

Apart from all this stuff with Alicia, that is. Ever since the fiasco at Christmas, Deanna had been on at him to let Alicia come home.

'When she sees sense and finishes with that layabout, she'll be welcome,' Rick said. 'Until then…'

'But she's our daughter and I miss her,' Deanna had pleaded. He longed to see Alicia himself, but he wasn't going to admit it. If she chose to disregard his wishes, then he had no choice. She was throwing herself away on that yob, and he was right to reject her till she saw sense.

After Christmas he'd gathered up all the photos of Alicia and pushed them into a drawer. But Deanna must have retrieved the one taken for Alicia's eighteenth birthday and replaced it on the bureau. Deanna was looking so tired that he hadn't got the heart to complain. In fact he often used to slip into the drawing room himself so that he could catch a glimpse of his daughter's beautiful face.

He forced his eyes back to the computer screen. He was spending too much time on this emotional claptrap. Work: that was the thing that mattered.

*

He thought he'd found a way to raise some funds, when the phone rang. He reached for the receiver, ready to tell Deanna he'd be on his way any minute now. He'd be in Rothbury before ten. He would open a bottle of wine and they could watch some television together.

'Hello Dad.'

'Flavia, I thought you were staying with Sophie.'

'It's not Flavia.'

'What?'

'It's Alicia.'

Rick's heart jumped. 'Alicia, thank God! I told Mum you'd see sense in the end. I'll pick you up. We can drive back together.'

'That's not why I'm ringing.' Alicia had always had a slight speech impediment, which he loved. When she was a little girl she would put on concerts, marching up and down in front of her parents on podgy little legs, while she lisped her way through Baa, Baa, Black Sheep and Twinkle, Twinkle, Little Star. Nowadays you could hardly detect the lisp, but this evening it was obvious. She was still his baby.

'Not tonight then,' he said. 'It would be better to warn your mother first. She'll be thrilled. When do you want to come? I can help you move your stuff.'

'Dad, listen a minute. I'm not coming back.'

'You're still seeing that slime-ball?'

'If you mean Gary, yes, I am.'

Rick felt the familiar throb in his brow. 'Then, what the hell are you ringing for?' His fist was clenched around the phone. 'I thought I told you—'

'Mum's been rushed to hospital.'

'What's happened?' He barked out the words.

'She couldn't get her breath and then blood started coming out of her mouth. I phoned for an ambulance.'

'Where was this?'

'At home.' Alicia's voice was barely a whisper.

'You were at home?'

From the other end of the line came the sound of Alicia crying. 'Dad, you've got to get here.' Her voice broke. 'I'm scared she's going to die.'

The room they'd put Deanna in was tiny. The walls sloped inwards, the feeling of claustrophobia emphasised by their khaki colour. The small window was too high for anyone but the tallest person to see out. Disinfectant hung in the air. Rick was back to that night his father died and they sat trapped together in a room much like this one, as they watched his life tick away. He shook his head. It wasn't that night. And it wasn't his father lying in the high narrow bed. It was Deanna, the woman who meant more to him than the whole world.

An oxygen mask covered most of her face and a drip was being fed into her left arm. Above the mask, her eyes were closed and the lids looked thick and puffy. Rick stared at her hands. They were clasped across her chest, one on top of the other in an attitude of prayer. It was as if she was already dead.

He felt stinging at the back of his eyes and he blinked. He wouldn't cry, especially in front of Alicia and Camilla. They both turned from the bedside as he appeared in the open doorway.

'Dad.' Alicia got up and came towards him. 'Thank goodness you're here.'

Rick sidestepped her arms and approached the bed. He looked down at Deanna, one hand on Camilla's shoulder. 'How is she?'

There was silence apart from the hiss of the oxygen mask.

'Camilla, how is she?'

Camilla looked up at him, her blue eyes that were so much like Deanna's, wide and scared. 'I don't know,' she whispered.

Alicia moved back to her place by the bed. She took one of Deanna's hands in hers. 'They haven't told us anything,' she said, her voice low and flat.

Rick turned away. 'I'm going to find a doctor.'

There was no one at the nurses' station. He leaned forward, his elbows on the counter and closed his eyes. He thought of Deanna this morning when he went in to say goodbye. She'd been sitting up in bed reading. Her face looked lined and thin. It was the first time he'd noticed how much weight she'd lost.

He sat down on the edge of the bed. 'I hate you being ill.'

'Honey, I could use your support right now.' She reached for his hand. Hers was cold and clammy. 'Cuddle me, please.'

He wrapped his arms round her. It was like holding a bird. She rested her head against his shoulder and the fur of grey hair tickled his cheek. It was starting to grow back after the chemotherapy and was cropped short. Rick couldn't escape the thought of her long blonde hair. He saw its golden strands, smelled its freshly washed scent, felt its caress as it lay across his chest when they woke in the mornings. It had been so thick and glossy. When they first met he would brush it for her. Long sweeping strokes, feeling her head beneath his hands move backwards and forwards in time with each stroke. She would sit at the big mirror in their bedroom and watch his reflection as he stood over her, with her eyes following his movements. When he couldn't bear to wait another moment, he would lift her into his arms and carry her to the bed.

He felt someone touch his arm and opened his eyes. A woman in a white coat, stethoscope hanging from her neck, was standing next to him. She looked too young to be taking care of someone so precious.

'What's happening?' he asked. 'What's wrong with my wife?'

'The lung has filled with fluid,' the doctor explained, gazing at a point above Rick's head. 'It's the organ's reaction to the tumour, I'm afraid.'

'What tumour? She hasn't got a tumour in the lung. She's had breast cancer.' He turned to the nurse who'd appeared at the doctor's side. 'Can you get someone with some medical knowledge to speak to me?'

The nurse tightened her lips. 'Doctor Hansard is one of our senior registrars. She knows as much about your wife's case as anyone.'

'Perhaps I can explain.' The doctor spoke again. 'Unfortunately your wife has developed metastases…'

'Metastases?'

'Secondary tumours have formed in the lungs. We've been trying her on a different sort of chemotherapy—one where you don't lose your hair—but the fluid is not a good sign.'

'How long has she known?'

'She saw Mr James, the oncologist, just before Christmas. He explained it all to her then.'

Rick tried to take in the doctor's explanation of the treatment. The fluid would be drained off. She would have a full body scan. She should be able to come home in a couple of days if they were happy with her blood count and they'd start her on another course of chemotherapy. He couldn't stop thinking how Deanna had known even at Christmas and kept it to herself. That was typical. She wouldn't have wanted to spoil it for anyone else. She had done that for them, and then Alicia had ruined the day with her pigheaded selfishness. He turned away from the doctor.

Alicia was standing in the door of Deanna's room. 'What did she say?' Her face was the colour of chalk.

Rick looked at her as if she hadn't spoken. 'That stunt you pulled at Christmas. That's what's made your mother so ill.'

'Please don't say that, Dad.'

'I'm going to tell you once more, Alicia. You're to give that prat his marching orders.'

'I can't do that.' Alicia's eyes pleaded with him. 'How would you have liked it if Grandad had told you to give up Mum?'

Rick bunched his fists. His nails dug into his palms. She had gone too far this time. 'Don't you dare compare you and that rat to your mother and me!' He could see the bed over Alicia's shoulder. Deanna's body caused only a slight swell in the covers. Camilla was resting her head on the pillow next to her mother's.

Rick felt his heart contract. Supposing Deanna didn't get better? He had to get his princesses back together. He tried to grasp Alicia's hand. 'I'm asking you… if you won't do it for me or your sisters… do it for your mother.'

She snatched her hand away. 'Don't do this emotional blackmail kick, Dad. This is for you. Mum doesn't want me to give Gary up.'

'Of course she fucking does!' he shouted and he saw Camilla lift her head from the pillow and stare at him.

'It's a good job Mum can't hear you,' Alicia said. 'No wonder she's got cancer. It's the stress of living with you.'

Twenty-five

Rick clutched his head. 'I didn't realise I was such a monster.' He reached out for his whisky glass and drained the last bit.

'You're not, Dad.' Flavia put her hand on his shoulder.

'But suppose it's true what Alicia said. What if Mum's illness is all my fault?' It was one o'clock in the morning and they were sitting at the kitchen table. Flavia had made Camilla a mug of drinking chocolate and she'd gone up to bed.

'Of course it's not. You fly off the handle sometimes, but Mum adores you—you know she does.'

'What made Alicia say that?'

'Dad, I thought you were an intelligent man. Alicia's angry with you about Gary. And she's worried about Mum—you know how close they are.'

Of all his daughters, Rick knew Flavia least well. She was the quietest of the three and often pushed into the background, sandwiched between the volatile Alicia and Camilla who, as the baby, was fussed over. He'd been so besotted with Alicia that he hadn't taken much notice of Flavia. Now he realised how calm and reassuring her presence was, like Deanna's.

After Alicia stormed out, Rick had phoned Flavia. She came to the hospital by taxi and took control. They sat by Deanna's bed until the doctor arrived to set up the drain.

'There's nothing you can do,' the nurse said after a while. 'I should go home and get some rest.'

In the car Rick struggled to fit the key into the ignition. He jabbed at the hole, but the key refused to slide in. His head dropped on to the steering wheel. Flavia had got out of the passenger seat and come round to his door. She had prised his fingers from the keys. 'I'll drive, Dad. You look done in.'

'Did you know Alicia has been coming home to see your mother?' Rick asked.

Flavia nodded.

'Why didn't Deanna tell me?'

'What would you have done if she had?'

'Forbidden it.'

She smiled. 'That's why she didn't tell you.'

'Alicia hates me.' Rick reached for the bottle and poured himself another drink. It was the only way he'd get any sleep tonight. 'I only want what's best for her. I can't let her throw herself away on that lout.'

'You can't choose for us, Dad, however much you care. What are you going to do if you don't approve of my boyfriend?'

He looked up from his glass. 'I didn't know you had one.'

She laughed. 'I haven't. Too many essays for that. But one day I will, and you might not like him. Nor Camilla's. Are you going to fall out with all of us?'

When Rick finally steeled himself to go to bed, he rolled over on to Deanna's side. He burrowed into her pillow, savouring the hint of her perfume. But the more he tried to capture her, the more she receded. He turned on his back and stared up at the ceiling. He'd opened the curtains before he got into bed, and moonlight streamed into the room. He placed his palms together, matching fingertip with fingertip. He'd been going to church since his father died, but it was years since he had prayed and the gesture felt strange. There couldn't be a God. His mind told him that, but his heart urged him to try. He turned his eyes towards the fierce silver disk in the sky and began to talk: 'Dear God—please let my darling get better.' He felt self-conscious at first. Suppose Flavia or Camilla heard? But he forced himself to keep going. 'I'm no good without her. I mess up all the time and she helps me out of it. I promise I'll be different if you let her get better. I'll make it up with Alicia. I'll let her see that wretched boy if he means so much to her. I'll keep my temper. Anything, God, as long as Deanna gets better. I'll even let George have Dad's piano. Just let her get better.'

Rick pushed open the door of Deanna's room the next day—thank God, his prayer had been answered. She was propped up against several pillows. Her face was unnaturally pale and her eyes were ringed with dark hollows, but the oxygen mask was gone, and she smiled as soon as she saw him. She held out her hand. 'Hi honey.'

Rick almost ran to her side. He slipped his arms under her shoulders so that he could pull her to him. He perched on the edge of the bed, cradling her against his chest. His chin rested on her head and the cropped hair scratched at his face. For once he didn't mind. He rocked to and fro, murmuring her name over and over again.

At last he eased her back on to the pillows. Her eyes, normally such a piercing blue, were faded, and her lips were dry and cracked. There were tears in her eyes, but she was still smiling. 'It's good to see you.'

'Good? It's fantastic!' He clasped both her hands in his. 'How are you feeling?'

'Better. Still got too many tubes.' She made a face at the array of equipment. 'But better.'

'You gave us a scare.'

'I'm sorry.'

'I've rung your parents.'

'How are they?'

'They're coming over. They're sorting out flights.'

'What about the girls?' she asked. The words were clearly an effort. A bubbling sound came from her chest as she spoke.

'I said I'd ring them with news as soon as I got here.' Rick glanced at his watch. 'They're at home. They weren't up to school.' He reached into his pocket. Deanna caught his wrist and glanced at the notice on the wall. 'No mobiles, darling.'

Instantly he felt his chest tighten. 'What do you take me for?' He stood up. 'I'm going outside. I'll be five minutes.'

'Give them my love,' Deanna called.

When he got back, he was full of apologies: 'I feel so tense.'

'I know.' Deanna stroked the back of his hand where it was resting on the bed. 'It's hard for all of us. Are the girls all right?'

'Relieved to hear you're so much better.' He drew up a chair to the side of the bed. 'Why didn't you tell me the cancer had spread?'

She shrugged and her nightdress slipped exposing her bony shoulder. 'You've got enough on your plate.'

'If you mean work, let me worry about that. You're my priority.'

She squeezed his hand. 'I'm glad. After Christmas… I did wonder. You've been kinda distant.' The two little furrows between her brows deepened. They looked as if they'd been there for some time, but Rick had only just noticed them. Her eyebrows had disappeared along with her hair. Now they were growing back, and he could see grey hairs coming through at the edges. He stared at the untidy straggle. Since Deanna's days as a model, she had been meticulous about such things, forever plucking and creaming, 'personal housekeeping' she called it. He never thought she needed to, but he enjoyed the idea that she worked hard to keep her golden lustre just for him. It hadn't done him any harm either to have such a beautiful woman on his arm.

He forced his attention back to what Deanna had been saying. He seemed to drift off from conversations all the time at the moment. *You've been kinda distant,* she'd said. It was probably the closest she'd ever come to complaining. 'It's Alicia,' he explained. 'When I think of my princess throwing herself away on that… that… there aren't the words to describe him. I'd kill him if I could get my hands on him.'

'Honey, I wish you wouldn't say such things.'

Deanna reached up to the locker beside her bed. She fumbled for the beaker. It was a blue plastic one, the sort with a lid and little holes to let the liquid out in drops. Rick remembered the girls having them when they were young. In fact Camilla had walked round with one permanently clamped to her lips for what seemed years. He'd complained to Deanna in the end. 'She'll be going to university with that in her mouth, if you're not careful.' He'd forgotten all about such beakers until that moment, when Deanna was forced to use one.

He recalled the previous night when he thought she might die. He'd have promised anything if only she could be all right. He felt embarrassed now even to remember that stupid prayer. Had he really said he would let Alicia see Gary if it meant so much to her? It must have been the whisky talking. He stroked Deanna's arm and she looked back at him with a wan smile.

'It's not nice talking like that about Gary,' she said.

'I'm sorry. It's you being in here. You know I'm hopeless without you.'

'Will you ring Alicia and tell her she can come in this afternoon?'

'Whatever you say, darling.'

'And I need her to be able to visit me at home when I get out.'

Rick took her hand and pressed it to his cheek. 'Anything, as long as you're happy.'

Deanna closed her eyes. 'I must sleep now.'

Rick planned to get home early that evening to be with Flavia and Camilla, but the meeting with the accountant dragged on. The verdict on his plans for expansion was more pessimistic than he'd anticipated and he was in a bad mood. He hadn't got round to ringing Alicia. It wasn't that he'd deliberately avoided it. There just wasn't a spare second. He thought about visiting Deanna again to say goodnight, but when he phoned the hospital as he was leaving the office, the nurse said Deanna was sleeping. He was dead tired himself and decided to head home.

The house was quiet when he arrived. A note on the kitchen table told him the girls had gone to bed and Mrs Crosby had left him some supper in the oven. Rick crossed to the dresser and pulled the bottle of whisky he'd started the night before towards him. He poured a large measure and tipping back his head, swallowed it in one go. The liquid burned the back of his throat. Without hesitating, he poured another, running his hand over his face. His skin felt rough and bristly. He pulled off his tie and slumped down on a chair. Putting his toe against his heel, he pushed off the shoe, then did the same with the other. The motor of the fridge whirred noisily and the ticking clock was relentless. He'd never noticed it before. He wished now he had called in at the hospital. He hated Deanna not being here.

Rick glanced across at the phone. The red light flashed. Perhaps she'd rung while he was on his way home and left a message. He needed to hear her voice. He pressed the retrieve button. There were two messages, but neither was from Deanna. The first was her parents. He listened to Bob's southern drawl. They'd got flights for the day after tomorrow. They'd arrive at Heathrow about six in the evening and then fly up to Newcastle. Would Rick be able to meet them? They'd like to go straight to the hospital.

Rick was fond of his in-laws. Roz fussed over him, treating him like the son she'd longed for, and Bob liked to talk business. To them, he was a successful entrepreneur who had given their daughter a good life. Not like his family, he thought, as the machine clicked on to the second message and his mother's insistent voice filled the kitchen. They saw him as a failure, and all because he couldn't play the wretched piano.

Eva's accent always seemed stronger on the telephone. She was worried, the message said. Rick poured himself a third measure of whisky as he half listened to his mother's concerns about the bungalow in Hexham. 'I got your letter. Is good, *caro,* that you want to take care of me, but is too soon after my Henry's death. Maybe… in a year or two…' Her voice tailed away. 'Don't be angry with your silly Mamma, *mio gioiello.*' The recording machine went silent.

Rick drained the glass and dialled his mother's number. She took an age to answer, and he sloshed more whisky into the glass while he waited.

'Hello.' She sounded breathless. 'Who is this?'

'It's Rick, Mum.'

'Oh, Ricardo. You give me fright. Is everything all right?'

'It's good. Everything's good.' He wouldn't tell her about Deanna, he decided. She'd be ringing every five minutes to see how she was. 'Sorry if it's late, but I've got your message about the bungalow.'

'The what?'

'The bungalow. You know the place I've bought for you up here.'

'I left you a message about that.'

'Yes, Mum, that's why I'm ringing.' Christ, what was the matter with the woman?

'It's all going to be fine. I don't want you to worry, Mum.'

'I'm not sure.'

'I'll come down in a week or two and explain everything to you. Okay?'

'Okay, *caro.*'

Rick went upstairs to his study, hesitating on the landing outside Flavia's room. He put his ear to the door. He wanted to go in and sit in the wicker chair at the foot of her bed. They could talk. She'd sit up in bed, hugging her knees. She reminded him more and more of Deanna. But her door was shut and he couldn't hear any sound.

He went to the study and sat at the computer. Some of the tension eased from his neck and shoulders as he felt the mouse nestling into his palm. He pointed the cursor at the email symbol. There were three new ones, all from his family. He was popular today. He clicked on the one from Grace.

Rick, I'm so sorry to hear about Deanna. Flavia emailed to say she'd been rushed to hospital. How is she? And how are you? I would have sent flowers, but I don't think they're allowed any more. Do give her my love. Let me know how things are, if you get the chance. Lots of love, Grace.

Rick was touched as he read his sister's words. Seven years older than her, he'd felt protective when she was young and he was glad that she was married and settled in Italy. He liked Franco. He admired his determination to make a go of his restaurant. If Deanna was well enough, he might take her to Ischia for a holiday this summer.

The second email was from Isabel.

Hi Rick, We need to talk. I went to see Mum today and she showed me your letter. She's terrified at the thought of moving up to Northumberland. She's lived in London ever since she came over from Italy and it doesn't seem right to uproot her. Can you come down for a few days to discuss it? Hope all is well with Deanna and the girls. Give them my love. Isabel.

Rick deleted the email. Isabel could be so annoying—even more than George, if that was possible. He'd seen the look she'd given him at Christmas when he mentioned buying a house up here for their mother. What gave her the right to know what was best for Eva? As if he didn't know his mother had lived in London ever since she arrived from Italy. That didn't mean she was better off there, did it?

He clicked on the next email. It was from his brother. What the hell did he want? They almost never communicated and they certainly hadn't exchanged any messages since the row about the piano.

Well then, you old bugger, how the devil are you? Still coining in the millions, I suppose? How's that darling wife of yours? I hope she's making good progress and I really mean that. I've always had a soft spot for Deanna—she's too good for you. Say 'Hi' from me.

The real reason for writing is that I gather from Isabel that there are plans afoot to move Eva up your way. That obviously precipitates action on the piano. I've got to go up to London in a couple of weeks and I'll talk to Eva. If she's okay with it, I'd like it shipped down here as soon as possible. I'll keep you informed. George.

Rick went downstairs and into the kitchen to pour another drink. His head already felt muzzy but the alcohol was deadening the ache in his guts. He crossed the hall to the drawing room. He went round switching on lights. He wasn't satisfied until light blazed from every lamp. He perched his glass on top of the piano. He'd been having lessons for several months now and was practising for an hour each day. He'd even given up running as much so that he could play before he went to work. Mrs Dobson had talked about Grade 1. Rick didn't want to take an exam, but Deanna had been all for it. 'You'll feel you're making real progress,' she'd said.

He pulled out the stool and sat down. He stretched out his fingers. He couldn't understand why it was difficult to move them across the piano keys to any order, when they knew the computer keyboard so well. He opened up his music book and played the first few notes of a Mozart minuet Mrs Dobson had given him to learn. He felt stupid playing 'baby pieces' as he called them and tried to practise when no one could hear. He reached the second bar before he stumbled and played a wrong note. He went back to the beginning. This time he managed several bars before he lost his place. He crashed his fist down on the keys.

Mrs Dobson had smiled when he told her he wanted to play the Moonlight Sonata. 'You'll have to progress before you're ready for that,' she said. He thought of his father's stubby fingers. 'I shouldn't have been a piano player,' he used to say, 'not with these fingers.' And yet, here Rick was, a piano player's son, and he'd never master the instrument.

Twenty-six

Isabel stood by the sink, arranging tulips. She snipped the ends from the stems and pushed each bloom into the narrow neck of the vase. Positioning it in the centre of the table, she moved back to admire her handiwork.

She'd returned from Italy determined to take control of her life. For too long she'd been the flimsy dinghy in raging seas, while her mother's demands, Brian's manipulation, even the children's whims buffeted her from peak to trough. The first step was to make the flat more attractive.

The vivid purples and pinks of the tulips made a pool of colour against the heavy oak units like a spotlight on a darkened stage. Pleased with the effect, she went into the lounge to survey the newly painted primrose-yellow walls. Rose had complained about the smell of paint making her feel sick, and Isabel opened the windows wide. The breeze blew through the flat and her spirits lifted, like ballooning sheets on a washing line.

She made herself go into the bedroom to finish unpacking her case—leaving items in there for a week hardly reflected her new resolve. She stacked the Italian dictionary on top of the magazines on the bedside table. It had been a surprise how much of the language she'd absorbed listening to her mother. She'd always rejected it, siding with her father as the non-Italian speakers in their family. Now that seemed ridiculous—she was going to take a class in the summer term.

She took a pair of trousers and a skirt from the bottom of the case and hung them in the wardrobe. Her hand brushed against the silky material of the dress hanging further along the rail. Grace had persuaded her to try it on in Naples. The red shift had skimmed over her breasts and hips, the gold trim round the neck and front of the dress sparkling against her pale skin. 'That's great on you, Bel,' Grace said. Isabel leaned closer to the mirror. She looked… well… elegant. '*Affascinante*!' the woman in the shop exclaimed. 'Does that mean what I think it does?' Isabel whispered to Grace. Grace had laughed. 'Glamorous. She thinks you look glamorous!'

But the confines of a shabby flat in north London provided an incongruous arena for glamour. When the dress was revealed, she was afraid its potency would evaporate.

She sat down on the bed and pulled the laptop on to her knees. She'd avoided looking at it for the last two days, ever since her email to Rick about their mother's reluctance to move. 'Don't worry, Mum,' she'd said when she read the letter from Rick. 'I'll sort it out for you.' And at the time she was pleased with the business-like tone, the 'this-is-something-that-needs-to-be-sorted-out-so-let's-get-on-and-do-it' approach she'd adopted in her email. But she knew from past skirmishes that, thwarted, Rick could be a tyrant, a bully, a despot, a persecutor—the more words she allowed into her mind, the more his lowering rage blackened her sky.

She clicked on her emails and checked the list—two. One had to be from Rick. She let the cursor hover over *view emails*. She clicked on the link. Two emails in the last two days. Both from Simon.

In the shower Isabel soaped her breasts. She ran her hands over her body as the hot water streamed down her back. She prodded her hipbones. All those years on diets, with Brian nagging her to do something about her weight, had little effect. Now, she was almost as thin as before she'd had Rose. She leaned backwards so that water splashed on her neck and shoulders and down on to her chest.

Her thoughts ranged over the flat, planning her next project. Perhaps she'd paint the hall, which was a dingy green. She was possessive about the little world she'd created. She could leave her music open on the piano; play her Beethoven CDs without having to look at Brian's long face; read in bed until the early hours with no one to complain about the light. She'd gone from seeing the flat as claustrophobic to relishing the freedom. Why should she let a couple of emails scuttle her confidence?

She wound a towel round her and went back to the bedroom. Opening up the laptop again, she pointed the cursor. Her hand hovered. Don't think about it. Do it. She clicked on Simon's first email.

Hi Isabel

Think you should be home from Italy by now. Hope you had a great time with your sister.

How about a drink and you can fill me in? Would be good to see you.

Simon

Was that it? She scrolled to see if there was more. But what was she expecting? She'd scurried away from him at the airport like Little Miss Muffet confronted by a tarantula. No wonder the poor man had kept his email brief.

Something caught her eye at the window, and she watched a little bird perch on the sill. She wasn't knowledgeable about birds, but this was surely a bluetit. She got up and sidled to the window, marvelling at the bird's vibrant mix of blue and green and yellow and white; at its survival in this urban environment. She stared at it and it blinked fearlessly at her.

She went back to the laptop and clicked on Simon's second email.

Hi again

In my attempt not to overwhelm you in my previous message, think I might have sounded too offhand. It would be really good to see you.

You've probably guessed that I'd like to be more than friends, but if friends are what's on offer—I'll take it! Give me a call.
Simon

Isabel read the email a second time and then a third. She conjured up an image of Simon's face: intense expression as he listened; the longing in his eyes when he spoke of his son; his mouth, wide with laughter; his fingers, long and sensitive, their delicacy marred by those maimed stumps. She picked up the phone and dialled his number.

That afternoon she took courage and told Rose she was going on a date. 'Cool, Mum. Nice move.' Isabel was surprised—enthusiastic approval from her daughter was the last thing she expected. But Rose put her hair up at the back in a comb and showed her a different way to apply her makeup, so that her eyes looked dark and smoky.

Rose gave the thumbs up when she saw Isabel in the red and gold dress. 'Wow, Mum! You look awesome.'

Isabel laughed. 'Will I do?'

'I'll say. Wait till I tell Dad.'

Isabel met Simon in a wine bar. He'd obviously made a big effort because he was there first and had a bottle of wine chilling in an ice bucket on the table. His hair was longer than before and she noticed the tendrils curling down his neck. Her fingers itched to stroke them. He hugged her and kissed her on both cheeks. Desire flooded her belly.

She slipped off her jacket and he gave a low whistle. 'You look lovely.'

She smoothed down the dress. 'I bought it in Naples.' She kept her gaze lowered; her hand stroking the creases she knew weren't there. 'It's a bit daring for me.' She made herself look up and he was smiling.

'You should be daring more often.'

*

Simon had found a table in a small room off the main bar. When they sat, a waitress came and lit the candle. It glowed in its glass bowl, casting soft shadows across the table. Simon poured out the wine.

'So, how was Italy? Ischia—is that the name of the island?'

'Yes, it's in the Bay of Naples. It's beautiful.'

'You seem more relaxed.'

'It's strange how quickly the stresses of home fall away when you're in a different environment.'

'I hope everything at home isn't stressful.' He reached across and touched her cheek.

Little tingles ran over her skin. 'Simon, about the airport…'

'It's okay. You don't have to explain.'

'No, but I ran off. It was…' What was she doing? She wasn't going to tell him, was she?

'Isabel, you're scared. I do understand. I'm scared. It's not easy when you've been dumped by someone else.'

Oh God. If only that's all it was. It was frightening to think of starting another relationship, but that was nothing. How much understanding would Simon need if she told him the truth? The thought of her *dirty little secret* caged her like barbed wire.

Simon smiled. 'Anyway, I want to hear about Ischia. How was your sister? Did you talk to her about George?'

Isabel nodded. 'But the strange thing was, she already knew.'

'Don't tell me your mother's revealed the secret to all of you, but sworn everyone to silence.'

'It's even stranger than that.'

Simon went to pour out more wine, but Isabel shook her head. 'I haven't had much to eat today.'

'We can soon remedy that. They do a wonderful selection of tapas here. How about we share some?'

'Sounds good.'

The waitress brought several plates to their table. Isabel realised how hungry she was. She'd been so excited about tonight, she'd hardly eaten.

'Hey, try some of that chorizo sausage.' Simon wiped his fingers on a napkin. 'It's really good.'

'I've got one of the little battered squid,' Isabel said. 'I didn't think I liked squid, but this is delicious.'

'They whet your appetite, don't they?'

'I'm going to have one of these bruschetta. I had them dipped in oil with tomatoes in Ischia—heaven.'

'I'm glad you're back,' Simon said. 'I missed you.'

'What have you been doing? Still busy with clients?'

'I gave myself some time off. And I think I've found a new hobby.'

Isabel smiled. He looked so pleased and proud.

'What are you laughing at?' Simon put on an aggrieved face. 'I try to tell you about my secret ambition, and you laugh.'

'I'm sorry. I haven't heard anyone say "hobby" for a long time. It seems to go with train spotting and stamp collecting.'

'Oh, right. I'm a geek, am I?'

'A nice geek,' Isabel said. 'Tell me your hobby.'

Simon speared another piece of chorizo with his fork. 'I've started writing a story.'

'What's it about?'

He frowned. 'I knew you'd ask me that. It's about two lights in a room. One's a reading light, and one's a table lamp with a tall elegant shade. They've got different personalities, and the reading light thinks it's not as pretty, but it's more important than the lamp that sits on the table providing a background glow. When the people who live in the room go to bed, the lights have an argument.' Simon stopped and looked at her. 'You think it's a stupid idea.'

'No, I don't. I think—'

'I can see it in your face. You think it's stupid.'

'Simon, I think it's great. I could never think up anything as imaginative as that.'

'Really?'

'Really.'

He leant across the table and kissed her. 'You are the most perceptive person I've ever met.'

'And you're the maddest.'

'So mad you wouldn't consider coming home with me?'

Isabel felt the blush spread across her chest and up her neck. She made herself think of cold things: an iceberg; freezing fingers in the snow; the wastes of Antarctica; winter wind whipping across her cheeks. It didn't work. Waves of heat rolled over her.

She met Simon's gaze. She'd keep her tone light like his. 'No, but mad enough to ask you to come home with me.'

He raised his eyebrows. 'That's either very mad, or one of the most sensible things I've ever heard.'

'So, do you want to come?'

'I'm all yours.'

Waking early, before the morning light pierced the bedroom curtains, she enjoyed the weight of his body next to hers. She turned on her side away from him, easing her hips into his lap. His thighs curled around hers and she snuggled back further until she felt his groin against the curve of her bottom. His breathing was light and rapid and feathers of air caressed her shoulders. In sleep, his hand slipped across her waist and reached up until it found her breast. He cupped his fingers round it, and she felt its heaviness settle into his palm. She allowed herself to savour the contentment of the embrace—still plenty of time before they had to get up.

*

Rose appeared at the door as Isabel was saying goodbye to Simon. She'd been staying overnight at Brian's and wasn't expected home for another hour. Isabel tightened her dressing gown round her. She was conscious of her nipples pushing against the thin cotton. She saw Rose's eyes flick to Simon's hand on her arm. 'Simon—Rose. Rose—Simon.' She managed to carry out introductions without too much stumbling over names. Rose shifted her bag on to her shoulder as she pushed past her mother into the hall. She was smiling. She didn't look too upset.

Simon's lips brushed Isabel's cheek. 'Well done,' he whispered into her ear. 'I'll ring you tonight for the verdict.'

Rose was bending down to look in the fridge when Isabel went into the kitchen. She took out a carton of milk, lifted it up high and the white stream cascaded on to the cereal. Drops splattered over the worktop. Isabel didn't say anything. She waited in the doorway, shuffling from foot to foot, her hands clutched in front of her.

'Well?' she asked when she couldn't stand the silence any longer. Rose turned and her long blonde hair swung across her shoulder. Isabel stifled a moment of envy. When had her daughter got so beautiful?

Rose spooned a mound of cereal into her mouth. She was holding the bowl close to her lips and she stared at Isabel over its rim. Their eyes locked and then Rose laughed. 'Your bit on the side? I wondered when I'd get to meet him.'

'You mean you knew about Simon?'

Rose dropped the bowl into the sink. 'You get loads of text messages and emails now. You never used to.'

'How do you know about my emails?'

'We share a computer, Mum. Remember?'

'Have you been reading them?'

Rose frowned. 'What do you take me for? Course I haven't read them, but you never log off from your emails, and I don't need to be a genius when the name Simon keeps coming up as the sender.'

'What do you think then? Do you mind?' Isabel sat down at the table. She hoped Rose might join her and they could have a proper chat.

But Rose picked up her bag and crossed to the door. 'It's cool, Mum, especially as I know you're only doing it to make Dad jealous.'

'What do you mean?'

'Dad asked me if you were seeing anyone and I told him there was some bloke sniffing round, but that you wanted him really.'

'You had no right to do that.'

'But that's what you've always said. As soon as Dad comes to his senses, we'll be back together as a family'

'Of course that's what I want, but your father—'

'He's come to his senses, Mum.'

'He has?'

'Yeah. He was talking about it last night after Anita went to bed. He's going to take you out next weekend.' She paused in the doorway and as she turned, Isabel caught a flash of something. She studied Rose's face. A small jewel glinted in her daughter's left nostril.

Rose grinned at her. 'It'll be another date. Only this time, it's for real.'

Twenty-seven

Grace met Lilian at their usual restaurant near Piazza Dante. She found her, as always, tucked in the furthest corner, nose in a book and an unlit cheroot between her fingers. She'd been a ferocious opponent of the smoking ban, but had finally given in when she'd been asked to leave a bar.

Lilian stood up as soon as she saw Grace. She barely reached Grace's shoulder and Grace had to stoop to apply her lips to each of her friend's cheeks.

'I was pleased to get your call this morning,' Lilian said. 'I haven't seen you for ages.' She waved the menu under Grace's nose. 'What would you like to eat? I've ordered two glasses of prosecco.'

'I'll have a pizza neapolitana.'

'Are you sure? You usually try something different.'

'Not today. When in Naples…' Grace wondered if she sounded too wistful—Lilian's antennae were sharp.

'Two of your wonderful pizzas, *per favore*.'

Grace watched Lilian's coquettish smile at the waiter, as she returned the cheroot to its case.

'*Prego*.' He responded with an extravagant flick of the white napkin, which he spread carefully on her lap.

'*Grazie, signore*.' Lilian snapped the menu shut and the waiter turned away. Grace was left to deal with her own napkin.

Last night she had woken suddenly. In the dim light she could make out the shape of someone sitting on the bed facing her. She heard breathing and had opened her mouth to scream, when Franco's voice came out of the darkness. 'It's me.' She reached out and snapped on the bedside light. Franco's shoulders were hunched, his head bowed. He was leaning forward on his elbows, his hands dangling between his knees.

'Whatever's the matter?' she asked.

He looked up at her then, and she saw what he held in his hands. It was her contraceptive pills.

Grace struggled to sit up. She drew the duvet up to her chin. 'Franco, let me explain.'

'You promised.'

'I know I did.'

'I go to England, you say. We have baby when I get back.'

She put her hand on his arm. 'Let's talk. I need to explain—'

'Talk. Explain. It's all about you. What you feel. What you want.' He banged his hand down on hers as if her touch stung his skin like a mosquito's. 'You don't care about me.'

'Of course I do. Because I'm not ready to have a baby doesn't mean…'

She watched Franco lift his arm. His hand was almost touching his shoulder. She saw the flash of his wedding ring. What was he doing? She felt the rush of air and pain as his fist slammed into her jaw.

She sipped the prosecco while the waiter placed their food on the table. Nothing compared with the taste of a Naples' pizza and this one might be her last. But still she picked up her knife and fork hesitantly: chewing was bound to hurt.

'So, what's new?' she asked.

Lilian dropped her cutlery as if she'd been dying for Grace to ask the question. She clapped her hands and her frizzy hair quivered. 'I'm going to the States.'

Thank goodness. Once Lilian picked a topic, she was off.

'Walt, my American professor—I must have told you about him—has gone home. His six months' sabbatical was up and he's invited me to visit him.'

Had Lilian told her? Grace couldn't remember. 'Really? Is it… you know?'

Lilian laughed, a loud trumpeting laugh that made the people at the next table look round. 'I know old witches like me shouldn't expect lust. That's for you young things. But…' she paused to shovel in another mouthful of pizza, '… he lives in Boston and I can manufacture lust for a month in Boston. Nathan went loads of times when he was in the diplomatic corps, but somehow I missed out on the trips.'

She reached down to the floor for her leather holdall. She fished around inside and found her diary. 'Let's make a date for lunch when I get back. What about July? I know it's busy for you but—'

'Lilian…'

'Shall we say the fourteenth?'

'I won't be here in July.'

Lilian licked her finger and turned over some more pages. 'Problems with your mother again?' she asked, almost absently. 'We'd better make it August, although lord knows how I'll keep my news until then.'

'I won't be here in August either.'

Lilian looked at her. 'Oh?'

'I'm leaving Ischia.'

'That *is* a surprise. I was talking to someone only the other day and they'd been over to your restaurant. Couldn't praise it enough.'

'It's not that—'

'It makes sense, I suppose. Franco could do bigger things in Rome or Milan. I always said he was ambitious. Mark my words—that husband of yours will go far.'

'I'm leaving Franco.'

Grace looked down, but she could feel the shock coming across the table. Lilian clasped Grace's hands in hers. 'My poor child,' she murmured. One of her rings bit into Grace's palm, but she didn't take her hand away. The discomfort gave her something to concentrate on.

She gestured to the waiter who was passing their table. '*Un litro rosso, per favore.*'

Grace shook her head. 'Not for me.'

'It's not for you! I'm the one who's had a shock.'

Grace tried to smile, but the movement trapped her face in pain. She pulled her hands from Lilian and cupped her chin in her hand. The cool palm was a comfort, but more than that, she wanted to conceal the bruises she could feel developing.

She accepted the large glass of red wine Lilian poured. It wasn't as if she had to worry about the *ristorante* that evening. She intended to stay in Naples until the last ferry left. She'd already sent Franco a text to say he should get Carolina to help him this evening. She didn't think he'd be too surprised.

Lilian drank her first glass almost in one go, her head thrown back. Grace stared at the necklace of lines circling her throat. Lilian poured a second glass and removed one of her thin cheroots from a silver case. She tapped it on the table. 'Don't worry. Just my comfort blanket.'

Grace noticed her initials had been engraved on the lid of the case. 'Is that new?' she asked. 'I don't remember seeing it before.'

'A parting gift from my swain,' Lilian said. 'But I'm more concerned about you. What's happened?'

Grace shrugged. 'Nothing, really.' Lilian was fun to be with, but the humiliation of Franco striking her was too raw to confide. 'No one thing, anyway, more an accumulation.'

'Tell me.'

Where to begin? Grace thought. 'There's the whole baby thing for a start,' she said.

'Still not sure about wee ones, eh?'

Grace remembered their earlier conversation when Lilian had told her how much she'd longed for children. She didn't want to hurt her friend, but she couldn't deny the way she felt. 'I feel pressurised. Franco, his parents, especially his mother, his brothers, even his sisters-in-law, all seem to think they've got a say in whether I have a baby or not.'

'The Italians are big on families. You must have known that when you married him.'

'I thought I loved him. It was all that mattered at the time.'

Memories of that first summer with Franco filled her mind. She'd been besotted. There was his wide easy smile, chocolate-brown eyes, the endearing halting English. Mostly there was his lean tanned body. She'd had several lovers, even lived with someone for a while when she was teaching in Suffolk, but nobody had been able to make her body ache with sexual pleasure like Franco. He'd arrive at her apartment on the second floor of the palazzo about midnight when he finished work in the pizzeria. Her windows would be wide open to catch what little air there might be. Waiting for him through the evening, she'd feel it was too hot to breathe, but the sultry atmosphere only intensified their passion. They'd cling together, slippery with each other's sweat.

'Grace, are you all right?'

Grace forced herself back to the present. 'I was remembering.'

'Is it only the baby?'

'Yes. No. He wasn't there for me the night my dad died, Lilian.'

'We all let each other down, child. It doesn't mean you can't still have a life together.'

'Somehow my dad dying so suddenly changed things. I've realised how short life is. I love Ischia. But I want more.' And would *you* want to live with a man who hit you? It would be a relief to ask the question. To see shock on Lilian's face. Feel her sympathy. But Grace couldn't. Saying the words would make it real. 'First though, I need to go home to be with my family. There are things we have to sort out.'

Lilian poured more wine. Grace had always joked that Lilian's capacity for alcohol was limitless, but now she tried to keep pace.

'Why don't you talk to Franco?' Lilian asked. 'Perhaps you can go back to England for six months.' Her face brightened. 'He could come with you. Didn't he always dream of a restaurant in London?'

'That's not what I want,' Grace said. 'I want to travel. I'm going to go to America. I wanted to years ago, but Dad stopped me.'

Lilian touched her hand. 'You seem different.'

'In what way?'

'Harder somehow. Is it only Franco?"

The side of Grace's face throbbed. Perhaps Franco had broken her jaw. It had been a pretty violent blow.

'Grace?'

She looked across at Lilian, at her weather-beaten skin, the knowing expression. What things had she witnessed? 'It turns out Dad was not my youngest brother's father.' She hesitated. 'George is my half brother.'

'And you didn't know?'

'No idea.'

'How did you find out?'

'I had a letter from an old friend of my dad's. And it seems Mum told Isabel the day Dad died.' Grace screwed up her napkin and flung it on the table. 'It means Mum had an affair when I was a baby.'

'These things happen.'

'If you'd known my parents… they worshipped one another.'

'You never really know what goes on in a marriage.'

'The worst thing is…' Grace stopped. What she was about to say, she'd hardly admitted to herself. 'I've spent all these years wondering if my father truly loved me. But now I don't seem to love him any more.'

'That's a bit harsh, child. If he loved George as his own, isn't he the good guy in this?'

'I know. If I blame anyone, it should be Mum.'

Lilian didn't reply and the silence stretched between them. She stood up. 'Let's find a table outside. I need some nicotine.'

The early summer sunshine felt warm on Grace's face, but the breeze was cool, and she pulled her jacket tight. They sat down at one of the tables on the pavement in front of the pizzeria. The waiter followed them out with the remainder of the wine and their glasses. Lilian lit her cheroot and her eyes narrowed against the thin column of smoke.

'Nathan had a child,' she said.

The announcement jolted Grace. 'I didn't know he'd been married before you met.'

'He hadn't. It was an affair.' She stared at the cheroot as if she was surprised to see it between her fingers. 'He confessed the day of our silver wedding.'

'How awful for you.' She'd always had the impression that Lilian and her husband were devoted.

'It was only a fling. Probably one of many, if the truth were known. The diplomatic life opens the door to that sort of thing. But this time there was a baby boy, Justin. He'd be about twenty now.'

'What happened?'

'It was in Yugoslavia, as it was then. His mother was a typist at the embassy by all accounts. I wanted to adopt the boy and bring him back to England, but she wouldn't hear of it. Nathan used to send money at first, but then she stopped writing. He went out there when the trouble first started in Serbia, but he couldn't find them.'

'Were you able to forgive him?' Grace was trying to imagine what it would have been like for her father when he found out about George.

Lilian shrugged. 'What could I do? I'd stayed behind in Scotland on that trip. My mother was ill and I didn't want to leave her. Nathan said he was lonely. I couldn't give a damn about the woman. I've never thought love is about sex anyway.' She stubbed out her cigar, squashing it into the ashtray. 'But the baby hurt. Nathan had a son and I didn't.'

'How did you cope with that?'

'I told myself providing the sperm doesn't make you a dad. It's the long haul—broken nights, the first day at school, cold football pitches on a Sunday morning—that's what makes you a dad.' Lilian started pulling on her jacket. 'Don't be too hard on your mum and dad. They probably had all sorts of reasons for not telling you.'

All at once Grace saw her father's face clearly. Since his death it had been impossible to get a picture of him in her mind. He was there, but out of focus. Now she saw his broad jaw, his slow smile, his eyes, which none of the family could agree on. She and George thought they were hazel, but Rick and Isabel insisted they were green. Whatever their colour, she'd thought they were the most honest she had ever seen. You could trust him utterly.

Lilian bent forward to kiss her cheek. 'Look after yourself, child.'

Grace walked down the hill and rounded the bend. The *ristorante* was in darkness. It wasn't even eleven o'clock and she'd never known Franco shut before midnight. In the stillness the only sound was the slap of her sandals against her feet. She could smell the heavy scent of pine from the wood on the hill above. To her left, the dark mass of sea was striped with lines of golden yellow from the castle lights. She wouldn't let herself look back at the bulky outline of the *castello*. Her eyes had sought it, first thing in the morning and before she went to bed; part of the daily ritual, like cleaning her teeth or kissing Franco goodnight.

She expected the front door of the restaurant to be locked, but it swung inwards with that familiar creak of the hinges. For most of the day and evening, it stood open, apart from in the middle of winter, and she and Franco kept forgetting to oil it. It was strange to think such things wouldn't be her concern any more. She stepped inside the restaurant and leaned back against the door, her eyes adjusting to the darkness. Only the swishing sound of the electric ceiling fans disturbed the silence.

'You're back.' Franco's voice made her jump. She reached up and turned on the wall lights. He was sitting at the far end of the restaurant. Grace always chose a table near the window so that she could see the sea, but Franco liked this one tucked away from public gaze. She walked between the tables, picking up a stray spoon that had been forgotten, until she was standing beside him.

He was hunched over, his chin in his hands. A coil of smoke drifted from a cigarette sitting in the ashtray in front of him. She counted three more stubbed out ends besides. He'd given up smoking when they got married. She hadn't asked him to, but he'd said, 'You always smell so fresh and clean, I can't do it any more,' and he hadn't smoked again. Until now. He didn't look at her and, not knowing what else to do, she sat opposite.

'You're late.' His voice was husky.

'I met some friends.'

'I thought you weren't coming back.' He looked up and their eyes met. His were puffy and red. She'd never seen him cry.

'How's your face?' he asked.

'Sore.'

He lifted his hand to her hair and stroked it back from her face. She heard his intake of breath.

'I'm sorry, *carissima*.'

'So am I, Franco. Sorry it's come to this.'

'I can make it up to you.' He caught hold of her hand. 'I didn't know what I was doing. I am tormented.'

She pulled her hand free. 'I'm leaving you.'

'For how long?'

She felt sick. Her head was spinning from all the wine and a hard knot had formed in her stomach. 'Forever.'

'Please. No.'

'I've made up my mind.'

'I know I've gone on about a baby.' He stretched out and she thought he was going to touch her again. She folded her arms across her chest.

'It's not only the baby. I can't do this any more.'

'Do what?'

'This.' She gestured to the room behind her. 'Us.'

'We'll change things. I'll change.'

Grace didn't answer. What could she say? She couldn't tell him that his pleading only made things worse. The Franco she'd fallen in love with had been vibrant, extroverted, always ready to laugh. That night when he'd arrived in the courtyard of the palazzo with the pot of bolognese sauce, it was the most romantic thing that had ever happened to her. Where had all that fun gone? Sexual attraction is a trap. Before you know where you are, you've tied yourself for life to someone you hardly know because of the way his hair curls or the little kisses he plants all over your body when you wake in the mornings.

Perhaps that was what happened to her mother when she met George's father. Their desire had been impossible to resist. In a way Grace hoped so. She couldn't bear to think of George being the result of some sordid fling like Lilian's husband's child.

'Please give it another chance.' Franco's voice came from far away. 'I love you. I'll do anything to make you happy.'

Grace shook her head. 'It's no good. It's over.'

'Please.'

Grace stood up. The chair crashed behind her on to the tiles. She glanced round. She remembered how she'd agonised over the exact colour for the floor. Franco had wanted pale marble, but she'd insisted on dark green, and she'd got her way.

'I'm sorry,' she said.

Franco looked up at her. She could see the yellow flecks in his eyes that caught the light and made them glow.

'Don't leave me. I'll tell Mamma to—'

'Franco… it's no good.'

He buried his head in his arms.

Grace ached to touch that funny wave at the nape of his neck. She knew exactly how it would feel. She went upstairs to pack.

Twenty-eight

The bedroom was darker. Grace turned on her side and felt for Franco. He was usually curled into a ball, his back a smooth curve. In the early days she'd snuggled up to him, pressing her breasts against his warm skin. Gradually he would stir, roll to her and take her in his arms. Now she was more likely to pretend to be asleep until he got up to go to the fish market. This morning something made her stretch out her hand to see if he was still there. And then, she remembered.

She wasn't in her light airy bedroom in Ischia. She wouldn't be able to throw open the shutters, step out on the balcony into a morning where the sun would bathe her bare arms and legs, where her eyes could feast on the *castello*.

'This is a record,' George had said the previous night as they climbed the steep narrow stairs. 'The third member of my family to stay in this room in the past year.' He laughed as he heaved her suitcase on to the bed. 'First no one visits me. Now I can't get rid of you all!'

Grace tried to smile, but her lips stuck to her teeth. All she wanted was sleep. Sleep would block the memory of Franco's sobs. Block thoughts of Maria, Vincenzo and Alphonso standing in a sombre line outside the *ristorante* when the taxi arrived to take her to the ferry, Franco inside, nowhere to be seen.

'Are you okay, Sis?' George had said. 'I've never seen you look so bad.'

'I need a good night's rest. I'll be all right in the morning.'

Now the morning was here. Outside the gulls shrieked. Rain pattered against the window. And she wasn't all right.

A throbbing pain attached itself to her head and was spreading down into her neck. The weight lodged in her stomach was worse. The single bed felt constricting and she was cold. Franco would be up by now, drinking his first cup of strong sweet coffee. She turned on her side and pulled the duvet over her head.

It was late morning when she woke again. She listened for sounds of activity. Unfamiliar with the house and its habits, she didn't even know what noises to listen for. Perhaps she could shut herself away in this little room, insulated from the world. Instead, with a great effort of will, she pushed back the duvet and forced her feet to the floor. She pulled on some trousers and a thick jumper and splashed her face with cold water. She risked looking in the mirror. Just as she'd thought. The side of her face was a mottled bluey green. Yellow patches leached into the other colours. She ran a comb through her hair and drew it forward across her cheek.

Downstairs, she hesitated. She had been so tired the previous night; she hadn't taken in George's instructions. She made for a door at the far end of the hallway. A young woman sat at the long pine table reading a magazine. As soon as Grace appeared, she got to her feet. 'Hi. You must be Grace. I'm Chloe.'

'Hello.'

'George said to say *sorry*. He's got classes all day. He asked me to look after you. Are you hungry?'

'A black coffee would be nice. Strong, please.'

Grace sat down at the table. Deep windows looked out on to a garden. A huge Aga took up most of one wall and several copper saucepans were strung along a cord hanging from the high ceiling. A bowl of fruit and a jug filled with fat pink roses stood in the middle of the table. A pile of books took up most of one end.

Chloe was busy boiling water and spooning coffee into a cafetière. With her dark hair scraped back into bunches and her blue dungarees, she looked like an overgrown child. Grace watched as she reached into the cupboard for a mug. She remembered George mentioning her in his emails, but she hadn't pictured her as so young.

Chloe brought the cafetière and a mug over to the table. 'I hope that's how you like it. I don't drink coffee, so I'm never sure if it will be all right.'

'It will be fine.' Grace pulled the sugar bowl towards her. From the look of the pale liquid she would need something to make it palatable.

'You're so like GP,' Chloe said. Her elbows were on the table, her chin resting in her hands.

'Who's GP?' Grace forced down a mouthful of coffee.

'Georgy Porgy. My nickname for George.' She laughed. 'It's a joke, you see, he's skinny.'

Grace couldn't imagine the brother she knew responding to the name Georgy Porgy.

'It's uncanny.' Chloe's gaze was fixed on Grace's face. 'It's like looking at George's double.'

'Everyone says we look like our mother.'

'But you're nothing like Isabel.'

'Do you paint, Chloe?' Grace hoped for a more neutral conversation.

'Yeah. But nowhere near as well as George. He's brilliant.'

'Do you teach at the art school as well?'

'I take one or two classes.'

'It's hard work, isn't it? I remember when I was teaching English in Naples.' Grace bit her lip. What on earth had she said that for? The last thing she wanted to talk about was Italy.

'George has helped me loads. I don't know what will happen when he leaves. I can't see Mark making a go of it on his own.'

'George is leaving?' Grace hated having to ask, but the question was out before she could stop herself.

'Hasn't he told you?'

'Perhaps he's mentioned it, but I've had a lot on lately.' There was something irritating about Chloe. The proprietorial way she talked about George for a start, as if she was the one who knew him best.

'He's going to Naples. He's fed up with teaching, even though he's so good. He just wants to paint.'

'Why Naples?'

'He feels comfortable in Italy, he says. Plus he'll be nearer you… Are you okay?'

Grace looked up and found that Chloe was staring at her.

'Only you look ever so pale.'

'I'm fine.' She moved her head to let her hair fall forward over her face again. 'What about you? What will you do if George goes?'

Chloe's eyes filled with tears. "I can't bear the thought of it,' she mumbled. 'I'm in love with him, you see.' She looked directly at Grace. 'Don't tell him, will you?'

When Chloe left to go to an art class, Grace went upstairs to her room. She fished around in her case for writing paper and began a letter to Archie Stansfield:

I'm in England for a while and I was wondering if you'd be willing to meet me. There are still lots of questions I'd like to ask you about my dad. As you've known him so long, I think you might be able to fill in some pieces of the jigsaw. I can get the train up to you, if you'd prefer.

When she'd finished, she had a shower and got changed. She wrote a note for George in case he came back and set off to explore Penzance. She turned left out of the house and found herself at the gates of Penlee Park. Recent rain had left the air fresh. The greenery was verdant. Grace breathed in, relishing the damp sweet scent that was peculiarly English. She wandered along the path, enjoying the sense of freedom. There would be no cries of 'Signora!' No constant calls for decisions at the restaurant. A sign to the right pointed to an open-air theatre. She passed tennis courts, their nets hanging low.

Before long she was through the park and out into a tree-lined street. She turned left and headed down to the sea. She slipped her letter to Archie Stansfield into a post box. When she reached the Promenade, she crossed the road and sat on the low wall which ran the length of the beach. The tide was in and little waves slapped against the wall. She shaded her eyes and looked out to where the horizon met a grey sea. Gulls swooped and squalled. One landed on the wall and perched a few moments before taking off, with a great fluttering of wings. She closed her eyes and behind the lids a picture of an azure sky, sunlight sparkling on sea of the deepest blue, the outline of a castle sprang unbidden. She forced her eyes open again.

She continued her walk along the Promenade, but every step was an effort. All she could think of was Franco. Sometimes he had a siesta between four and five. Was he lying on their bed now? The shutters would be closed. They would often make love when they woke from their short rest, their bodies languorous. Grace could almost taste the slightly salty sensation of Franco's skin on her tongue.

Further along the Promenade, she came across an open-air swimming pool. 'Jubilee Pool,' the sign said. It had been opened in 1935, the year of George V's Silver Jubilee. She watched people splashing in water, which looked remarkably green against the blue terracing and white walls.

The open-air pool that her parents had taken them to as children flashed into Grace's mind. She remembered a magical place, with fountains, chutes, green open spaces and a diving platform. Once, when she was about ten, she'd clambered up the metal steps, determined she was going to jump. She got to the top at last, but she couldn't bring herself to step out on to the diving board.

People began to push past, their wet bodies brushing against hers. She saw her father on the ground, shouting something and gesticulating for her to come down. But the way back was crowded with people. She started to cry and the boy at the top of the steps laughed. 'Cry Baby Bunting!' he jeered. He had pale skin and his shoulders were burned a livid pink. He had red hair and huge freckles spattered his face and arms. She'd hated red hair from that day. At last Rick's face had appeared at the top of the stairway. 'You stupid little girl!' he shouted, but he'd taken her hand, turned her to face the steps and climbed down ahead, his steadying hand at her waist all the way to the ground.

George was home when she arrived back at the house. 'You look done in,' he said as she opened the kitchen door. 'What have you been up to?'

'I went for a walk.'

'Bit of a shock—the bracing sea air—after Ischia.'

She slumped at the table.

'Have you had anything to eat?'

She shook her head.

'I'll fix you cheese on toast. It's my speciality.' George took a blue and white striped apron from a drawer. He eased it over his head and tied the strings round his waist. '*Ecco fatto*! I have nothing to declare but my genius!'

Grace watched as George sliced bread, slotted it into the toaster and began grating cheese. All his movements were graceful and elegant, feminine, almost. She couldn't help scrutinising him for signs of Henry. Some fleeting expression, a tilt of the head, maybe. She so wanted Archie Stansfield to be wrong. But there was only his hands, she thought, as he placed the food in front of her. Those same short stubby fingers that her father had and which didn't at all fit the rest of George's slim physique.

She picked up her knife and fork and took a mouthful. The cheese was soft and spongy. It melted against her tongue. 'This is good.'

'What else did you expect?' George sat at the table. 'Sorry I had to abandon you today. Mark's covering for me tomorrow, and I'll take you to St Michael's Mount.'

'You don't have to do that,' Grace protested. 'I'll be fine on my own.'

'I don't think you will. I've never seen anyone so in need of love and affection.'

Grace concentrated on her cheese on toast.

'I'm not going to ask what's happened,' George said. 'But I hope the other one came off worse than you.'

Grace didn't dare look up. 'Did you know Deanna's been in hospital again?' she asked.

'Yeah. Eva said something about it last time I rang home. I thought she was on the mend.'

'I don't know if she's going to make it.'

George fiddled with the pepper mill, twirling it round and round. 'She'll pull through. She must be tough to have survived all these years with Ricky Boy.'

'You know he hates to be called that.'

'Why else would I do it?'

Grace sighed. Her brothers' hostility was worse since Henry's death. 'What is it, Sis?'

'Please give up the idea of Dad's piano. Rick will never back down and it will only cause more stress for Deanna.'

'Why should I let that bastard have it? He can't even play the damn thing.'

'He's having lessons.'

'Credit me with some sense, Grace. He might be a wizard with computers, but he's got no chance learning to play the piano.'

Grace chased the last piece of toast around the plate. George had made up his mind. She tried a different tack. 'Chloe said you're thinking of moving to Italy.'

'Chloe's got no business gossiping about my plans.'

'I don't think she meant any harm. Are you?'

'I haven't finalised it yet, but probably.'

'Why?'

'Why not?' George went to the fridge and poured out a can of beer. 'I love the light. The language. I've always felt more at home in Italy.'

Grace felt her heart leap. Did he feel an affinity with Italy because he'd been conceived there? 'Whereabouts are you going?'

George came back to the table. 'Near Naples. Not all that far from Mum's village. Plus, I'll be near you.'

Grace thought she detected something wistful in her brother's face. But it was gone in a flash and his usual smile was back.

'If you're going to Italy,' she said, 'what's the point of having the piano? You'll only have to leave it behind when you go.'

'I'll have it shipped over.'

'Why not buy one over there. New pianos are supposed to be better anyway.' Grace felt excited at the thought of a possible solution. 'You could buy a grand piano. Go to Venice instead. I can see you in some palazzo, music echoing across the Grand Canal.'

'I don't want a grand piano.' George's mouth tightened. It was an expression Grace had seen on her mother's face. 'I don't want a Steinway or a Broadwood or any other piano you care to mention. I want Dad's.'

Grace winced at the word *Dad*. It would break his heart when he knew the truth.

'That man meant the world to me.' George prodded the table with his forefinger. 'He believed in me when everyone else had written me off as a waste of space and—'

'I didn't mean—'

'I don't want to hear any more pleas for poor Rick.' George got up and poured his beer down the sink. 'I played duets with Dad on that piano for more than thirty years. It belongs to me.'

Grace arranged to go up to London. She had to face her mother and Isabel with the news that she'd left Franco. The morning she was due to leave, a letter arrived from Archie Stansfield. He was sorry it was short notice, he wrote, but he could come to London the following day. Would she be able to meet him, as she'd suggested? He was catching the ten twenty-five train to Euston. It should arrive just before one and he would wait for her by the barriers. If she couldn't make it, his phone number was 01625…

Before she left for London, Grace asked George if she could use his computer. Her email to Isabel was brief:

Sorry I haven't been in touch. I need to talk to you face to face. I'm in England. I've been staying with George, but I'm coming up to London today. I'll stay at a friend's tonight, and tomorrow I've arranged to meet Archie Stansfield. If it's okay with you, I'll come on to you after. We've got to decide how we break the news to Rick and George. This secret has gone on too long as it is.
Love, Grace

Twenty-nine

Isabel studied Rick across the kitchen table. His hair, which he normally wore short, sprouted from his head in an untidy mess. He ran his fingers through it constantly. He had developed a nervous tic and kept screwing up his nose, like a rabbit. His gaze raked the room, back and forth, up and down like a searchlight. The big pine table, which Isabel had insisted on keeping from the old house, took up most of the space. You had to move the rocking chair to reach the cupboard and plates and saucepans were piled on a worktop because there was no room to store them. Most of the time the kitchen didn't seem as small and inconvenient as it had when Isabel first moved here, but now, with Rick's eyes on it, she squirmed in her seat.

'How is Deanna?' she asked.

He blinked furiously. 'Doing great.'

'And the girls?'

'They're good. Flavia's got her last exam next week.'

Isabel wanted to ask about Alicia—the memory of that scene on Christmas Day still haunted her—but the expression on Rick's face silenced her.

He picked up his briefcase from the floor and set it on the table. He clicked the locks open and took out a notebook. 'I've made an inventory of the stuff in Mum's loft. There's a huge amount she'll have to get rid of. There won't be room in the bungalow.' He licked his forefinger, flicking through the pages of his notebook.

'About this bungalow,' Isabel began. She knew the points she wanted to make off by heart, but then she saw Rick's expression change. *Don't let yourself be intimidated.* The voice in her head spoke sharply. It was the same with Brian. Despite his rough edges, he was a lot like Rick, domineering, irritable, obsessed with work. But she'd changed. She hadn't been through all the doubts and self-questioning, simply to slip back when the first test came. No. She forced herself to ignore the look on Rick's face.

'Rick, did you get my email?'

'What email? Do you know how many I get a day?'

'I've got no idea. But this one was about your mother.'

Rick raised his hands. Isabel flinched. But they moved to his head. He ran first one, then the other through his hair.

'Rick…'

He slammed the notebook into his briefcase. There was a wild look in his eyes that frightened her.

She heard the voice in her head: *Do it. Don't give up now.* 'Mum's not happy about leaving London.'

'Isn't she?'

'Everything she knows is here.' She swallowed. 'She's lost Dad. She needs to be with all his things around her.'

Rick snapped the locks of his briefcase shut. 'She'll have us up there.'

'But you're busy with work. The girls will be doing their own thing and Deanna needs to concentrate on getting well again. She's not going to want the worry of Mum.'

'Deanna's fine. I told you.'

Isabel made one more attempt. 'You've got to see it from Mum's point of view. She checks through his books and his old records every day, reminiscing. I've seen her do it.'

'She can't dwell in the past. She's got to move on. Get on with her life.'

'But Dad was her life.'

As she said the words, the thought of the time when that hadn't been the case flitted into Isabel's mind. Once Eva had cared so little for Henry, she had climbed into bed with another man. Become pregnant with his child.

'I'm having work done on the bungalow,' Rick was saying, 'so it's not ready anyway. She can have another few months to get used to the idea and shift some stuff. We'll move her up next spring.'

'And the piano?' Isabel crossed her fingers under the table as the question dropped into the room.

'You know I'm having the piano.'

'I thought you might have reconsidered. It means so much to George.'

Rick pushed his chair back from the table. 'George. George. George. Why is everyone so concerned with him? All his life, he's messed up.'

'He and Dad spent hours playing together on it.'

Rick stood up. 'I'm not wasting time on this any longer. We'll talk to Mum about it tonight over dinner. And you'd better support me, Isabel. She listens to you.'

Isabel sipped her coffee and pulled a sheet of paper from her bag. It was quiet in the coffee shop and she might as well write her shopping list while she waited for Simon. Honeyed chicken, new potatoes and salad for dinner, she decided. She'd have enough to do dodging Rick's potshots without having to worry about complicated food. Rick was impossible. Every exchange resembled a high-powered board meeting, and he had to win the vote at all costs. Poor Deanna—putting up with him all these years.

She checked her watch. Simon had improved his timekeeping, but he was still inclined to arrive after they'd arranged, overflowing with apologies. She tapped her pen against her lip imagining what his excuse would be today. He'd used most of the traditional ones and was now on to the *dog ate his homework* variety. She hoped he'd get here soon. He would be able to advise her on a nice wine for tonight. She'd wondered about inviting him. He'd be sure to charm her mother and his presence might be a check on Rick. Besides, she was longing to show him off. But she needed to do something about Brian first. She'd already put off the meeting with him twice, and Rose kept asking when they'd all be moving back in together.

She'd almost given up hope when Simon finally arrived. She was worrying about Grace—why she was in England; why she'd gone chasing off to George's; why she'd arranged to see Archie Stansfield again—when she saw Simon push open the door.

She waved.

He rushed towards her. 'Isabel, I'm so sorry.'

She laughed. 'Did the elephant tread on your toe?'

'Sorry?'

'I'm wondering what your excuse is this time.'

He swung his jacket over the back of the chair and sat down. 'I knew you wouldn't believe me. My meeting overran.'

'It's okay. I'm teasing you.' She reached out and smoothed down the bit of his hair that insisted on sticking up at the back.

In the weeks since they'd first made love, Isabel had spent most of her free time with Simon. Walking in the park, going to concerts, cooking and eating together—every activity shared made her like him more. He was kind and generous, giving of his attention, and more importantly for Isabel, of himself. 'I've learnt,' he told her. 'I'm not going to mess up another relationship.' More often than not, they met at his flat. It was even smaller than Isabel's, cluttered and chaotic, but at least they could be sure of privacy. Rose hadn't said much after their accidental meeting, and Isabel couldn't decide if that was a good or bad sign. 'Too early to chance bumping into her again,' she'd explained to Simon.

They finished their coffee and Isabel got up to cross the road to the supermarket. Simon caught hold of her hand. 'Stay a few more minutes.'

She glanced at the time. 'I haven't got long. There's the shopping and I've got to prepare dinner. I don't want anything to go wrong.'

'I'll help with the shopping—I haven't got another client until five.' Simon looked up at her. 'Please. I want to talk.'

'Ten minutes and I must go.' Isabel put her bag on a chair and sat down again. 'I've left Rick in the flat on his own, and I'm not comfortable with him being there.'

Simon put his palms together as if he was offering up a prayer. 'Okay. I've prepared a speech…'

'Simon, you're making me nervous. I'm already on tenterhooks about tonight. I don't think I can cope with a speech.'

'I'll make it quick.' He felt in his jacket pocket, no doubt for his cigarette packet. 'I'm not going to get all lovey dovey —not because I don't want to, but in case I scare you off.' He stared intently into his empty coffee cup. 'I like you. A lot. But I know you've still got feelings for Brian—'

'My feelings—'

'No. Let me say it. I wake up in the night worrying that you'd rather be with him and I'm second best.'

She ran her hand up and down his arm. 'You're a lovely man, Simon. You could never be second best.'

'I'm sorry but I've got to ask—are you completely finished with Brian?'

'We're not divorced yet if that's—'

'That's not what I'm talking about. Be honest with me, Isabel.'

'I've still some issues to resolve with him,' she said. *Please don't ask me what.* Her mind tapped to the beat. *Please don't ask me what.*

'And then you'll finish with him?'

'I hope so.' Would that do? Would he be satisfied?

A frown passed over Simon's face. 'One last question. Are you still in love with him?'

A patch of sunlight had been inching its way across the floor of the coffee shop since Isabel arrived. Without her noticing, it had reached their table. Its brilliance illuminated the red and white checked tablecloth, the cream cups and saucers, the milk jug. 'No,' she said. 'I'm not.'

The shopping took longer than Isabel expected and it was nearly five o'clock by the time she pulled up outside the flat. She'd hoped Rick would have gone back to Eva's and she could have the place to herself to prepare for the evening, but his car was still parked outside. He'd asked if he could work on her computer as his laptop had crashed.

She opened the boot of the car and took out the shopping. The plastic carriers were heavy and their handles bit into her fingers. She pushed open the front door. 'Hello!' she called. There was no reply. Rose's door was ajar and she could hear the noise of the television from the lounge. She piled the shopping on the kitchen table and examined her fingers. The plastic handles had left grooves in the skin.

'You're back.'

The voice made her jump. She looked round. Rick was standing in the doorway, holding out a sheet of paper.

'You gave me a fright!' She laughed, but then she saw his face. 'What's the matter?'

'This.' He waved the paper at her. 'Perhaps you'd like to tell me what it's all about?'

'What is it?'

He came closer. His eyes were bloodshot and a high colour stained his cheeks. He loomed over her. She knew he hardly ever drank, or she'd have sworn she could smell whisky on his breath.

'It's an email from Grace. It was sent from George's computer at eight o' clock this morning. I would have thought you'd remember it, but as you can't, I'll read it to you.' Isabel's chest grew tight as Rick read out the email. She put her hand on the table and steadied herself. She was sure she'd deleted the email. She was always careful in case Rose came across something she shouldn't. She printed messages she wanted to save and deleted them immediately. Rick was looking at her, waiting for an answer.

She'd have to bluster her way out of this one. 'What the hell were you doing going through my emails?'

'That's not the issue here.'

'I think it is!'

'What is this news? This secret you and Grace are keeping.' Rick slapped his hand against the sheet of paper. She remembered his raised fist on Christmas Day. It was only Deanna who had stopped him then.

He wouldn't rest until Isabel told him. He'd always been able to ferret secrets from her when they were young. He was glaring. 'I'm waiting.'

'It's not my secret to tell,' Isabel said.

'Right. Whose secret is it?'

Isabel turned to her shopping bags. She took out the chicken breasts. 'I need to get these in the fridge,' she said. She opened the fridge door and rearranged some stuff on the shelves. She put the chicken on the second shelf. The cold air from the fridge stung her cheeks. There was nothing else for it. She was going to have to shut the door and turn around.

Behind her, she heard the bleep of Rick's mobile. Isabel clutched the handle of the fridge. Saved by the bell. She risked a glance over her shoulder. He was checking the caller ID. He clicked a button and the bleeping stopped. She'd have to tell him. There was no way out. Once she'd panicked in an exam. She couldn't answer any of the questions. She was going to fail. She stared at the paper again: the black print was fuzzy. She couldn't read a word. She looked down at the floor. It wasn't far to fall. Isabel wouldn't be the first person to pass out in an exam…

'About this secret then.'

Okay, this was it. Behind her, at the open kitchen window, she heard Samson yowling. She turned to face

Rick. 'The secret relates to George. It's Mum you need to talk to really—'

'Isabel, cut the crap and get on with it.'

From across the hall, came the sound of the phone, and the murmur of Rose's voice.

'The day Dad died—'

'Mum.' Rose appeared in the doorway behind Rick.

Isabel tried to signal with her eyes: *get me out of here, Rose. There must be something you need me to do. Something you want.*

'That was Nonna, Mum. She said Flavia's been trying to ring you, Uncle Rick. Can you call her ASAP?'

Rick jabbed at the screen of his mobile. 'Flavia!' he barked, his eyes fixed on Isabel. 'What do you want? I'm busy here.'

Isabel watched as the colour drained from his face. 'When? Where?'

She heard a murmur coming from the other end of the phone.

'Stay with her. I'll be there in three hours. Four, max.' He glanced across at Isabel. Then turned away. 'Flavia... tell her I love her.'

He snapped the phone shut. He swayed forward on to his toes. Isabel stretched out a hand. She wouldn't be able to catch him if he fell. She remembered that look on his face when their father shouted at him for playing the wrong notes. Perhaps he'd let her put her arms round him. But then he seemed to regain his balance. He straightened his jacket.

'I've got to go. We'll continue our conversation at a more opportune moment.' The mask was back.

'What is it, Rick? What's happened?'

'Deanna's been taken to hospital.'

'Is it serious?'

Rick pushed past her. 'She'll be all right. I'll make sure of that.'

Thirty

Isabel listened to young Jonathan Hayward practising his scales. He'd been coming to her for lessons for a year and his progress was slow. He'd begun the scale of D at least five times, but kept losing his place and having to go back to the beginning.

'Right, Jonathan.' She tried to keep her voice bright. 'Let's leave the scales for today. Perhaps you'd like to work on them for next week?' He didn't answer and his face remained set in its sullen lines. She knew he was only here because his mother insisted. Probably most of his friends were out playing football.

She turned the pages of Jonathan's piano book. 'This is the piece I asked you to prepare. How did you get on?'

Jonathan mumbled a reply.

'Let's hear it, shall we?'

He held his fingers over the keys.

'It says *allegro*. What does that mean?'

The boy shrugged his bony shoulders.

'It means brightly, cheerfully. Let's see how cheerful you can be, shall we?'

Isabel half-listened to Jonathan's hesitant playing. If she had to sit through one more child murdering a piece of music, she'd scream. She glanced at her watch. The lesson would be over in ten minutes and then she was due to meet Brian.

He'd rung to arrange it the day before. 'I'm not accepting any excuses or postponing this time,' he said. He wanted to meet at Kenwood House: 'I know how much you like it there.' But that was the last place she wanted to go with him. It was special. Whatever happened today, she wanted to keep the memory of her first meeting with Simon intact. She suggested the pub opposite Waterlow

Park. 'It's been refurbished,' she told Brian. It was a lively place and they'd blend into the hubbub.

'The pub it is then,' Brian had said. 'See you there about one.'

Brian was already at the pub when she arrived. At the last moment she'd decided to walk and she'd cut it fine. He kissed Isabel on the lips, and she had to resist the urge to wipe her hand over her mouth. 'I've got a bottle of champagne on ice,' he said.

She raised her eyebrows. 'Champagne?'

He scanned her face. 'Not jumping the gun, am I?' He pulled out a chair.

'Have you been reading some etiquette book?'

'Can't a man make a fuss of his wife once in a while?'

'Not when he's dumped her for his bit on the side!'

'Ouch! That hurt,' Brian said. 'I know I deserve it. But I'm going to make it up to you. Let's order some food and then we'll talk.'

Isabel watched Brian as he stood at the bar. He was wearing a yellow cotton shirt she hadn't seen before and for once his jeans looked freshly washed instead of stained with grease. Although he employed numerous mechanics to work in his chain of garages, at heart he was still a 'spanner boy'. There was nothing he liked better than fiddling with engines and he wasn't too fastidious about showering and changing afterwards. But today he'd made an effort. She looked at his thick red neck and broad shoulders. He had the physique of someone who spent their life in physical labour. Isabel thought of Simon's body. That pad of fat starting to form around his waist. His slight sloping shoulders.

'I've ordered chicken and salad sandwiches.' Brian looked pleased with himself. 'On granary bread, as you like it.'

'Great.'

He pulled his chair closer. 'Let's cut to the chase, Bel. We can get this wrapped up before the food arrives. Then we can really celebrate.'

'How do you mean?'

'It's time we stopped this nonsense. You want me. I want you. The kids want us to get back together.'

'You began this *nonsense*.'

'I don't blame you for giving me a hard time. When I think…' he broke off and a smile played round his mouth in a way Isabel would have sworn he'd practised if she hadn't known him better. He looked up again. His eyes gleamed as if he was a convert to some evangelical movement. 'When I think what I've put you and the kids through and all for some moments of madness.'

'Moments of madness. Is that all Anita and the baby mean to you?'

'Of course not. I'll see her right. Make sure she and little Mark have got enough dosh. But as for shacking up with her… I don't know what I was thinking of.'

Isabel twisted the stem of her glass. She'd scarcely touched the champagne. This was the moment she'd been waiting for. Since that night Brian had told her he was leaving, she'd imagined this day. She'd spent hours with her father discussing how and when he might come back. 'I'm sure he loves you really,' Henry had said. 'He's just like the greedy boy at a party who wants all the sweets. Then he'll be sick.' They'd laughed at that. She remembered after her father died, meeting Grace at the airport, telling her *I'm going to get my husband and son back, whatever it takes*. And now, here he was, not quite pleading, but almost, to be together again. Her plan had worked. She'd got what she wanted.

'I've seen a new house for us,' Brian was saying. 'Right on the edge of Hampstead Heath. Six bedrooms, three reception, a huge garden. You always said you wanted a bigger garden at the old house.'

'That sounds nice.'

'You'll love it! I'll ring the estate agent when I get back to the garage. We can go and view it tomorrow. If you're not doing anything, that is,' he added as an afterthought. 'What do you say? You still haven't actually agreed.'

She tried the champagne. Bubbles fizzed in her throat and made her cough.

'What do you want? The full works?' Brian's champagne glass remained untouched, but he was already half way down the pint of beer he'd bought when he ordered the food. 'You always were difficult to please.'

He glanced round the pub. It was crowded with lunchtime drinkers and there was a buzz of conversation. He stood up. 'Okay, if this is what it takes.' He steadied himself against a chair and sank to the floor on one knee. The people standing round cleared a space for him.

'Brian, get up. You're embarrassing me!'

'Answer me first.' He gazed up at her with that wheedling look that had always been a prelude to sex.

Isabel was saved further mortification when the food arrived and Brian stood up.

'I want an answer, though, Bel.' He took a huge bite from a sandwich. 'You and me and the kids together again, right?'

The granary bread seemed to stick to the roof of Isabel's mouth. 'I don't think it's going to work.' There, she'd said it.

'What?' Bits of lettuce and tomato escaped from Brian's mouth. 'You've been angling for it ever since I left.'

'At first, maybe, but it's different now.'

'And what do you propose telling Rose and Josh? I've given them all the info on the new house and they're dead chuffed. There's even room for a swimming pool.'

Isabel dropped her half-eaten sandwich on the plate. It felt as if a chunk of bread was lodged in her throat. 'You can't buy them, you know, Brian.'

'Don't be ridiculous. They want to see their mum and dad happy again. We owe it to them.'

So, his knife had finally sliced open her weak spot. She did have a responsibility to give Rose and Josh their family back. She imagined their excited voices as they rushed from room to room in the new house choosing which would be theirs. Rose would be able to invite her friends back instead of going out every evening because she was ashamed of where she lived. Josh would laugh again and ask her to help with his homework, like he used to. And she'd loved Brian once. Maybe she could again.

'I can see you want to say yes.' Brian downed the rest of his beer. He drummed his fingers on the table. She watched them beat out their tattoo: one, two, three, four; one, two, three, four; little, ring, middle, fore; little, ring—a picture of Simon's damaged fingers flared in her mind. She'd never seen the violin in his hands. Never been able to hear him play. But it would have been beautiful. He'd lost so much because of those fingers. And yet they revealed everything about him: strong; sensitive; vulnerable; brave. *Are you in love with Brian?* he'd asked. 'No,' she'd said, 'I'm not.'

She looked across at Brian. 'I'm sorry. I don't want to be with you any more. I can't do it, not even for the children's sake.'

Brian caught hold of her hand. 'I can't complain if you play hard to get after what I've put you through.' His palm was hot and felt slimy. 'And if you need a bit more persuasion, think of lover boy's face when he hears about your dirty little secret.'

Grace was sitting on the wall outside the flat when they pulled up. She jumped down and rushed to the passenger side, half hugging, half pulling Isabel out of the car. 'I've been waiting for ages.'

'Why didn't you phone?'

'I couldn't get a signal on the wretched mobile. Anyway, you're here. I've got so much to tell you.' She leaned into the car. 'Hi Brian.'

'What's this?' he asked. 'A flying visit?'

'Something like that.'

'How's Franco?'

'He's fine.' Grace took Isabel by the arm and steered her to the house. The contact with Brian was over, as far as she was concerned. As Isabel passed Brian's window, he reached out and caught hold of her wrist.

'You go on, Grace. Here's the key.' Isabel turned back to Brian. 'Ring me tomorrow and we'll make the arrangements.'

Brian squeezed her hand. 'I might not say it much, but I love you.'

'What on earth's happened?' Isabel asked.

'You'll never believe what Archie Stansfield's told me.'

'But what are you doing in England? I didn't know you were coming.'

'I've got to tell you about Archie Stansfield first. I'm still reeling.'

They were in the kitchen and Isabel was mixing drinks into a glass jug. She measured out the Pimms and added lemonade. She dropped ice cubes and shreds of mint into the jug, carefully slicing up a lemon. She reached up into the cupboard and took out two tumblers. 'Shall we sit outside? It's such a lovely day.'

Simon had helped her buy garden furniture last weekend and she set out the glasses and jug on the wrought iron table. She put up the umbrella and positioned two chairs in its shade. She sipped her drink as Grace related what Archie had told her: the summer when their father was seventeen and fell in love with Dottie, his friend's sister.

'We know she was pregnant,' Isabel said. 'But I still can't believe it was Dad's.'

Grace tapped her glass against her lips. 'Prepare yourself, Bel. You won't like this.'

'Hurry up. I'm scared.'

'Dottie kept quiet about the pregnancy for months. Almost pretended it wasn't happening, Archie said. Her mother guessed something was up, but she denied it.'

'What happened when her mum and dad found out?'

'Archie said they went mad. It wasn't only the shame of it; Dottie was clever. She was studying at night school and she wanted to be a teacher.'

'Was it Dad's baby?'

'He was her only sweetheart.'

'So, they could have got married.'

'Apparently Dad wouldn't. He was working for his music scholarship—'

'This is awful.' A band of metal seemed to have attached itself round Isabel's head. She pushed her chair further into the shade.

'And Granny and Grandad wouldn't hear of it. They'd set their heart on Dad going to music college and you remember what Granny was like—no one ever argued with her. Dad didn't even go to see Dottie.'

'It gets worse by the second.'

'Dottie was sent to an aunt who lived miles away in Kent. Her parents told everyone she'd got a job down there as a cook in a big house. Nobody believed them, and the village blamed Dad for not facing up to his responsibilities.'

'So everyone turned against him?'

'Seems like it. And there's more.

'The baby was a boy and she called him Henry.'

'Oh no!' Isabel closed her eyes and felt tears squeezing between the lids. Her father's son. Henry. 'Did she keep the baby?'

'They made her have him adopted.'

'So we've got a half brother somewhere?'

'We've got two half brothers, Bel.'

Isabel fished a slice of lemon from her glass and sucked. Its sourness gave her something to concentrate on. She bit on something hard and found herself chewing the pip.

She poured them each another glass of Pimms. 'Imagine —a son of Dad's somewhere. I wonder where he lives.'

'I haven't told you the end of the story yet,' Grace said. 'After the baby was born, Dottie came home, but she was like a different person, Archie said. Dad had gone to London to college by then, but he wrote to her once via Archie. She never even opened the letter. Archie found it in her bedside drawer. He burnt it afterwards.'

'After what?'

'Archie cried when he was telling me, even after all these years. Dottie wouldn't go out of the house. She used to sit in her bedroom all day with the curtains pulled. After about six months, her father lost patience with her. "Lass will have to snap out of it. Moping about the house with a face like a wet week." He arranged for them all to go on a coach trip to Blackpool to see the lights. At the last moment Dottie refused to go. Archie wanted to stay with her, but his father wouldn't hear of it. "Do her good—a day on her own. Let her think about trouble she's caused." When they got back about midnight, she was nowhere to be seen. Archie went out looking for her. His parents went to bed. "She'll turn up in the morning, right enough." Archie searched all night. He found her at first light, down by the river where she and Dad used to go. It had been their hideaway. She was hanging from a tree.'

There was a scrabbling noise from the other side of the fence and Samson appeared from next-door's garden. He balanced on the fence and then skidded down the side, heading straight for Isabel. She leaned forward and scooped him into her arms, burying her face in his fur. He'd been lying in the sun and was warm.

'I can't bear it, Grace,' she said when she felt able to talk. 'To think what Dottie must have gone through.'

'I've been trying to get my head round it ever since Archie told me. Poor man—he's obviously never got over it.'

'He must have hated Dad.'

'He said he hit him.'

A dull fire of anger caught in Isabel. Her father's actions repelled her. 'I'm surprised he didn't rip him apart.'

Grace smiled. 'If you could see him, Bel. He's such a mild little man.'

'I remember in Archie's letter he said Dad kept writing to him afterwards—wanting forgiveness. That was some load of guilt Dad had to carry for the rest of his life.'

'Perhaps he took George on to try to make amends.'

Isabel ran her hand over Samson's fur. He arched his back and settled again on her lap. She tried to imagine that past world. The decisions that were made. The consequences that followed. They could wonder and surmise, but however much they probed what had gone before, the truth would never fully reveal itself. The past titillated—the *what* could be uncovered, but in the end it retained its secrets: the *why* and the *how* remained hidden.

'I suppose…' she said, unable to resist, like going back to a crossword you have to complete '…if he'd refused, Mum might have left him and taken us with her, so he'd have lost more children.'

'Or she'd have been forced to give her baby away. Like Dottie.'

'Do you think Mum knew about Dottie and the other baby?' Isabel asked.

'She must have known something because she let Archie know Dad was dead.'

Isabel heard a snuffling noise from Grace. She looked across and saw she was laughing.

'Grace! How can you?'

'Sorry. I've just had a thought… Dottie and Dad's baby was adopted…'

'Yeah. We've been through all that.'

'No, listen, Bel. The baby was adopted, but he's still Dad's son.'

'Technically, yes. What are you getting at?'

'You remember that night Rick and George had the big row about the piano?'

'Remember it? I thought if Rick ever got his hands on George—'

'Rick said that as Dad's eldest son, the piano was his.'

Isabel started to laugh too. 'Now there are *two* eldest sons.'

'What about us?' Grace said. 'We're his daughters. I'm sure you'd like the piano, Bel.'

'I've just remembered…' Isabel stared at Grace over Samson's back. 'Rick saw the email you sent yesterday. Kept on and on about the secret. He nearly got it out of me about George. If Flavia hadn't phoned—'

'He knows, Bel.'

'He knows?'

'There was so much other stuff to tell you, I haven't had a chance. Rick phoned while I was with Archie. He was at the hospital, but Deanna must be improving, because he'd got the bit between his teeth. Demanded to know what my email was about.'

'I should have warned you.'

'I decided there was no point stalling. So I told him.'

'What did he say?'

'Nothing. He put the phone down on me. I wouldn't be surprised if he's on his way here now.'

Isabel pushed Samson to the ground. Indignant, he stared up at her and stuck his tail in the air. She stood up and reached out a hand to pull Grace to her feet.

'Where are we going in such a hurry?'

'We'd better get round to Mum's,' Isabel said. She gathered up the jug and glasses. 'Tell her what's happened in case Rick arrives. As far as she's concerned, I'm the only one who knows about George.'

Thirty-one

Eva was in the dining room when they arrived. The table was piled high with books and letters, bills and magazines. Discarded scraps of paper littered the floor, like confetti after a wedding. Their father's records were strewn around, their covers abandoned. Eva was sitting in the middle, a sheet of paper clutched in her hand.

'Mum! What's happened?' Isabel knelt next to her mother. She stroked her arm. Eva closed her eyes and rocked backwards and forwards.

Grace put a hand on Eva's shoulder. 'What's wrong, Mum?'

Tears rolled down Eva's cheeks. Her hair was loose about her shoulders. It looked dull and lifeless, the once-glossy sheen gone.

Isabel took a packet of tissues from her bag and held one out. 'Talk to us. Has something upset you?' A thought struck her. 'It's not Deanna is it? Has Rick phoned?'

Eva clenched the tissue in her hand, but she made no effort to wipe her eyes.

'I'll make some coffee,' Grace said.

Left alone with her mother, Isabel prised her fingers from the sheet of paper. 'Let me take that.' She tossed it on the table with the rest of the debris. Isabel massaged the fingers to bring back the blood.

Grace arrived with a tray of coffee and biscuits. She placed a cup in Eva's hands. 'Drink some. It will help.'

Obediently Eva took a few sips. She looked up at Grace. 'It's good. Just how I like it.'

'What's happened, Mum? Why are you so upset?'

Eva looked from Isabel to Grace, her brown eyes like an ill-treated dog's. 'I don't want to live in Northumberland,' she said. 'It's so cold. So dark. I would die in the winter.'

'You don't have to go, if you don't want to.'

'Rick says I'll like it when I get there.'

'We'll talk to him. Make him understand.' Grace drew her mother's hair back from her face; it lay limply across her back.

Eva shook her head. 'He won't listen. I tried to tell him when he was down here, but he was making lists. Told me what I had to get rid of. I gave up in the end. I've never been able to argue back in English. I can't think of the words quickly enough.'

'It's all right, Mum. We'll do it for you,' Isabel said. 'We know how much this house means to you. Where you're surrounded by Dad's things.'

'But that's just it.' Tears brimmed in her eyes again. 'I'm so lonely without Henry and I miss Italy.' She caught at Grace's hand. 'I thought maybe I could come to Ischia. Live with you and Franco.'

Grace and Isabel exchanged glances.

'I wouldn't be any trouble. I promise.'

'No, I know you wouldn't,' Grace said. 'But Bel and I need to talk to you about something else.'

'What is it? You're not ill, are you? Or you?' Her gaze moved to Isabel. 'I couldn't bear it if anything happened.' She started moaning. 'It would be too much after Henry.'

'There's nothing wrong with us.' Isabel took the coffee cup from her mother's hands and placed it on the tray. 'But we need to talk. You know what you told me the morning Dad died? About George.'

Eva glared at Isabel. 'Not that again!' She sat up straight and jerked her head upright. 'I told you it would break your father's heart to hear you going on about it.'

'You can't keep a secret like that forever. It's bound to come out sometime.'

'Not unless you tell anyone.'

'You can't gag me, Mum. I'm not Dad.'

'I don't know what you mean.' Eva's voice had grown shriller. 'It was your father who insisted we kept it a secret.'

Isabel shrugged. 'Whatever you say. But I might as well tell you, Grace and Rick know.'

Eva's face shrivelled, lines and wrinkles appearing as if she was ageing in front of them. 'You took it on yourself to tell them after all.'

Isabel didn't answer. It didn't seem the moment to mention Archie Stansfield.

But Eva wouldn't leave it at that. 'Now you'll see the trouble you've caused.'

'Me!' The accusation stung Isabel. 'I'm not the one who had a child outside my marriage.'

In the split second before it struck, Isabel saw her mother's hand coming towards her. She heard the dull slap and felt the pain almost in the same moment. She cupped her face in her hand.

Eva stood up. She staggered and caught hold of the table.

'I can't believe a daughter of mine could be so cruel. I would never have spoken to my mamma like that. I loved her too much.'

I can't believe a mother would slap her own daughter. Isabel cradled her cheek—if only she was brave enough to say the words out loud.

'I'm sorry you're upset, Mum, but we all know the secret —apart from George—and it's not Isabel's fault, so don't take it out on her.'

Isabel heard the determination in Grace's voice: she was going to stand up to Eva.

'And the first thing Rick will ask is *who is George's father?*' Grace folded her arms. 'It will be easier if we already know. We can pacify him.'

Eva took another tissue and blew her nose. 'All right,' she said at last. 'I'll tell you.'

Isabel's mouth went dry. She swallowed several times trying to find saliva. She couldn't look at Grace.

'But first I must ask him. See if he agrees.'

Isabel snapped her head back to stare at her mother. Eva's face was spread in a broad smile as if she had given her daughters a wonderful present.

'Ask him?' The words shot out of Grace's mouth like bullets. 'You mean you're still in touch with the father?'

Eva looked from Isabel to Grace, her mouth pouting and her eyes cast down. '*Sì*. Why wouldn't I be?'

Isabel couldn't believe it. Her mother didn't care. It didn't matter to her what her daughters knew or thought. Her metamorphosis from helpless widow to arrogant coquette was breathtaking.

Grace picked up a chair and banged it down next to Eva. 'Sit down, Mum.'

Eva's hands fluttered at her throat. 'I no understand. Why you shout?'

'Come on, Mum. Don't start doing the broken English, the poor me act.'

Eva's eyes flashed, but she sat down. 'I didn't know you could be so hard.'

'I must have got it from you. Now, who *is* George's father?'

'Henry idolised Giorgio.'

'We know that, but he wasn't his biological father, so who was?'

Isabel stared up at George's portrait of Henry. Her father's eyes met hers. He could never have imagined this scene would occur only a few months after his death. He must have thought he'd taken his secrets to the grave. Perhaps they were wrong. Perhaps they shouldn't be pushing Eva. George had a right to know, but maybe she and Grace didn't.

'Okay, you want to know…' Eva pinched her lips together spinning out the silence… 'It was Eduardo.'

'Uncle Eduardo?' Isabel had been waiting, her body tensed, for a name. She thought she was prepared for anything, had primed herself not to react, but she couldn't help the yelp of surprise.

'Your cousin?' Grace looked equally shocked. 'That creep.'

'My second cousin.'

'Second, third, fifty times removed. Who cares?' Grace stood over Eva. 'He used to visit us. He paid for your trips to Italy.'

Eva nodded. 'He wanted to help us. He had money and your father didn't.'

'But you made Dad tolerate him.'

'Henry was grateful Eduardo let me come back. And when Eduardo visited, he could see little Giorgio.'

The phone rang. None of them moved; locked like actors in the scene they'd just played. Isabel turned to her mother, but she had her hands clamped to her ears. The ringing bounced around the room. Someone was going to have to answer. She looked at Grace. Her sister's eyes were fixed on the portrait.

'Make it stop! Make it stop!' Eva whimpered.

The ringing finally pierced Grace's reverie. 'I'll get it,' she said.

The phone sat on Henry's bureau in the sitting room. Isabel listened to the soft rise and fall of Grace's voice. She didn't dare look at her mother.

It must have been only a couple of minutes, but it was like forever before Grace came back. 'It was Rick,' she said. 'Deanna died at ten o'clock this morning.'

Thirty-two

Isabel woke. Her heart drumming, soaked in perspiration. There'd been a voice. It was calling. She sat up straining her ears. Nothing. Only Samson's soft breathing from the foot of the bed. Rose was at Brian's, and Grace had stayed with Eva.

Isabel fell back on the pillow. She turned her head towards the clock: five a.m. Not even twenty-four hours since Deanna had died. After Rick's call, Eva had cried. '*Triste. Molto triste*,' she muttered over and over. Grace made more coffee and they talked about Deanna. How beautiful she was. How Rick had adored her. What would happen to the girls. 'Poor *bambini*.' Eva sighed. 'She was a good mamma.'

Isabel lay on her back in the darkness. Sometimes weeks passed and nothing happened. You got up—you looked after the children—you worked—you prepared food—ate—you went to bed. Day after grey day slipping into each other, like one foot and then another into quicksand. Then comes a day like yesterday: Brian. Dottie. Eduardo. Deanna. She turned on her side and curled into a ball. Samson crept further up the bed and settled against her left hip. She ran her hand over his head and down his back. His body vibrated with purring under her touch.

Ringing reverberated in her ears. She reached out blindly for her alarm, but the noise persisted. She forced her eyes open and squinted at the clock. It was nearly eleven. The ringing stopped and started again. Samson lifted his head from his paws. She struggled out of bed, sleep still clawing her. There was a figure at the front door. She pulled it open. 'Simon!'

Isabel stared at him. She smoothed down her nightie and tried to flatten her hair. She hadn't taken her make-up off last night and mascara must be smeared across her cheeks.

'Can I come in?'

Isabel opened the door wider. 'I was going to phone you when I'd had a shower.'

'I've been texting you all morning.'

'I overslept.'

She could see the fine criss-crossings of wrinkles around his eyes. He looked as if he was going to kiss her, but she stepped back. 'I must freshen up,' she said. 'Go on through to the kitchen.'

Simon was looking out of the window. He'd had his hair cut since she'd seen him the other day and a line of pale skin ran across the back of his neck. She wanted to put her lips to it.

He turned. There were dark circles under his eyes, stubble where he hadn't shaved.

'You didn't phone last night,' he said.

'Sorry.'

'I got your message you were meeting Brian. I've been imagining all sorts.'

'Sorry I didn't ring. Deanna died yesterday.' She took a step towards him and his arms went round her.

'Isabel, my love. I'm so sorry.' His voice crooned close to her ear.

She rested her head against his shoulder. A tiny curl of hair in the V of his shirt tickled her face. She wanted to scratch it, but she didn't move. Her throat ached. A thread had worked loose on his shirt, and she held it between her fingers as if she might pull it. He stroked her hair, his hand cupping her head.

*

Simon made tea and they sat down at the kitchen table. He'd brought a bag of croissants and their warm doughy smell filled the room. Yesterday's sunshine had disappeared and rain clouds hung low. Isabel was glad. She needed to find corners to hide some of the pain away. The fierce sun would have forbidden that.

She told Simon about Deanna. She told Simon about Dottie Stansfield. She told Simon she was angry with her father. She told Simon she was angry with her mother. She didn't tell Simon about Brian.

They were still sitting at the kitchen table when the front door slammed. 'Hi, Mum.'

Isabel jumped up. 'It's Rose!'

'What's the panic?' Simon pulled a mock-surprise face. 'She's met me before.'

'You don't understand—'

Rose appeared in the doorway. 'Oh, *he's* here.'

Isabel saw her gaze take in Simon, the mugs, the two croissants left on the plate. 'Simon's popped round,' she said.

Rose turned her back on Simon and slipped her arm round Isabel's waist. 'Dad told me about Auntie Deanna.'

'Yes, I rang to ask him to tell you and Josh.' She knew his eyes were on her, but Isabel couldn't look at Simon.

'It's sad, isn't it?' Rose said. 'She was really cool.'

'Yes, it's sad.'

'What's going to happen to Flavia and Camilla?'

'They've still got Uncle Rick.'

'There was this girl in my class whose mum died. Her dad couldn't cope and she had to go and live with her granny.'

Isabel risked a glance at Simon. The petals of the yellow roses in a vase on the table had begun to fall. She saw him pick one up and tear it into tiny pieces. They lay scattered round his hands like specks of golden blood.

Rose said 'I feel bad because Auntie Deanna's died—'

'We'll talk about it some more, when Simon—'

'I mean I feel bad because they must be really miserable, but I'm happy about you and Dad.'

'Not now, Rose.' *Please shut up, Rose. Shut up. Go.*

'Dad told me last night. He said we can see the new house at the weekend. It's going to be ace.'

'Isabel?'

She tried to compose her face before she turned to Simon. Expressions came and skittered away: affronted disbelief, misunderstanding, confusion. One of those might have done, but when she turned to face him, she felt her mouth, stupidly, lift in a smile.

Simon stood up. There was no answering smile. 'What does she mean, Isabel?'

'I can explain. Rose, give us a minute, will you?'

Rose muttered and flounced out of the room. Her bedroom door banged shut.

Isabel took Simon's hands in hers. 'I'm sorry. I was going to tell you.'

'Go on. You know what a good listener I am.'

'Don't make this harder than it is.'

'What is it you've got to tell me?'

'Simon, you mean so much to me. You've changed my life.'

He pulled his hands from her grasp. He leaned forward, his palms flat on the table.

She forced herself to look at his fingers. To look at his left hand. At the two stumps that had destroyed his musical career.

'You're going back to him, aren't you?' His voice was flat.

'It's for the children.' She felt weak and futile, but her skin tingled as if she was on top of the big wheel.

He pushed past her, and she watched him go down the hall and out the front door. He didn't slam it.

Rose jumped out of her room as if she'd been listening behind the door. 'Wow, Mum. What was all that about?'

'Leave it for now. I'm tired.'

'But what did I say? You were only seeing him to make Dad jealous, weren't you?'

Isabel didn't want to talk to her daughter. She didn't want to go and see the new house. She didn't want to plan a new garden. She didn't want a swimming pool. Simon was walking down the path and along the pavement. He was getting into his car and starting the engine. He was arriving home. He was packing up the clothes and CDs and toiletries she'd left at his flat and putting them in a box. Isabel was going to live with Brian.

Grace phoned in the afternoon. 'Are you coming over? I could use some help here.'

'Sorry. I took a headache tablet and I fell asleep.' Isabel had been lying on her bed, dry-eyed and awake. She ached all over—she must be getting flu.

When she arrived at her mother's house, Grace was sitting at the dining room table. She looked as if she was writing a letter but she turned the sheet of paper over when Isabel came in. Her face was pale and her eyes were puffy.

Isabel sat down opposite her. 'Where's Mum?'

'In bed.'

'How is she today?'

'Weepy.'

'Have you spoken to Rick?'

Grace was doodling on the paper in front of her. Intricate shapes of circles and interlocking triangles filled the page. 'No, but Flavia phoned.'

'How are they all? Did she say when the funeral is?'

'End of the week.'

'Only gives us three days to make arrangements.'

The circles and triangles darkened as Grace traced over them again. 'Rick doesn't want us there.'

'He can't stop us going.'

'Flavia said it would be better if we didn't. She's afraid it might tip him over the edge.'

'What do you think we ought to do?'

'I don't know. Even Deanna's parents aren't going to be there. Poor things, they'd only just flown back to the States, and her father's had a heart attack.'

'All the more reason for us to go,' Isabel insisted. 'I've always loved Deanna.'

'I didn't get much sleep last night.' Grace pen wavered and aimless lines spattered the page. 'I'm too tired to think.'

Isabel caught hold of Grace's hand, squashing the pen between their fingers. 'Please stop doing that.' She pointed to the web of doodling. 'It's making me feel queasy.'

Grace threw the pen down. 'It's making me feel better!'

Isabel wondered what was going on in her sister's mind. Sometimes you knew. You looked at a face and it smiled at you and you knew the person inside the face was happy. Simple. But other times, that inner world was a thicket, dense and unyielding.

'What's wrong?' she asked. 'It's not only Deanna, is it?'

'I've left Franco.'

Isabel thought back to her time in Ischia. She remembered Grace telling Franco that she and Isabel were visiting the *castello*, remembered his comment that his wife was *innamorata di Vittoria*. It was a light, teasing moment, something any man might have said. But afterwards something like hatred had flickered across Franco's face: there and then gone.

'I'm sorry, Grace,' she said. 'I know how much it hurts.'

'I was the one who left and now I keep worrying about him.'

'I thought you were crazy about each other.'

Grace shrugged. 'Things change.' She picked up the pen again and drew in more lines, each one blacker than the last.

Isabel watched her sister's intense concentration. 'I was always jealous of you, you know,' she said.

'Why?' Grace took a second sheet of paper and the circles and triangles continued.

'You were the beautiful one. You were clever. Then you met Franco and it was all so romantic…'

'Romantic? You try working in a restaurant sixteen hours a day.'

'But your whole life is more glamorous than mine. Solid, dependable Isabel.'

Grace began to sob. Isabel looked at her dark head where her forehead rested on the table. Her arms were crossed and she was clutching her shoulders. Isabel stretched out her hand to touch Grace's hair. She knew it would feel soft and springy. She'd washed it for her, combed the tangles, helped her put it up for her wedding. She knew the feel of her sister's hair as well as her own. But the gulf between her hand and that black hair was wide. Despair is solitary and seals us from others. Isabel drew her hand back and waited.

'Sorry about that.' Grace blew her nose on the tissue Isabel offered.

'Did I set you off?' Isabel asked.

'No, I've needed to cry since I got on the ferry in Ischia. It wouldn't stay in any longer.'

'Do you want to talk about it?'

'I'm sick of thinking about it, never mind talking. I'll tell you another time.' The skin around Grace's eyes was the colour of bruises. 'Sorry, Bel. You don't need this. Especially with all the trouble you've had yourself.' She blew her nose again. 'I haven't even asked you what happened with Brian the other day.'

'We're getting back together.'

Grace put her arms round Isabel and hugged her. 'I'm pleased for you. I know how much you wanted it.'

'Yes.'

'You don't sound very excited.'

Isabel managed a little lift of her lips. 'It's complicated. Like you said—I'll tell you sometime.'

'I don't know about you, Bel, but I could do with a glass of something.'

'It's only five o'clock!'

'I'm going to raid Dad's wine—if George has left any. Desperate times, desperate measures.'

She came back with a bottle of merlot and some cheese crackers. She poured two glasses. 'I think you're right. We should go up for Deanna's funeral.'

'What about Rick?'

'He'll have enough to do coping with his own feelings. The girls need people to support them as well.'

'I feel so sad for them. They adored Deanna.'

Grace bit into a cracker. 'Rick says Alicia isn't allowed to go to the funeral.'

'He can't do that.'

'Flavia said he's blaming her for Deanna's death.'

'That's madness!' The scene at Rick's on Christmas Day reared up in Isabel's mind: all of them frozen in that tableau of horror. 'I didn't tell you,' she said. 'Rick and Alicia had a terrible row at Christmas when Mum and I were up there. He hates her boyfriend.'

'He still can't keep her from her own mother's funeral.'

Footsteps sounded overhead. They heard the loo flushing.

'She's up,' Isabel said. 'I'd better go and see her.'

'Hang on. I want to tell you this first.'

'If you're going to drop another bombshell, I don't want to know!'

Grace sipped her wine.

'Go on,' Isabel said. Her mother would start calling in a minute and she'd have to go.

'You said you didn't want to know.'

'Get on with it.'

'I got her to tell me some more about Eduardo this morning.'

'That goat! We've heard enough about him already.'

'It's worse than we thought.' Grace finished her wine and poured some more. 'Apparently, Mum and Eduardo were childhood sweethearts. Her brothers thought he was no good, so they sent her to London. To get her away from him.'

'But she told me they sent her here because there was no money. It was after the war, and her father had died. Her brothers said she'd have a better life in England. So, she came over to Great Aunt Rosa's.'

'And there was Dad waiting—like a lamb to the slaughter.'

'Grace!' They heard their mother calling from upstairs. 'Grace!'

'Oh no!' Grace covered her face with her hands.

'It's okay. I'll go,' Isabel said. 'But I've remembered something Mum said to me about Brian.'

'What was that?'

'She said he'd come back. "Make him pay a little and then forgive him".'

'And?'

'Grace! Are you there?' Eva's voice was more insistent.

'Suppose she found out about Dottie and the baby,' Isabel said. 'Perhaps she stayed on in Italy after Nonna died to punish him.'

Grace laughed. 'And Eduardo and George were the thumbscrews!'

Thirty-three

Grace and Isabel checked into the hotel in Newcastle. It had been a long drive and Grace was glad she'd insisted on a hire car—Isabel's old Volvo would never have made it. Brian wanted to drive them, but Isabel said he needed to stay with Rose and Josh. That was one relief. The thought of being trapped with Brian for all those hours had filled Grace with dread. Eva cried off too: 'I couldn't face another funeral—not after my Henry.'

Their room was bright and spacious with a view over the river. Isabel went to have a shower and Grace stood at the window looking down at the water. Bridges spanned the river on each side. She'd seen pictures of the Millennium Bridge and was sure that must be it up on the left. She remembered Alicia telling her she worked nearby. She looked at her watch—Alicia should be here soon.

Grace had never been to Newcastle, and she couldn't have imagined her first visit would be for Deanna's funeral. She swung her bag on to the bed and took out her new dress. She hung it from the wardrobe door and smoothed the creases. It was dark green with long sleeves and a straight skirt. She'd bought it the day before, as she'd only packed the essentials when she left Ischia. Flavia said Deanna had wanted everyone to wear bright colours, but Rick would be sure to have different ideas, so she was playing safe with dark green. 'Don't say anything to your dad, but Isabel and I are coming,' she told Flavia. 'Thank you, Auntie Grace. Mum would be pleased.'

Isabel came out of the bathroom, a towel wrapped round her head. She'd hardly spoken on the journey up and was really annoying, checking her phone every five minutes.

'Did Brian say he'd call you?' Grace had eventually asked.

Isabel had shoved the mobile in her bag. 'It's not him I'm looking for.'

Grace looked up from unpacking. 'Good shower?'

'Heaven, especially after the rubbish one at the flat.'

'Expect you'll soon have a designer bathroom.' Grace caught the frown on Isabel's face. For someone who'd got what they wanted, she didn't seem happy.

Grace pushed her underwear into a drawer. 'I meant to ask you…' she put her clean bra on top of the pile, '…what happened to that man—Simon, wasn't it—the one you met on the blind date?'

'It didn't work out.' Isabel's tone was studiously neutral. 'You know how it is.'

'Yeah, shame though. George said he was nice.'

'I'll give George his number, shall I?'

Oh, tetchy. She'd hit a raw nerve.

Grace left Isabel and Alicia in the bar of the hotel and set out for Rothbury. Up the A1 and then branch off. It looked easy on the map and Alicia said it should take no more than forty-five minutes. Forty-five there, forty-five back, half an hour at the house—she should be able to spend time with Alicia later. The trip was the last thing she needed after the long drive from London, but the thought of Rick's reaction if they turned up tomorrow unannounced urged her on.

At least it wouldn't be dark for some time. She wouldn't have to cope with the swoop and burn of headlights. She took the left fork and followed the steep curve of the road. Despite its unfamiliarity, it was nothing compared to the precipitous inclines that circled Ischia, some clinging to the island's perimeter. The road that climbed to Fontana was even worse. She remembered the bus chugging up it early one morning, and her gripping Franco's hand. They'd got up at dawn to climb Mount Epomeo before the heat grew too intense. The sky was sharp and clear, its blue stinging her eyes. When they stopped at a bar on the way down and ate a late breakfast of ham and eggs, Franco had toasted her with his cup of strong sweet coffee: '*Non posso vivere senza di te, carissima*,' he'd whispered. The words played in her head: it's not possible to live without you, my darling.

She gripped the steering wheel. Her eyes wanted to close and she turned the radio on. A deep female voice filled the car with the lyrics of lost love. The road ahead narrowed and she had to swerve to avoid a car breasting the hill and coming towards her.

She reached Rothbury and made her way through the village. Alicia's directions were clear. She turned the car into the drive and the gravel shifted under the tyres. Isabel was right—it *was* a mansion. She parked outside the front door and surveyed the house. A face peered from one of the upstairs windows. Her heart fluttered.

She crunched over the gravel and the front door was pulled open. Thank goodness. It was Flavia standing there. They hugged. 'I'm so sorry, Flavia,' she said. 'I'm so sorry.' Flavia felt brittle-thin in her arms. She put her finger to her lips and pulled Grace inside, leading her into the kitchen.

'Dad's in his study. We'll go up in a minute. I haven't said anything.'

'Where's Camilla?'

'She's staying the night with her friend, Imogen. It's a bit bleak here and Imogen's mum said she'd look after her.'

Flavia's face was pinched and tired-looking. Poor child. It was too much for her to carry on her own.

'How are you feeling?' Grace asked.

Flavia looked down at the floor. She had on a pair of pink slippers with hearts on the fronts. 'I'm okay,' she said. 'I'm trying to be strong for Dad.'

'And who's being strong for you?'

'Mum. I talk to her when I'm in bed and she helps me.'

Grace followed Flavia up the staircase with its oak banister and pale yellow carpet. Huge, highly-decorated vases stood on the landing. Hand-painted probably. The opulence of the house amazed her. She remembered Franco's outrage when she ordered the quilted cream canopy for the restaurant: 'Are you mad?' he'd yelled. 'That's our income for three months blown!' She'd shut the office door so no one would hear the tirade.

Flavia led her along the corridor and they stopped at a wood-panelled door on the other side of the landing. Flavia knocked and a laugh bubbled up in Grace's throat. It was like being called to the headmaster's office.

'Yes.' True to the image, Rick's stern voice came from inside.

Flavia pushed open the door. 'Dad, Grace is here.'

This was the moment Grace had dreaded. Rick would be angry. He would shout. He would say he didn't want her here. He would tell her to *get out.*

But none of that happened. Rick was sitting behind a desk, the lower half of his face illuminated by the computer's ghostly light, the upper half in shadow. 'Grace,' was all he said.

She went towards him. She couldn't help it. He'd hate her for it, but she put her arms round him and held him to her. His cheek was against her heart. She wondered if he could feel it beating. He didn't say anything, but he let her hold him. It was a comfort of sorts.

She looked across at Flavia, still clutching the door. She motioned to her to go and the slight figure slipped from the room. She let her arms fall from Rick's shoulders, and he seemed to slump without the support.

'Isabel has come up with me, Rick. We're at a hotel in Newcastle,' she said. 'We're coming to the funeral.' She waited for the outburst, but Rick seemed not to register her words. 'I know you said not to, but we need to say goodbye to Deanna.'

'The church will be full,' he said.

'I'm sure it will.' It was like cajoling a small child into bed. She decided to be blunt. Better than an explosion tomorrow. 'Alicia's coming with us. She loved her mum, Rick.'

He nodded. 'Tell her not to bring that jerk.'

'She won't.' Grace leant forward and kissed his forehead. It felt hot and slick with perspiration. 'We'll see you tomorrow. You don't have to do this on your own, you know.'

Rick looked up at her. 'Deanna was my life.'

Alicia had already left when Grace got back to the hotel, and Isabel was in bed reading a magazine. Grace crawled into bed, shivering with exhaustion.

Isabel put down her magazine and turned out the light. 'How was Rick?' Her voice came out of the darkness.

'Very quiet. He surprised me.'

'Perhaps he'll come through okay.'

'He must.'

'Good night. Hope you sleep.'

'Night, Bel.' Grace lay on her back and listened to Isabel's soft breathing. She felt peaceful in a weird way. Perhaps it was sharing a room with her big sister.

Grace, Isabel and Alicia arrived early at the church, the atmosphere between them stiff. There'd been a battle at the hotel when Alicia turned up with Gary. He'd obviously made a big effort and was wearing a dark suit, and his piercings were gone from his nose and ears.

'I'm sorry, Gary,' Grace said, 'but I can't let you come.'

Alicia's eyes filled with tears. 'But Auntie Grace, he's borrowed a suit specially.'

Grace held up her hand. 'It's not fair to your dad, Alicia. Not today of all days.'

Gary put his arm round her. 'It's okay, babe. Me brother will drive me over. I'll wait for you by the bridge.'

Alicia had been silent in the back of the car all the way to Rothbury.

Rick was right—the church was full. Full of people, even an hour before the service was due to begin. Full of flowers, hundreds and hundreds of creamy pink roses in huge displays at the entrance, in front of the altar, along the aisles. Full of light, the red and gold banners of it streaming from the massive stained glass window. Full of music. 'What is it?' she muttered to Isabel as the organ swelled into sounds that reverberated on the walls. Isabel made a face. 'It's that Bach Toccata—Dad used to hate it.'

They hesitated at the beginning of the main aisle.

'We'll wait with you here till they arrive,' Grace said to Alicia. 'Then you can follow the coffin with your dad and sisters.'

Alicia caught hold of Grace's hand. 'I can't,' she said. 'Suppose he says no.' With her straw boater, a wide black band circling it above the brim, her blue and white checked dress, she looked young, little more than a schoolgirl. Grace swallowed hard. If she started to cry, Alicia would never be able to do it.

She saw Isabel put her arm round Alicia. 'Come on, Alicia. Be strong for your mum.'

'I can't… I can't do it… I'm going to find Gary… I'm —'

The organ crashed into a crescendo of chords. Sounds rose and billowed through the church and into the far reaches of its ceiling. The noise was deafening, but at least it stopped Alicia. She stiffened, head tilted back, like a deer catching the scent. From the corner of her eye, Grace saw the cortege pull up outside.

Grace and Isabel walked back up to the house. It felt like a party or a carnival as other mourners thronged the hill, the women with their bright clothes—as Deanna had wanted—

like a cloud of butterflies against the dark branches of the men's suits.

Grace put her arm through Isabel's. 'That was wonderful, so sad and so awful, but wonderful too.'

'I'm glad Rick let Alicia sit with them,' Isabel said. 'You did well to persuade her to wait for them.'

'I was afraid she was going to have a real wobbler when she said she couldn't do it.'

'She's rushed off now though. Can't see her coming back to the house.'

Grace thought about the straw boater she'd glimpsed bobbing towards the river. 'Do you remember when Rick used to call them his three princesses?'

'Over-the-top, typical Rick,' Isabel said. 'Like the funeral itself, but you could tell he'd done it all for Deanna.'

Grace laughed. 'I couldn't believe it when they started playing *Islands in the Stream*! I didn't think Rick had a sense of humour.'

'Deanna loved Dolly Parton,' Isabel told her. 'And when you listen to the words—especially that first line—they're perfect for Rick and Deanna.'

'Why's that?'

'I sometimes wonder if Rick went to America because he was so unhappy.'

'That's a bit melodramatic. He got that job offer with IBM.'

'But when I think about it now, Dad was horrible to Rick. I remember once Rick telling him about a football match. He'd scored three goals and come home full of it. But I heard Dad send him away: "Can't you see George is practising his scales?" he said.'

Grace felt a rush of air behind her and a hand on her back. 'Is that my name you're taking in vain?'

She swung round. 'George! What are you doing here?'

George kissed her and Isabel on the cheek. 'Same as you, I imagine.'

'You mean you were at the funeral?' Isabel asked.

'Of course. Had to make sure my sister-in-law had a good send-off. And Ricky Boy did her proud, I must say.'

Grace turned to walk the last bit to the house. Just as she thought they'd got through the worst, George turns up with his *Ricky Boy* taunts.

George fell into step beside her. 'What's up? Did I say something wrong?'

Back at the house, Rick spent most of the time sitting in an armchair by the window in the drawing room. He didn't talk much and every time Grace looked in, he had fresh glass of whisky in his hand. There was such a crush of people, with luck, he wouldn't even notice George.

Grace stood out on the lawn talking to some of Deanna's friends. 'Tragic'… 'such a lovely person'… 'I'll miss her so much'… their love made Grace want to cry.

She was standing at the French windows consoling Mrs Crosby—*I loved her like me own daughter*—when she heard shouting from the drawing room. She pushed past the group gathered in the centre of the room. Rick was still in the armchair, his head dipping forward on to his chest, a glass hanging from his hand. George stood over him, flapping a sheet of paper.

Isabel appeared beside her. 'What's going on?'

'Search me, but we've got to get George out of here.'

As they moved towards the two men, George caught sight of them. 'Don't you dare try and shut me up! The bastard's gone too far this time.' He flicked the paper in Rick's face.

The movement brought Rick round. He opened his eyes and shook his head, like a threatened stallion. He half rose from the chair, but George pushed him back.

Grace caught hold of George's arm. 'What is it? What's wrong?'

George flicked the paper again. 'Ask him. Ricky Boy.'

'Rick.' Grace bent towards her brother. Alcohol fumed in her face. 'Do you know what he's going on about?'

Rick stared up at her with glazed eyes.

Isabel grabbed her arm. 'Look.'

Grace whirled round. George had climbed on the coffee table and held the sheet of paper out in front of him.

People were crowding into the room, wondering what the commotion was. Their horrified faces flashed in front of Grace. Flavia materialized next to her. 'Make him stop, Auntie Grace,' she pleaded. 'Make him stop.'

Grace stood one side of George and gestured to Isabel to stand on the other. 'Get down, George.' She raised her voice above the hubbub. 'You're making a show of yourself.'

'The letter,' George shouted. 'You wait till you hear the fucking letter.'

Isabel stretched up for the paper, but he held it out of reach. 'This is Deanna's day, George. It's not only Rick you're hurting. Think of the girls. They've lost their mother.'

George ignored them. He lifted his arms. Grace could see the paper shaking in his hands.

'I'm sure you'd all like to hear this letter.' George's voice was lower now. The silence in the room was intense. 'This is a letter to me. It's a letter from my late father.' His gaze dropped to the paper. 'It says *My dear George, you and I have shared the closest friendship possible between father and son…*' George paused and looked up. His eyes focused on the people packed into the room. 'How lovely, you might be thinking. What a lovely sentiment for a father to express to his son. And I would have thought the same…' He slapped his hand across the paper. The noise shattered the silence. 'If I'd ever seen the letter. Which until today, I hadn't, because… because…'

Grace closed her eyes. Thank God, he'd stopped. He'd run out of steam. She opened her eyes and sensed a ripple of movement in the people packed into the room. Please let someone intervene.

'Because…' Oh, no, his voice was louder again. He turned to point at Rick. 'This bastard! This fucking arrogant bastard had the letter and kept it a secret. Let me read you another bit, which is, I presume why he stole the letter. *I want you to know the piano is yours. It's possible Rick will claim it, but he's never played it, nor wanted to, so it's my wish you should have it.*' George jabbed his finger again in Rick's direction. 'That, my friends, is what my father thought of my esteemed brother.'

Thirty-four

When Isabel and Grace got back from Northumberland, Eva was waiting at the gate. 'I've been looking out for you ever since you phoned.'

'Mum, its miles away. You know that,' Grace said.

Isabel heard her irritation.

'My poor *bambini*. You look *esausta*.'

'We are exhausted. It's been a hard few days.'

'Come in, come in. I have pasta for you.'

They sat at the table in the dining room and ate the pasta pomodoro that was one of their mother's specialities. She'd bought brown crusty rolls, and she scrutinised every mouthful.

'I love to see you eat!' She clapped her hands and Isabel heard bracelets jangling on her arm. She was almost herself again.

'So, tell me, how is my Ricardo? He must be *desolato*.'

Eva was reverting more to Italian every day. 'He is.' Isabel supposed *desolato* summed up Rick. 'You know how much he loved Deanna.'

Eva shuddered. 'I understand so well. When my Henry died—'

'Please don't Mum.' Grace was close to tears. 'Can we recover from this funeral before we have to relive Dad's.'

Isabel saw her mother pout. She hadn't even got into her stride.

'Was it in the Catholic church? I told Ricardo he must make sure he had a Mass.'

'Deanna wasn't Catholic, was she?'

'No, but the requiem Mass is beautiful and you can have the incense—'

'But why would you want it if you weren't Catholic?'

'Grace, *mia cara*, you're very cross with your poor mamma today.'

'I've been to a funeral. I've driven hundreds of miles and I'm tired.'

'Of course! Of course!' Eva stood up. 'Silly me. You must have a sleep. And you must want to speak to Franco. He'll be worried about you.'

Isabel signalled across to Grace: *you haven't told her, have you?* Grace shook her head: *no, and don't you say anything.*

Isabel pushed her chair back. 'I must get off. I need to check on Rose and Josh.'

'Before you go…' Eva put her hands together. She'd painted her nails again, Isabel noticed. 'I want to take you both out for dinner tonight.'

'Mum, you've fed us a mountain of pasta.' Grace kissed Isabel. 'I'll see you in the morning. All I want to do is sleep.'

'Tomorrow night, then. I want you to be wide awake.' Eva smiled. 'I've got some news.'

When Isabel pulled up at the flat, she noticed Brian's car parked further along the road. That was all she needed.

He was in the lounge with Rose and Josh watching television.

'Hi, Mum.' Josh sat on the floor, close to the screen. She was always on at him to sit further back. 'Come and watch this, Mum. It's ace!'

'Hi. How are you, Rose?'

Rose was curled up on the sofa next to Brian. 'Yeah, I'm good. How was the funeral?' Her gaze didn't move from the screen.

'Oh, you know.' Isabel dropped her bag on the floor.

Brian got up and came over. 'Hi, gorgeous.' He put his arms round her and pulled her close. 'How did it go?'

'It was very sad to see Rick and the girls without Deanna.'

'No point grieving now—he didn't appreciate her while she was alive.'

'And you've always appreciated your wife, have you, Brian?'

'Ouch! No, you know I haven't, but I'm lucky I've got another chance.' He leaned forward and kissed her on the mouth. Wet smeared her lips, and she had to clench her fists to stop herself wiping them.

She tried to ease out of his grasp, but he held her tighter. 'Brian, you're hurting me.' The smell of his after-shave assaulted her.

He laughed. 'Can't a man show his wife a bit of love?'

'I thought you were going to keep Rose and Josh tonight,' she said. 'I'm shattered.'

'Change of plan. We're going out to celebrate instead, aren't we, kids?'

'Oh, Brian—'

'No excuses. I signed the contract today for the new house.'

'That's great news. But let's not tempt fate. We ought to wait till we get completion.'

'We'll celebrate again then!'

'I can't go out tonight, Brian. It's already late.'

'Tomorrow, then. Don't suppose another day will make much difference.'

Isabel pulled away from him. She couldn't stand his crotch pressed up against her another second. 'My mother's taking Grace and me out for dinner tomorrow night.'

'Am I invited?'

'It's family only.'

'I am family, aren't I?'

'Just be patient, Brian. It will give me a chance to tell them we're getting back together.'

Isabel was still in bed the next morning when Grace came. She'd been awake early and finally fallen into a restless sleep, plagued by dreams and tormented half-awakenings. She dreamt she received a parcel. As she unwrapped layers of brown paper and plastic, a rotten smell drifted from the package. When she unpeeled the final layer, she had to rush to the sink to be sick. Inside the parcel were two fingers, putrid and decomposing. There was a card, spattered with blood, in Brian's writing: *From Lover Boy.*

She woke to hear loud banging at the door. She stumbled to open it. Grace was standing there.

'I've been out here for hours, Bel, ringing and knocking.'

'Sorry, I didn't hear you.'

'So I gathered. Are you going to let me in now you have opened up Fort Knox?'

Isabel pulled open the front door. She bent down to retrieve the post, which was all bills.

'You look as if you need coffee.' Grace walked down the hall to the kitchen. 'Rose and Josh with Brian?'

'He kept them overnight.'

'And most of today. It'll soon be lunchtime.'

'I'll get dressed,' Isabel said.

When she got to the kitchen, the smell of coffee greeted her. 'Just what I need.' She sat down at the table. 'What brings you round? Escaping Mum?'

'George rang me this morning.'

'Oh God! What did he say?'

'He's driving up—'

'But he's only just arrived back there from Newcastle. Is Mum dragging him up for the dinner?'

'Be better if it was. He'll be here about nine this evening, and he's got a removal van coming in the morning.'

'A removal van?'

Grace dropped a spoon on to the draining board. It landed on the stainless steel with a clatter. 'He's taking the piano.'

Isabel covered her eyes with her hands. She couldn't do this any more. She wasn't strong enough. The blackness helped, but sounds wouldn't be silenced. She could hear a tap dripping in the bathroom. The distant ringing of next-door's phone. Samson scratching at the back door.

She opened her eyes. Grace was leaning on the worktop, her head bowed. There wasn't anything to say. She pulled the post towards her, more for something to do than curiosity. She shuffled through the envelopes. Caught between two bills was a postcard. She recognised the picture. She glanced over at Grace to see if she'd noticed her shock. Grace hadn't moved. Isabel stuffed the postcard to the bottom of the pile and started going through it again, studying each envelope. A gas bill. A letter from the bank. An invoice from a music publisher. One that said 'To the Occupier.' She reached the bottom. She couldn't put it off.

The postcard showed a picture of a young woman playing a guitar. Vermeer. Isabel stared at her ringlets, her yellow dress, her fingers on the guitar. She turned the postcard over. *I hope you're okay*, Simon had written. *I've packed up your stuff—what do you want me to do with it? I can send it, or I'll bring it over. It's the only thing that's keeping me going—the thought I'll see you one last time. S x*

Isabel could hear Simon's voice in the gallery at Kenwood House: 'You can almost see the strings vibrating under her fingers.' She wanted to go back to that day. She wanted it to be the day she'd met Simon. When she might have passed him in the street with scarcely a glance. When she didn't know what a broken heart felt like.

Isabel took a taxi to the restaurant. It was a new one called Luigi's, and she'd heard it was expensive. Apparently it was popular with the Hampstead set. Whatever her news, Mum was pushing the boat out. Perhaps she was going to sell up and move to be nearer Rick after all. Perhaps, with Deanna gone, she thought he'd need her.

Grace had suggested getting to the restaurant early. 'Get back before George arrives,' she said.

'Have you told Mum he's coming?'

'No. He can explain himself what he's up to.'

'I never thought he'd actually do it,' Isabel said. 'I can't imagine the house without Dad's piano.'

'And what the hell is Rick going to say?'

Eva and Grace were already there. Eva beckoned her over. '*Cara*, you look wonderful.'

Isabel had chosen her red and gold dress from Naples, the only posh one she owned.

Eva was wearing a floor-length turquoise gown with a deep décolletage—it looked more as if she was going to a ball than a dinner with her daughters. It was the first time she hadn't worn black since Henry died.

She ordered a bottle of champagne, flirting outrageously with the waiter.

'Order anything you like.' She batted a hand towards the menu Grace was holding. 'It's all on me tonight.'

They ordered their food, and the waiter poured their champagne. Eva raised her glass. 'Salute. I am so lucky to have such beautiful daughters.'

Her mother had never called her beautiful before, Isabel thought.

Grace raised her glass, but she didn't drink. 'What's your news, Mum? Are you going to tell us now, or have we got to wait till the end of the meal?'

Eva clasped her hands together. She was wearing a gold charm bracelet Isabel didn't remember. It already had a cross, a car, a high-heeled shoe and a lipstick hanging from it. 'Now. I'll tell you now and we can celebrate properly.'

'Let's hear it then.'

'I'm going home to Italy.' She clapped her hands and the golden charms danced and sparkled.

'You haven't got a home in Italy,' Grace said.

'Eduardo has bought a new house. And I am going to live there with him.' Eva looked from Isabel to Grace.

Isabel didn't dare meet Grace's eyes, but she saw her fingers clenched round the stem of her glass.

'Let's get this straight.'

Isabel was glad Grace kept talking. Her tongue felt as if it was too big for her mouth and she was sure no words would come out.

'You're going to live in Italy with Eduardo?'

'He's lonely. I am lonely. And he loves me.'

Isabel stared at her mother. Her hair was newly-dyed black and shone harshly under the lights. Brilliant red lipstick outlined her mouth.

'This would be the same Eduardo your brothers sent you to England to escape.'

'*Sì*.'

'The same Eduardo you slept with while you were married to Dad.'

'*Sì*, but your father—'

'The same Eduardo who is George's father?'

'*Sì*. It's *miracoloso*.'

Isabel went back to the house in the taxi with Grace and her mother. Her eyelids wanted to close, and she longed for home and the oblivion of sleep.

Grace had persuaded her to come when they went to the Ladies at the restaurant: 'I can't do this on my own, Bel.'

'But you handled Mum brilliantly. I could never have pinned her down like that.'

'I'm tired. I can't take much more.'

That makes two of us, Isabel thought, but she agreed to go.

She was already regretting it as the taxi pulled up at her mother's house. She started to apologise—'I don't feel well, Grace'—but Grace had opened the door and was out on the pavement before they'd even stopped.

'What the hell?' Isabel heard her shout.

Eva screamed. Someone's broken in!'

Isabel stumbled from the taxi. Lights streamed from every window. The front door stood open and next-door's dog began to bark. Isabel followed Grace through the gate and up the path. A figure huddled on the step by the front door. 'Grace, don't…' she began, as Grace bent over the crumpled form. In the glow of the streetlight, Isabel saw a face peering up. It was Flavia. She was sobbing: 'It's Dad. It's Dad.'

Isabel pushed past Grace and Flavia and stepped into the hall. 'Don't let Mum come in,' she shouted over her shoulder.

'Rick?' she called. The silence was unnerving. Where was he? What was he doing? She strained to hear the smallest sound. She could almost feel his presence on the other side of the dining room wall. She listened again and heard him breathing, a thin rasping. She looked back. Grace and Flavia stood framed in the front door. Eva was on the path behind them. 'Be careful, Bel,' Grace shouted.

She turned back to the dining room door. 'Rick?'

The silence was broken by something infinitely worse. A blood-chilling howl came from the dining room It was the cry of a creature from the wild. A cry of anguish. Her scalp crawled as if spiders had invaded it.

The wailing died away. What should she do? She needed to go in and talk to him. Tell him she understood. He'd lost Deanna, and there was nothing to live for. The sky was black. The grass was black. The sun was black. If snow fell from the sky, it would be black. But light would come again. However obdurate the blackness, a rainbow would glow, the clouds would lighten.

Another terrifying howl erupted.

Isabel flung open the dining room door. Rick was standing in front of the piano. Blood streamed from a wound on his forehead. His face was the colour of brick dust and his eyes bulged. Obscenities gushed from his mouth. His arms were raised above his head. In his hands was an axe.

Isabel screamed. The axe crashed down on the piano. She covered her ears against the noise of splintering wood and mangled notes. A terrible symphony of sound. Rick raised the axe above his head again. It slammed into the piano a second time, slicing a deep gash in the smooth polished surface. He hauled the blade from the wood. Grunts reverberated from somewhere deep inside him. He steadied his position, shifting his weight from one foot to the other. He swung the weapon above his head. It crashed on to the keys. Isabel's head filled with the cacophony. The ivory splintered and cream particles shot in all directions. Rick panted. Spittle foamed at the corners of his mouth.

The axe smashed down a fourth time. The top caved in. A piece of wood flew off and its sharp point pierced Isabel's cheek. She clutched her face. The axe began its arc again. 'Rick!' She dragged at his arm. 'Stop!' His shirt was wringing wet. He turned to her. The axe was above her. She stared up at the shiny blade. The corner was a foot from her head.

'Isabel, get back!' She felt arms grasp her from behind. Push her to one side. It was George. She watched as he reached up for the axe. His hands were on it. His fingers tried to prise Rick's away. A flash. Rick. The steel blade. George. They turned and twisted. The weapon between them. Light glinted as the blade scythed downwards. She saw George stagger. He fell on his knees, blood spouting from his head.

Eva pushed through the others to stand in front of Rick. The axe was still in his hands. '*Il mio bambino*,' she sobbed. 'What have you done?' She clung to the piano, now a mess of broken wood. 'You wicked boy. Your father's piano.'

Isabel heard screaming. 'Get an ambulance!' she screeched. 'The police!' It was her screaming. George was on the floor, blood streaming down his face. Grace shoved her to one side. She dragged the cloth from the table and held it down on George's head.

Eva was cradling the piano.

'Mum. It's George. He's hurt.'

Eva looked round and her eyes focused on George on the floor for the first time. Grace had ripped the tablecloth in two and bound it round George's head. Still the blood pumped out.

Eva got down on her knees, her head close to George's. '*Carissimo*,' she crooned. '*Mio tesoro*.'

George opened his eyes. He must have rallied at the sound of Eva's voice. He fixed his eyes on his mother. 'Bitch,' he said. 'Bitch.' And he closed his eyes again.

The ambulance men and the police arrived at the same time. The policemen approached Rick. One lifted the axe from his hands, and the other snapped handcuffs on his wrists. 'We'll need you to come with us, sir.'

A paramedic knelt beside George. He put his fingers to the pulse in his neck. He looked up, shaking his head. 'I'm sorry. He's gone.'

'Oh… Oh…' The sound of Eva's weeping filled the room. '*Mio tesoro*.'

Isabel bent and stroked George's hair. It felt soft and silky.

A hand touched her shoulder. 'Come on. You'd be better away from here.'

She looked round at the paramedic. 'He's dead.'

'I'm afraid he is.'

'My brother's dead.'

'I'm really sorry.'

She stared at her hand stained red. 'There's so much blood.'

'Bel, let's go.' Grace's voice came from a long way off. 'There's nothing more we can do tonight.'

'But there's so much blood.'

Thirty-five

Isabel stepped out of the taxi. She hesitated, her hand gripping the door handle.

'You all right, miss?' the driver called.

She wondered if he'd seen the blood on her face and jacket. She'd swilled water over herself, but there must still be blood on her. She could smell its rusty odour. 'I'm fine.' Her teeth wouldn't stop chattering. 'Is this okay?' She shoved a ten-pound note in his hand.

'Thank you very much, miss. You go carefully now.'

She hadn't realised how scared she was until she opened the front door of the flat. She was sure it had never been so dark. She turned on the light and listened. She stood with her back to the door. Listening. The doors leading off the hall were all firmly shut. But what was behind them? Who was lurking there? She rushed through the flat, drawing curtains, turning on lights.

The chair tapped against the kitchen unit every time she rocked backwards. Tap. Tap. Tap. The sound, the normality, comforted her. Tap. Tap. Tap. Samson jumped down from the table and climbed on to her lap. Tap. Tap. Tap.

Isabel had vomited after Rick and George had been taken away, and she couldn't stop shivering.

'It's shock,' Grace said. 'I'll take Eva and Flavia to a hotel. You go home.'

'I'll come with you.'

'Bel, you're not in any state to cope with Eva after what you've been through. Get Brian to come over. You shouldn't be on your own.' She wrapped her arms round Isabel. 'I'll ring you first thing in the morning.'

Isabel wasn't sure if she'd fallen asleep. The overhead light glared into her eyes. Tap. Tap. Tap. She stretched. Her arm was numb where Samson had been lying on it. Tap. Tap. Tap. The movement of the rocking chair was making her feel sick again. She pulled her mobile from her bag. She scrolled down contacts until she reached S. She pressed her thumb on Simon's name. *Call.* She clicked on *Call.* The ringing trilled against her ear.

There was no answer. He wasn't going to answer. He was asleep. He was out in a noisy bar and couldn't hear his phone. He'd seen her name flash up on the phone and was punishing her.

'Isabel?' His voice was muzzy with sleep. 'Are you okay?'

'I'm sorry… can you come over?'

'What's the matter?'

'Please. I need you. Can you come?'

'God, you sound terrible. What's happened?'

'Simon, please.'

'I'm on my way.'

Thirty-six

Isabel sat on the floor in front of piles of clothes, books and papers. She'd thrown so much away when she and Brian split up, but here she was again weighed down with possessions. She'd also inherited George's painting of Henry. It was propped in the hall, packaged in bubble-wrap and thick masking tape. She didn't know what she was going to do with it, but her mother hadn't wanted it and she couldn't bring herself to get rid of it.

One of the problems was her piano music. Some of it went back to pieces she'd played when she first started having lessons aged four. She didn't see the point of keeping them when she was going to get rid of her piano. Simon had tried to persuade her not to. 'There's room for it in my flat,' he'd said again last night, 'and once we move somewhere bigger…'

But Isabel had made up her mind. She couldn't imagine she'd play again.

Now that she'd decided, she couldn't wait to leave the flat. There were too many memories: of her life, and the one her parents had shared not far away. All her affection for that house where the family had grown up was gone. She'd hated having to go back every day to help her mother pack. But now Eva had left for Italy, and the house was for sale.

She'd clung to the idea of a family which—in reality—had never existed. That was why she'd been so devastated, she realised, when Brian left. She'd felt such a failure not being able to reproduce the idyllic marriage her mother and father had shared. But that image was now exposed as a sham. And knowing Simon had taught her that her relationship with Brian had been based on lies and secrets. Not of the kind that Henry and Eva had shared. But smaller ones that wore away at fulfilment. The worst secret was the one she'd kept from herself—Brian was not the husband she dreamed of having.

Her new life wasn't going to be easy. Rose and Josh were both going to live with Brian. Rose wouldn't have anything to do with her. She'd become hysterical when Isabel told her that she wasn't getting back with Brian, that they weren't moving to the big house. She'd punched and kicked like a toddler. 'I hate you!' she screamed in Isabel's face. 'You're a cheat and a hypocrite.' Brian had grinned as he listened to the tirade. He'd put his arm round Rose and walked her to the door. When they got there, he turned back to Isabel: 'That just about sums you up, don't you think?'

Isabel sorted her clothes into two piles. She'd lost so much weight that she was taking most of them to the charity shop and the pile she was keeping would fit into one suitcase. She snapped the locks shut on the case and stood it in the corner with the trunk and boxes already waiting to go. She stretched backwards, easing the ache in her spine.

Sitting down on the bed, she reached for the envelope in the top drawer of her bedside cabinet. She drew out the two sheets of paper. They were creased and dog-eared where she'd read and reread them. The first sheet was a letter she'd received from Chloe a few days after George's funeral.

Isabel and Grace had already started organising the funeral, fending off constant demands from Eva for a requiem mass, a choir, a mahogany coffin—'Everything must be *perfetto* for my Giorgio', when a letter arrived from a solicitor in Penzance. He was in possession of a document, signed by George, which stated that in the event of his death, George wanted a simple ceremony with only his friends from the art school there, and afterwards his ashes were to be scattered in the sea. Eva had spent a day crying in her bedroom. '*Perche*? *Perche*?' she asked whenever they went up to see if she was all right. 'Why is he punishing me? What did I do?'

Isabel smoothed down the page with Chloe's loopy schoolgirl handwriting:

Hi Isabel

I've been sorting out George's room and I came across a diary he kept for a few weeks last year. There's one entry he wrote while Henry was staying down here. I think you'd be interested to read it—it explains a lot about George.

I hope you're beginning to recover from the trauma of George's death. From what you said on the phone, it must have been terrible. I hope his brother has to stay in prison for the rest of his life for what he did.

I miss George more than I can tell you. I loved him so much, and he'd asked me to go to Italy with him. I don't really know what I'll do now, but I can't see how the art school will survive without George. I go down to the sea where we scattered the ashes nearly every day. I know it's silly, but I feel closer to him there.

'Come on, Chlo,' he used to say. 'Put your sparkle on—we're hitting Penzance.'

Let me know how you are, and come and see me if you're in Penzance.

Chloe x

The letter always made Isabel want to cry, but it helped to know George had someone like Chloe. The other sheet of paper was more difficult. She almost knew it by heart:

14 March

Wow, it's been some weird day. Navel-gazing doesn't usually do it for me, but today the old man told me something that's rocked my boat, capsized it, you could say.

He suggested going down to The Admiral for a quick pint before dinner. He's going back tomorrow and I thought it'd be nice to have a chinwag before he hops it back to the smoke.

He downed the first pint straight off and then he ordered another. I'm not a great beer drinker, but I thought why not? It's his last night and he's bought my portrait of him. Christ knows if he likes it—he paid a tidy amount.

So, I'm half way down the second pint, feeling nicely sozzled and planning the third, when he comes out with it: 'I've got something to tell you, dear boy.' If a lottery win depended on it, I couldn't have guessed what that something was.

It's funny but even writing this—when it's only me who's going to see it, and I already know what the SOMETHING is—it's hard to put it down in black and white. Here goes: the old man is not my father. Even reading that back gives me the shivers. Okay, so he's looked after me, bought me clothes and food, taught me the piano… everything… you name it, he's done it for me. Except for that vital bit of business, which somehow he missed out on—her fanny was feeding some other prick. And what a miserable little prick she chose! He said she wanted it kept secret because her brothers would kill her if they found out. They'd got some sense—those old Italian uncles.

He told me no one else in the family knows, but I don't believe him. He's joined at the hip to Isabel—there's no way he wouldn't have told her. I expect they all know. I expect they laugh at me behind my back. Bastards and bitches the lot of them. Mind you, it's my dear mamma who's the biggest bitch. I'll tell her so one day as well.

Isabel stood at the cooker stirring a sauce to go with pasta. Simon would be here soon, and although it had only been a few days, she couldn't wait to see him again. His wife had finally agreed that his son could come down from Scotland to visit. 'I'd like you to meet him,' Simon had said. 'So would I, but let's take it slowly. You don't want to do anything to mess it up.' He'd put his arms round her and kissed her. 'Oh, wise woman.'

*

The phone rang. She lowered the heat under the pan and picked up the receiver: it was Grace.

'How's Rick?' Isabel asked. Grace was staying up in Rothbury with the girls. Rick had been charged with manslaughter and was being held in a secure psychiatric unit until it was decided if he was fit enough to stand trial.

'I went to see him yesterday. He stared out the window the whole time. I don't know if he even recognised me.'

'What do the doctors say?'

'They think it will be a long road, but they're hopeful he'll recover from the breakdown.'

'And the girls?'

'Camilla wanders round the house like a lost soul. But Alicia went to see Rick the other day.'

'Gosh, was he okay with that?'

'She said she held his hand and he smiled at her.'

'That's a breakthrough. But it's a shame about Flavia's university place.'

'It's only deferred,' Grace said. 'She might still go next October.'

'What about Alicia's boyfriend?'

'Gary comes over most days. He's a lovely boy, Bel. Really looking after Alicia.'

Isabel smelt burning and carried the phone over to the cooker. She'd caught the sauce just in time. 'And you're staying up there? No hope of reconciling with Franco?'

'I'm filing for divorce.'

'Still planning to go to America?'

'One day. I've waited this long, I can wait another couple of years. But we're rattling around in this big house. I've been thinking of shutting it up and moving to that bungalow Rick bought for Mum.'

'Worrying about that seems a long time ago.'

'I'd better go,' Grace said. 'I can hear Camilla calling me. Oh, forgot to ask—have you heard from Mum?'

'Eduardo phoned to say they'd arrived. Apparently Mum got a film star's welcome.'

'She'd have enjoyed that.'

'Just before you go, Grace…' Isabel hesitated. Now it had come to it, she didn't know how to tell her sister. What her reaction would be.

'Come on, Bel. I've got to see what Camilla wants.'

'I've decided I'm going to look for him.'

'Who?'

'The baby that was adopted. Our half brother.'

'Wow! That's a big decision.'

'I've talked it through with Simon, and he agrees I should.'

'It will have repercussions. Look how it's blown our family apart.'

Isabel could tell Grace didn't approve, but she'd made her mind up—it was something she had to do. 'It was the secrecy that caused that. I need to find him if I can.' Isabel took a deep breath. 'I think it might help heal some of the wounds.'

'I can hear you're determined, so go ahead and I'll support you.'

Isabel shredded lettuce and sliced tomatoes. She added some basil and sprinkled black pepper on the salad. Brian hated basil. 'Smells like cat pee,' he used to say. Simon liked the same food she did. Simon. He would be here soon, and she was hot and grubby from packing. She left the sauce simmering and went to the bathroom. It didn't take her long to shower and then it was time to decide what to wear. She picked out the dress Simon had bought for her birthday. It was a rich midnight blue and the velvet was soft against her skin as she slipped it over her head and reached over her shoulder to pull up the zip. She picked up a brush and glanced in the mirror. The dress set off her hair and eyes. Even she could see she looked good these days. She thought of Simon's face when she opened the present. His eyes had that warm soft look that made her shiver. She leant over to kiss him and he pulled her closer. 'I love you,' he'd said.

Isabel stopped, hairbrush in mid-air. Heat flooded through her body as she remembered. The sex with Brian. She still hadn't told Simon her *dirty little secret.* She thought of what he'd said about her parents: 'The trouble with secrets is that they come back to haunt you.'

She'd been telling herself for weeks that she had to confess about Brian. But the time was never right. It would have to be this evening or she'd need to keep quiet forever.